The Fabulous Wizard of Oz

Kaye Draper

Cover design by Rainbow Danger Designs

I value every one of my readers and friends who support me in the crazy, wonderful adventure of writing. Thank you to all my patrons. A special thanks to Kate McKenney, SG, Verity St Clair-Prime, SW, Danna, Lilith R., M. Woodson, and Sandi Devlin for helping me create. Thanks to Frank Boston for the alpha reading and constant encouragement. And thanks to my proofreading team for making things pretty. I couldn't make this dream into a reality without you!

Chapter 1

"Well, it's definitely not fucking Kansas," I muttered, doing my best to keep my rickety old landing pod pointed in the right direction. The thing was a complete piece of junk. I had no idea how it had even managed to fire up for the short trip from the ship to the planet's surface.

Of course, the Elite Allied Republic of Terran Humans—or EARTH for short—probably didn't care if I survived the trip. Why waste good machinery on banished failures they were trying to make disappear?

They had provided the junk pod and just enough fuel to make it from the republic's fleet ship to the planet. There was no other habitable option in this area, so it was do as told and land on Ozma-4, or run out of fuel and die in empty space inside my tiny metal can.

Honestly? I was tempted to choose the die alone in space option. Oz was a backwater colonial planet in the middle of nowhere. They had limited tech and resources, and a weird governing system that didn't make for easy planetary advancement.

The "four" in Ozma-4 was a nod to the four planets who had tried to colonize the place and take over. Why they bothered to try to colonize the place was anybody's guess. Though it probably had something to do with a hush-hush resource of some kind. That was usually how these things played out. But there was nothing nearby except one poor, probably forgotten space station provided by the Interstellar Morals and Discipline committee.

No one would know where I was. No one here would know *who* I was. Which was the whole point. I was too well-known to be executed, even after my shady discharge from the diplomatic branch of EARTH's military. So they decided to make me disappear instead. Somewhere no one could find me, but where EARTH could still come retrieve me if they needed me for something.

Wanted by everyone and no one all at once. Story of my freaking life. And I'd lost half my fake nails somewhere along the way. "Insult to injury," I muttered.

The display screen lit up and an alarm started pinging. "Shit, shit, shit."

I had made it through the atmosphere. So at least dying alone in space was no longer an option. But of *course* I was about to hit turbulence. According to the limited information I'd been given while in my holding cell, Oz was known for its erratic weather. It was particularly infamous for its cyclones. Growing up in Kansas, back on Earth—the planet, not the military force—I was no stranger to tornados. But our weather was more predictable there, monitored and mitigated by environmental controls. I guess I was about to see what my ancestors had to deal with before that cozy little bit of planet-wide tech existed.

I double checked that I was strapped in as tightly as possible, then hit all the appropriate buttons to ensure I had some chance of surviving a rough landing. Propulsion was still firing, for now.

I tossed my low pigtails over my shoulders and closed my eyes. It would be fine.

"Girl, you've survived worse things in your life than a bumpy ride," I said in my best stage voice. Right before the fuel ran out and my propulsion died.

The viewscreen and electronic systems still worked for the moment, which afforded me a spectacular view of just how fucked I was. A swirling wall of debris whirled across the screen. But I was saved having to stare at that for long. With no propulsion to keep it on track, the little pod pitched sideways, rolled over, and began to spin.

I let out a shriek that would make the most fabulous queen on the stage green with envy. Then I clamped my mouth shut and tried not to puke.

Dying was bad enough. I didn't want to leave this life covered in half-digested EARTH ship rations. I was a fucking *lady.* I was going to go out with dignity.

And probably soiled underwear. But you know, you can only do so much.

I didn't have much with me, and most of it was secured against entering atmosphere, deceleration, and landing. But of course, I'd forgotten to secure my fucking lip balm. The recycled plasti-tube hit me right between the eyes, the stinging blow just one more note in the symphony of abuse my body was taking in this spinning nightmare.

It seemed like the falling, the tumbling, and the weightless feeling in between jolts of motion might last forever. Until it stopped.

The emergency landing safeties were on, so I didn't die on impact. But it sure as fuck felt like it. Even cushioned as I was, embraced by the impact safeties on my seat, I managed to bite my tongue hard enough my mouth filled with blood. Every bone in my body felt bruised.

I was also rendered temporarily deaf by the sound of impact.

I sat there for a moment, frozen while my heart tried to remember how to beat and my lungs remembered how to breathe. Now that motion was at a standstill, the safety on the headrest of my seat disengaged with a little hiss and click, allowing me to turn and lean over the seat. I spit out the mouthful of blood that had accumulated, careful not to stain my blue cotton dress. Then I disengaged my safety harness with shaking hands.

“There’s no place like a new home,” I said in my best falsetto. Time to go greet the locals.

I stumbled out of the destroyed pod and took a look around. The twister had moved on, its damage done, for now. I had been aiming for a town, but it looked like I’d been blown off course. In the distance, I could see a road leading toward what looked like a distant cluster of buildings.

Normally, I’d appreciate the wild, vivid colors around me, but after the trip I’d just had, it was all a bit much. I took my eyes off the bright foliage—and was that an aquamarine road? Yes, yes it was—to find a good place to vomit.

That taken care of, I went back inside and rinsed out my mouth and patted my face with a bit of water from the canteen I’d been given. Then I grabbed my knapsack out of the overhead bin, tracked down my escaped, murderous tube of lip balm, and stuffed it and whatever useful crap I could salvage from the pod inside the bag.

I had turned to leave when a dull thud brought me to a halt. Huh. At first, I thought the dull banging in my head was just the result of my eventful landing and my rattled brain. But no. There was something clanging around under the boards. Sighing, I crouched down and worked a service panel free. I let out a surprised squawk and fell backward to land on my skirt-clad ass when a metallic ball darted out at me.

"What the hell? *Toto*?" I yelped in surprise. I grabbed the hovering metallic device and examined it in disbelief. The EARTH goons had taken away all of my tech. They even deactivated my translator implant. Add that to the list of illegal shit they'd done to get rid of me. Removing translators and tossing someone out on a foreign planet was a huge people's rights violation.

They had *definitely* removed my trans orbital takeaway orb—or TOTO—before they shoved me into this death trap. Touted as the best traveling companion in space, TOTOs were able to connect with nearby space stations, download information about your current location, and serve as communication devices. They were invaluable for diplomats and emissaries visiting foreign planets.

I'd had my own device designed to look like a pufferdog from a small, water-covered planet I had visited in my travels as a diplomat. The creatures were so ugly they were cute, reminding me of some weird cross between an Earth puffer fish and a terrier. It annoyed people to no end that a smart, high-ranking, in-demand diplomat like me went toting around a piece of tech that looked like a children's toy.

There was no way EARTH had just let me keep Toto when they flung me onto Oz.

I held up a hand to get Toto to back off. "Messages," I said, knowing there had to be more to this than some crazy oversight on behalf of my kidnappers.

I was not disappointed. Toto rolled over to show me the display screen in its belly and a familiar face appeared. Freddie. My one friend at the EARTH academy. The one person I'd actually stayed in contact with once I graduated and worked my way up the ranks. He was a technical systems engineer. And he had probably risked everything to get this damned TOTO to me.

"Daniel," he said, voice hushed on the recording, looking over his shoulder one last time. "This is all bullshit, mate. Not sure what the hell you did to piss these guys off. But I'm working on it, I promise. I've got you covered." He shuffled the screen around and looked over his shoulder again. "I know it's not much, but you'll at least have the replicator and the communications device. Press your TOTO's nose to your port on your implant node. That should shock them back awake."

He drew in a breath. "Look, these assholes are gonna wipe your records, Dannie. I backed them up, saved a copy to your TOTO. You just have to link him up to the nearest Interstellar space station. Go over EARTH's head to IMAD, okay? EARTH is dirty. But I'm pretty sure IMAD is clean. And…well, Oz could use you anyway, yeah? I made sure that's where they sent you. There's—"

A rush of air announced the door opening behind him and Freddie went all relaxed and bored as he flipped Toto over and picked up a micro screwdriver.

"What's taking so long?" a gruff voice demanded.

"Hold onto your panties, dude," the technician huffed. "Delicate work here. If I tear into this thing too fast, I'll either ruin the data you want to get at, or I'll trigger the factory backup mechanism. Pretty sure you don't want that, yeah?"

The gruff voice again. "Get that data to my chip, then destroy that thing, kid. Any fucking around and I'll have you stripped from your cushy little job."

"Understood, sir," Freddie sniped, his voice dry. Then the message cut off as he apparently put Toto into sleep mode or something, rather than junking him the way he'd been instructed.

I had to wonder though, just what personal data the higher-ups had been so intent on stealing. I had wiped all my work-related files from the device the moment I left EARTH service. Five years ago.

Ah well, no use worrying about it at the moment. First, I needed to get acquainted with my new temporary home. Following Freddie's instructions, I asked Toto to turn my translator back on, then pressed his shiny little dog snout to the lump below my left ear, where my node interfaced with my brain.

The fucking jolt of electricity that zapped me probably cost me some brain cells. But hopefully that warm rush I felt in my blood meant the nanodes were back online.

Once I was back outside, I stood there waiting for the slight dizziness to fade while I studied my surroundings. If I wanted to find civilization, it looked like I had a lot of walking to do.

"Toto," I said tiredly. "Coms up. Please send an encoded message to the nearest IMAD station. Request to speak with the commanding officer regarding treaty violations and a civilian in distress." Ex-military, technically. But let's not give the big guys a reason to hate me on sight.

Toto gave a soft bark, and I smiled. That was one of my very first modifications, replacing the bland chimes and beeps that came standard—it drove people up the fucking *walls* when my weird-looking TOTO device barked.

But the smile was wiped off my face soon enough. Toto gave a low whine and it's AI voice, programmed to sound like a stuffy upper crust Andiluvian butler informed me, "Apologies, sir. Unable to establish a link."

I scowled. "Did you suffer damages in the pod crash, hon?"

"No, sir. I am undamaged. However, there is interference in the atmosphere. Possibilities include weather, undocumented mineral interference, or security blocking."

I sighed. My luck. Probably leftover clouds and atmospheric crap from the recent storm. It was unlikely that any mineral or planetary influence would have gone undocumented. There could be planetary security codes to prevent tech theft, but you usually only saw that on really rich, tech-savvy, industrial planets.

"Well, Toto," I said with false cheer. "Looks like we're gonna go for a walk, boy." Looking down at my feet, I sighed.

EARTH's little soldier boys had snatched me right off the drag stage in the middle of a performance. My cute, old-fashioned midwestern girl look was made all the more fabulous by my six-inch stilettos with the platform soles. They were covered in shimmering silver sequins that matched the silver and rhinestone ribbons in my pigtails and my glittery silver eyeshadow.

The shoes were fucking *fierce*. But they weren't exactly hiking shoes. And the few personal belongings in my bag didn't happen to include a change of clothes. Fucking EARTH. They really knew how to ruin a girl's day.

Arriving in the middle of nowhere on a backward colonial planet in full drag was definitely a metaphor for my life. Or something.

I shook my head and glanced back at the pod. I had checked every nook and cranny for usable paraphernalia, so I knew there wasn't a pair of hiking boots hidden in there somewhere. But still. I was tempted to go look again. I couldn't walk all the way to town in these shoes. And hiking across an alien planet barefoot was just asking for death by some slow parasitic infection.

I sighed. Then I went around the side of the pod to sit on a rock and get to ripping the heels off my beautiful shoes.

I rounded the side of the pod and froze. Oh. *Oh no….*

My eyes were riveted to the pair of *legs* that protruded from under my pathetic transport. Thankfully, there wasn't too much in the way of visible gore—I'd seen enough of that in my active duty with the EARTH military. I didn't need any more nightmare fodder. But still, squishing someone to death with your landing pod wasn't exactly something to inspire warm fuzzy feelings. They must have had some great personal shields, to only be a *little* squished.

"Fuck," I breathed. "I'm sorry."

Then I really focused on what I was seeing, and the part of me that had been trained to survive during weird alien situations kicked in.

"Really sorry about this," I said again. Then I knelt and carefully, efficiently removed the poor thing's black hiking boots.

They were a bit tight, and the soles were needlessly chunky, but they'd do the job.

I stuffed my fabulous silver heels into my knapsack. Muttering the galactic prayer for civilians killed in battle, I saluted the dead person and turned toward the eyeball-burning aquamarine road, my little TOTO hovering along beside me.

Chapter 2

The weirdly colored road seemed to serve an actual purpose. The surface, which was made to look like old-timey rough cobblestone or brick, turned out on closer inspection to be a relatively smooth composite. The color was explained when I passed the first intersection, the perpendicular road a bright purple color. There were no road signs, so I was guessing the color was part of some local navigation system.

It was a long, hot hike, the weather comparable to a Kansas summer—but not quite so scorching. The scenery was pretty, with rolling hills of vibrant flowers and greenery flowing into distant gem-bright mounds of forest.

Toto did have some basic information about the flora and fauna loaded into his memory. He was able to point out a few edible flowers along the way. The pink blossoms were surprisingly spicy. Huh. The weird place was growing on me already.

It took me most of the day to reach the distant town. I encountered a few large, strange-looking wheeled vehicles driven by even stranger-looking people, but I didn't think it was wise to chance hitchhiking. Oz was supposed to be a peaceful planet, but I knew next to nothing about its culture and customs. The place had been colonized by not one, but *four* other governments. From what I understood, each area had its own governing body, though they all took part, to some degree, in planet-wide politics and rules.

It was the way a lot of planets started out, but eventually most ended up ruled by one governing body—usually their own, unless the natives were really primitive. The time of hostile take-over had dwindled a few decades ago with a couple of interstellar peace treaties and the formation of Interstellar Morals and Discipline—IMAD—which worked in the interest of native peoples, particularly on newly discovered planets.

Once, I'd been a part of all that. EARTH's most sought after diplomat when it came to negotiating tricky situations between natives and colonizing races. But even the most supposedly forward thinking, open-minded organizations have their prejudices. My outside the box thinking had been just a bit too outside the box for the higher ups within EARTH's ranks.

And my insistence on *honesty?* In my line of work, it was an unforgiveable flaw. When the last group of people I advocated for had lost out to greed and power plays, I had turned in my resignation. It was that, or be dishonorably discharged. Maybe even made to disappear.

I had walked out on my career, my cushy life as a diplomat, and all my years of honest, heart-felt service. I'd been angry. Jaded.

But I was free.

The drag artist career had just been the icing on the cake. One final middle finger at the uptight system. I gave up on intellectual career pursuits and doubled down on being *me*. I had always been good at acting, at playing whatever part was demanded of me—and I loved to dress up. The only thing that really changed when I left my diplomat career was the stage. It became lights and glitter, rather than conference screens and meeting rooms. And the part I played was one I truly enjoyed playing, rather than a role designed to ensure that I didn't offend anyone's cultural beliefs or political views.

Not all species were as accepting of gay males in positions of power as Earthlings and their far-reaching EARTH planets had become. But after leaving EARTH, I was free to be my own fabulous self, no matter how I chose to express that.

Too bad it didn't last.

I enjoyed five years as a whopping success on the drag stage. And five years of slowly learning how to be a new version of myself, exploring all the facets of me that I'd had to keep under lock and key before. And just when I was able to relax and enjoy life…bam! EARTH showed up and spouted some nonsense about violation of article number 37B of my severance contract, and blah, blah, blah….

I hadn't done anything wrong. Someone just wanted to get rid of me. They wanted to get me as far from Earth and my old connections as possible.

And I had not a single fucking clue why.

Sure, I knew things. In my position, I had to be a master at reading people and politics, at knowing the ins and outs of every situation and what motivated all the players. I probably knew something that could ruin someone's life. But who? And why had they suddenly decided that I was a problem *now*, after I'd been out of the political game for years without any issue.

I might never know. Of course, I was going to try to figure it out, eventually. But for now, I had to focus on just surviving. On figuring out my current surroundings and how to best integrate myself into this culture. I'd keep my head down and get myself established. Maybe get a job, some housing, make some friends. Try to find some allies.

Then I'd start working on my whys and hows—if I even cared enough to put the effort into solving the puzzle. Who knew? It might be safer and easier to just stay here in the middle of nowhere for the rest of my life.

I stopped outside the gates of the little village. And yes, I mean *literally* little. It had looked further away. My brain just assumed the height of the buildings was a trick of perspective. It wasn't.

My eyes were probably embarrassingly wide as I took it all in. I mean, look, I'm not the galaxy's most inconspicuous person. Especially not at that moment, in full stage makeup, a blue cotton dress covered in rhinestones, white knee-highs with little silver bows on the tops, and chunky-soled hiking boots. And after a long day's hike, I probably *also* looked dirty and deranged. But this place….

I warily eyed the bubblegum pink walls. Why did a little village in an idyllic countryside need walls? Were there dangerous animals out there? Were the townsfolk in the middle of a feud with the neighboring burgs? Toto had no info on the little village. Good thing I had made it here in a single day's walk. I shuddered to think what unknown threat came out at night and necessitated a wall.

I had been in military service for ten years, but I was never a fighter. I had basic training, sure, but I was a diplomat, a spoiled, pampered talking head. I was under no illusion that I was some hardened soldier who could survive in any terrain.

I put Toto to sleep and tucked him away in my knapsack for safe keeping. Then I squared my shoulders and walked through the gates. I was stopped by a pair of men in bright yellow uniforms with short jackets and enough tassels to make even the most over-the-top queen flinch. The outfits clashed a bit with the men's slightly greenish skin. They both came up to about the level of my sternum.

Which I supposed explained the short buildings and the tiny, thatched cottages all around the outskirts of the village.

"Name, direction, and business," one of the guards said, gesturing at me with a glittery baton thing that I was fairly certain was a pretty little taser.

Well, looked like the translator implant was working, at least. There was just that slight millisecond delay between hearing and understanding. And when I spoke, I knew I'd have to get used to the way the nanodes altered my words on the way to my mouth before I spoke to them.

Brain manipulation at its finest. Getting the expensive, military class device installed had been part of my diplomat onboarding, absolutely necessary for being able to negotiate with species who didn't speak interstellar standard. I could have refused brain augmentation and settled for lower rank—many did, fearful of the procedure. But I thanked the damned stars I'd been a reckless kid fresh out of school. Because it was saving my ass now.

I gave the guards a curtsy. I was dressed the part, might as well stay in character. "Dotty West," I said in a husky alto. "I was sent here by EARTH to…relocate." I wasn't exactly sure what EARTH had told the local governments about me—probably nothing. Technically, it was illegal to cast off your exiled refuse without letting the other planet know. Usually, they'd say something like "relocation" or "refugee" or "asylum." They'd use words meant to convey "We don't want them, so we dumped them on your garbage planet, but they aren't hardened serial killers. Good riddance."

The guards immediately stiffened. "West?" the nearest one nearly shouted. "What do you want here?"

I arched my perfectly—at one point yesterday—plucked and penciled brows. "My last name is West, yes. Like I told you, I was sent here by the EARTH military. You know, the organization encompassing a little blue planet and its resultant colonial planets? Loud. Lots of money and angry humans?"

I got a wand thing pressed into the small of my back in response. "Come on."

I sighed, but didn't argue. I was bigger than the guards, but they had the weapons. Plus, I really didn't even know what we were fighting about. So, I just let them march me through the gates and into the center of the village. Going peacefully would probably mean talking to someone in charge without spending a night in jail.

The buildings got weirder and more colorful as we went. We passed other denizens of the place, all of them vaguely humanoid but uniformly small of stature and dressed in the most amazing colors and shapes.

I frowned. It was a bit strange, not seeing any other non-Ozma species here. It seemed to be nothing but natives. On a planet that had been colonized—even one as potentially divided as this one—you would normally expect to see a mix of various types of people. Most planets that interacted with the EARTH planets or IMAD had a varied population from all over the galaxy, a cacophony of sizes, shapes, colors, and languages that was both dizzying and exciting to my traveling diplomat's heart.

So, this…this was odd. Apparently, the natives were more reclusive than I thought.

The townspeople stared openly at me as I was directed to the short, light pink stone building in the center of town, but when I looked around, I saw nothing but happy, smiling faces. The doorway and ceiling of the pink building were tall enough for me to enter without ducking, but just barely. Interesting, because I was pretty sure I would have had to bend down to get into most of the other houses and buildings we had passed. Why was this building built for tall people?

This place seemed to be an office of some sort, with a little reception desk at the front. One of the guards nodded and hurried off, probably to return to his post. The other one addressed the waiting secretary in his smart cobalt blue suit with the rhinestone collar. The residents of Oz certainly had *flair*, I'd give them that.

"We need an immediate audience with the good witch," the guard intoned.

I stifled my smile. Ah yes, the witches. To the natives, advanced technology or innate biological ability to manipulate energy was probably viewed as magic. Although, from the little I'd read about the planet during my lovely little pod trip, the term "witch" here meant something different than it did back on Earth. A person of power, and a person *in* power. It was a title of office, as much as a designation for a magic worker.

It was an astounding and wonderous thing, when humans took to the skies and encountered alien races. Some humans, like mystics and the odd scientific anomalies, were able to manipulate energy in ways most could not. But they were the exception to the rule, the wild stories or interesting rarities. But space travel revealed that there were whole *species* out there who could utilize energy in a way that could only be explained to humans as...magic. While some tight-laced scientist types insisted on calling it energy manipulation, the common interpretation in standard intergalactic translator speak was "magic."

My Terran biases made it hard to wrap my mind around the concept. But apparently, the people of Oz didn't have the same problem. Every culture had its nuances. I just took it all in without judgment. As much as possible. If there was one thing my time traveling and working with the diplomatic branch of the EARTH military had taught me, it was to expect my mind to be blown at every turn. Weird was just…normal, really.

Soon enough, I was ushered into a plush office where I was greeted by a redheaded bipedal person in a glittering purple pantsuit. Her presentation said "female" to my Terran sensibilities, but I knew that was more about me than her. Other species didn't necessarily have Terran anatomy or Terran ideas about gender. She wore a headband that reminded me of a tiara, and long strands of diamonds glittered in her long earlobes.

"Welcome to Moonkin City, she said with a warm smile and that twittery sort of voice some people had. "I am Lady Stella-donna, Witch of the North. Please, sit down and tell me how you've arrived in my little city."

I sank down into a chair what was just big enough for a human male of medium stature, setting my knapsack aside. Right. The directions. North meant this was head of the planet Nibfar's colonial interests here on Oz. They called her the "good witch" because her people were known to be fair and peaceable, and she got on well with the natives. That probably explained why this village was so filled with native people. I relaxed a bit.

The four planets with colonies on Oz were Nibfar, Svaarnia, Eton, and Valklon—known on-planet as North, South, East, and West respectively because of their original areas of colonization. North and South were known to be generally friendly and welcoming. The East colony was fairly neutral, from what I understood. But the West colony was rumored to be cold, suspicious of everyone, not willing to negotiate or work well with the others.

I had been sent to the north. But I couldn't be exactly sure that was where I had landed, what with my exciting entry into the Ozma-4 atmosphere and all. That cyclone had been downright demonic.

If this person was Stella-donna, then I *had* actually made it to the north area. I was in a place where I stood a good chance of being accepted and making a place for myself. I could work with this. So, I truthfully explained my situation.

Well, most of it. Sort of.

It wouldn't do to be *too* naïve—no matter what my current girly-girl, midwestern costume implied. I had been sent here for some political reason I didn't fully understand. Looking into Stella-donna's perfect, smiling face, I made a snap decision.

No one here knew me as anything other than Dotty West—which, yeah, in retrospect, that last name was unfortunate, but what's a girl to do? So, I would just *be* Dotty. No one needed to know about Daniel Xavier Westerfield the Eighth, decorated and once-beloved ex-EARTH diplomat. Maybe that way I could stay off people's radar until I figured out what had gone so wrong and why I was here.

So, I told Stella-donna I had hitched a ride with an EARTH ship by way of some questionable connections with a friend in the military service. I had been looking to escape my boring life (and a bad breakup) back on Earth, I told her in my best airhead voice, but I had been found out by the EARTH ship's captain. I told her how my escape pod had crashed when he kicked me off his ship, and that I was currently stranded on Oz without much in the way of resources.

Stella-donna took all of this with the calm patience of an understanding parent when faced with a weird, wild youth. “There is nothing worse than a broken heart,” she said, commiserating with my bad breakup story. “It makes us do things we’d never otherwise consider.”

Crazy things like run away to a distant planet, she meant.

I smiled sadly at her. “That it does.”

She reached out and took my hand, giving it a squeeze. “We will make you feel at home here, Dotty, you’ll see. Oz is a wonderful planet, where you can be at ease. We’re not driven by the greed and capitalism you’re used to. Here, we are all about living happily in the moment.” She winked. “I think you’ll find all your worries just melt away when you’re surrounded by people who want nothing more than to be happy. The native way of being is contagious.”

I grinned back at her. “I hope so. Because I’m sure sick of my old ‘way of being.’”

I didn’t mention the outcome of my unfortunate crash landing. I needed to figure out what the local views were on involuntary manslaughter and whether they favored the death penalty for offenders before I went there.

“I’m sure you’re tired from your travels,” the witch of the north said sweetly. Rising, she gestured toward the door. “Come, I’ll direct you to an inn where you can rest and fill your belly. We’ll deal with everything else tomorrow.”

I nodded. Dusk was falling fast. I was grungy and starving. Not to mention, sore and tired. “I’d appreciate that. But…I don’t have much in the way of money. Just a bit of EARTH-issue coin." It would be tradable on a larger, more advanced planet. But the currency was probably close to worthless here.

She smiled that motherly smile again and patted me on the back, the lines at the corners of her eyes crinkling. "Never fear. For now, you are our guest. We'll work out the rest later."

I didn't like not knowing what I'd end up owing these people for my food and lodging, but it seemed that they valued hospitality and kindness here. So, I'd take the charity for the night, at least. "Thank you."

Then I was handed off to a moonkin assistant to show me to the inn. She was wearing an orange vest with a high, stiff collar over a diamond patterned blue and green unitard. "Work it, girl," I muttered under my breath.

All things considered, my first day exiled on an alien planet could have been worse.

But we'd see what tomorrow had in store for me. I had a feeling it couldn't be this easy.

Chapter 3

Thankfully, there was one inn in town that was able to comfortably accommodate a small-to-average-sized human male. I hadn't been looking forward to sleeping with my feet dangling off the bed or scrunched up like a shrimp…but hey, anything was probably better than sleeping outside with whatever the city walls were built to keep out.

My clothes were taken away to be laundered, and after a blissful soak in steaming, bubbly water enhanced with whatever "magic" or tech they used around here to produce such things without obvious electricity, I fell into bed naked and slept like the dead.

The bath had helped ease the encroaching muscle soreness caused by crash-landing then walking for hours to reach the city, and my nanodes no doubt sped up the healing. But when I woke up in the morning, everything was seized up. I groaned and rolled out of bed, dragging a sheet around my hips before going to answer the knock at the door.

A sweet-cheeked woman in a neon green dress with a frilly puce apron looked up at me with a smile, holding out my clean, folded clothes. "Your laundry, uh…ma'am."

I thanked her and took my things, closing the door behind her. As I got dressed, I ran a hand over my face, glad that one of the few belongings in my knapsack was my dilapidator and my cosmetics. For once, I was glad I'd been at the drag show when they snatched me. It meant my bag contained all the things I needed to remain Dotty, rather than transforming back into plain, boring old Daniel.

I pulled on my now clean bustier, booty shorts, thigh-highs, and cotton dress. Then I yanked on my borrowed hiking boots once more. Freshly electrolocized and wearing an almost *demure* amount of makeup, I packed up my things and headed out to see what I could make of the place.

The inn fed me breakfast—some sort of sauteed vegetable matter with what I wasn't going to examine too closely, but suspected was cooked insects on top, and a side of something fruity. I pulled Toto out far enough to discreetly check for toxins, not surprised when he told me not to eat the cute little blue flower petals that were sprinkled over everything. Just because an alien race could eat something did *not* mean a human cold.

I picked the flowers off, re-scanned just to be sure, then I ate the rest like a ravenous beast and said thank you to my hosts. It might have had a strange appearance and texture, but the food tasted fine. I was an ex-diplomat…I was used to accepting what was offered to me, smiling, and eating as politeness dictated. I did get a couple of weird looks over the discarded flower petals on my plate, but it wasn't like I was going to poison myself just to be polite.

Breakfast finished, I headed out to explore the little village. I had to duck my head to enter the shops, and I didn't have the money to buy anything. But I looked my fill, taking in the way people interacted, how they spoke with one another, all the little customs and mannerisms that could tell you so much about a place.

One thing I could say of Moonkin City—they certainly *were* happy folk.

I nodded to the smiling man on the sidewalk as I crossed the road toward an elaborate fountain in the square. Something was bothering me. I knew it was probably just a cultural thing. But these people were *smiley*. I mean, I was from the American Midwest on Earth…we were known for our weird, almost dangerous hospitality and our penchant for smiling at strangers, but these people were over-the-top, even to someone of *my* upbringing.

I was just about to go hunt for Lady Stella-donna, when a man in a purple suit with a tall, curly red mohawk appeared at my side. "Excuse me, miss Dotty," he said with a polite smile and a nod, "but the good witch would like a word with you. She says she has papers for you to fill out so we can get you a place to stay."

I hadn't exactly said that I wanted to *stay* in this little village. But I supposed it was a start until I learned more about the culture and figured out where to go from here. I nodded to the man and stood.

He held out a little napkin-wrapped pastry with more of those little blue flowers baked into it. "She sent this, in case you hadn't had breakfast yet."

I took the pastry with a polite nod, but tucked it into my pocket to throw away later, unwilling to risk offending the guy by telling him their delicacy was inedible.

We had almost reached the offices of the good witch when a fireball erupted directly in our path.

My companion squeaked and took off running, his little legs pumping as fast as they could, the long tails of his violently purple jacket flapping behind him. I glanced around to find that everyone had either disappeared or collapsed down into a prone, prostrating position at the arrival of the fireball.

I had quite a bit of practice not externally reacting to internal alarm bells. I stood at ease while I tried to assess the nature of this new emergency, ignoring the sensation in my gut that urged me to run and hide.

A sharp, commanding voice rang out in the square. “Stella! Come out, come out, you grinning bitch!”

The fireball died down, the trailing smoke it left behind clinging to the long black skirts of the person who stood in the square. She—at least I was assuming they were a she—was tall, with light blue skin, angular features, and an epically long, knife-edged nose. A jaunty black hat with a glinting, deep green jewel in the band sat atop her glossy blue-black hair.

Now this…*this* was what a witch was supposed to look like. She was like something from a storybook my nanny had read to me as a child.

And here I was, standing right between her and the building where Stella-donna resided. Our eyes met, her angry silver gaze burning into me.

“What are you?” she demanded, pacing forward. Wow, the skirts of her long black dress and loose strands of her long blue-black hair even billowed behind her when she moved. Impressive showmanship.

I held up my hands and gave her my best diplomat’s smile, then remembered I was in drag and added a cocked hip for good measure. “Just a visitor, Sweetcakes.” I shuffled to the side. “I’ll just…”

The door behind me opened with a bang, and Stella-donna, paragon of goodness and mom smiles glided out to stand beside and slightly in front of me. “What are you doing in my city, West?” she said, her voice just as sweet and syrupy as ever.

West. Interesting. So, this was the “wicked” witch. The problem child of the colonies. I stayed where I was, eager to learn more about the dynamics here. Even if part of me was really starting to wonder if magic was really real, and if maybe getting out of the line of fire might be a smarter course of action.

I shoved the military training aside. There was tea about to be spilled here, girl. I was *not* going to miss this show.

“My sister is dead,” the wicked witch snarled, her long-fingered hands clawing inward with her rage. Those hands had too many fingers, but I didn’t have the attention to spare for counting. “Her body was found under a space pod!” Those searing gray eyes narrowed further, darted to the side, pinned on me. “And here you are with an alien guest, North. Harboring a murderer?”

Shit. Should have got while the getting’ was good, Dotty.

“I have no idea what you’re talking about,” Stella-donna said calmly.

Then she glanced at me like a sweet, patient parent waiting for their kid to spill their guts over that broken window and the rogue baseball, or something. I swallowed. “Well, um. You see, I was going to explain this all to you today, Lady Witch. I simply needed to get my bearings and assess the local norms and customs.”

The wicked witch snarled, and a green flame appeared in her hand.

I held up my hands and played at being a complete airhead. “I’m sorry! Really, I am. It was an accident. I barely made it to the surface *alive*. My pod lost thrusters and I was caught in a tornado. You know? Cyclone? Twister thing? Surely someone saw that storm yesterday!" I glanced around, but all the moonkins were still hiding. "Anyway, I crash-landed, and when I left the site, I may have noticed that there was…a casualty."

Stella-donna's sweet expression simply looked saddened as she patted my shoulder. "An unfortunate accident."

But the wicked witch of the west? She looked like she was going to strip the meat from my bones with her bare hands. "You killed my sister! And you just…failed to mention it to the local authorities? Who sent you? Who do you work for?" She paced closer. "If this bitch sent you, you wouldn't be stupid enough to hide here in her town, would you…."

Stella-donna held up her hands. The moonkins had slowly started to come out of hiding, watching in clusters from behind every convenient bush, sculpture, or brightly painted trash bin.

"There you go, West," the good witch said soothingly, "jumping to conclusions again. Surely you can see this was an accident. How could our new friend here have known your sister would be passing by? How could she have purposefully maneuvered her injured craft to land on her in the middle of one of the storms? You know how sudden and unpredictable the cyclones are."

The wicked witch snarled and lobbed a green fireball at Stella-donna's head. The good witch gestured, and a burst of purple glitter extinguished the flame. "Your magic won't work here behind my protections, West," she said sweetly. "Nothing but smoke and magic tricks. Now scurry on home to stew on your conspiracy theories and your bitterness." She clapped her hands. "Be gone!"

The wicked witch pinned me with that silver glare. "I will learn the truth," she promised in that dark alto voice. "You can't hide here in this happy little village forever."

She turned her glare on Stella-donna. "And you! Be warned. I *will* find a way through your protections and glamours one day. Then your head will part ways with your body."

The fire flared again, and when it was gone, so was the wicked witch of the west.

I let out a shaky breath. As far as getting off to a good start in my new community, this was just going off with flying colors, wasn't it? "Fuck."

Stella-donna regarded me with a soft, sad smile. "I'm afraid you've made a powerful enemy, Dotty. Though I'm surprised she is so convinced this horrible thing was done on purpose." She patted my shoulder, then leaned in, her sweet voice conspiratorial. "Did you perhaps…take something off the body? A token or charm belonging to the witch?"

She frowned. "It is strange that the witch of the east would be passing so close to the center of our territory without my knowledge. Perhaps she was carrying something to the west and that's what has the wicked witch so upset."

I shook my head. "I didn't see anything," I said immediately. "But it wasn't like I really saw much of the body…you know, it being under my pod and all."

I wasn't going to mention the boots. Because, come on. I doubted the wicked witch of the west was on a rampage because of a pair of stolen hiking boots. I mean…wasn't it a little odd that *Stella-donna* thought it was strange for the wicked witch of the west to be mad that her sister had been murdered by falling space debris? I know *I'd* sure as shit be irrationally angry if that was my relative lying pancaked out there in the field….

I was silent as the witch of the north called an impromptu meeting with the mayor, right there in the square. Then both of them announced to the gathered citizens that the “wicked” witch of the east was dead.

I had never heard anyone but the witch of the *west* described as evil. All the reports I’d read labeled the colony to the east “neutral” at worst.

But the citizens of Moonkin took the news of my accidental murder with apparent joy. They beamed their biggest smiles, and food and drink flowed in the town square as an impromptu celebration erupted.

“The precious things,” Stella-donna whispered to me as I looked on in confusion. “They’ve been so oppressed by the constant pressure from the other colonies around us, especially the east and west. Let them have their moment of joy.

Her pretty face was full of understanding, and she turned to smile along with the townspeople when they came up to speak with her.

But when I tried to draw away, to find a quiet moment to think in peace, she caught my arm. “Dotty,” the smiling redhead said, pulling me into a quiet corner between a decorative shrub and a little bench. “I think you should leave.”

I looked up into her cornflower blue eyes. “Do you?” I said innocently. “But West said she’d be after me the moment I left the village.”

Her smiling facade dropped, and she gripped my shoulder in one warm hand, giving it a squeeze. “You’re sure you took nothing from the witch of the east?”

I shook my head. “I did *not*…riffle the corpse for valuables or magic trinkets!” What was going on here?

She nodded. “Then you have no reason to fear the witch of the west. Her bark is worse than her bite, I promise.”

She smiled again. “Tomorrow we shall see you off. Perhaps you’ll find one of the bigger cities suits you. I hear the Emerald City is fond of taking in…refugees from other planets. Maybe you’ll fit in better there?”

Her words said “refugees,” but her tone said “refuse.” Clearly, I’d outstayed my welcome.

I plastered on my best politician’s face and called on my best acting skills. Smiling a sweet smile, I nodded. “If there are other Earthlings there, maybe I’ll feel more at home. Thank you for your help!”

She patted my shoulder and returned to the festivities.

My gut churned. What the hell was going on here?

Chapter 4

I had trouble sleeping that night, my mind whirling with all the random, useless scraps of information I knew about the planet of Oz and everything that had happened since I arrived. I dragged my butt out of bed before the sun was fully up, then pulled Toto out of my knapsack. He barked at me happily, but once again failed to connect with the IMAD space station. I let him float alongside me so my pack wouldn't be so heavy, double-checked that I had all my stuff, then headed downstairs.

The inn staff had been so welcoming just yesterday, but today they were cold and off-putting. They handed me a lukewarm piece of toast and flatly refused my request for something to take with me on the road. No poison flowers this time, at least.

I had a sinking feeling in my gut. I could read the situation. I knew what was coming.

I stepped out onto the street, surprised to see so many people up and about this early in the morning. They were too happy and dopey most of the time to seem like the kind to rise early and eagerly get to work. I certainly hadn't gotten the impression that rising early was the done thing, yesterday morning. But now, eyes followed me, and I started gathering a crowd of onlookers as I made my way through the center of town to the gates.

"Good morning, my sweet hunk of manly meat," I said to the short, round guard at the gate. "Which way to the Emerald City?" I batted my lashes at him for extra effect.

He grunted. "Follow the yellow brick road," he muttered, pointing.

I flinched, hunching my shoulders when something hit me in the back of the head. A moldy bread roll tumbled past my feet. Yep. As I suspected, the townsfolk were pissed.

I held up my hands. "Going," I called out. "No need to waste the foodstuffs."

A squishy pink fruit hit my shoulder, the juice dribbling down my arm in sticky rivulets. Damned thing better not stain my dress!

They all laughed. I glanced over to find the path back into the village filled with grinning, jovial faces. Ha! See? I *knew* those fucking smiles were wrong.

They weren't just overjoyed at the thought of pelting me with shit and running me out of town. No. That would have been different—the awful, but unfortunately common mob mentality. But the Moonkins wore the *exact* same expressions as they always wore. It was as if…as if they literally couldn't feel anything but blissed out as they went about whatever they were doing.

Even pelting a stranger with produce.

Okay...

I turned and jogged down the yellow road in the direction indicated by the guard. Hopefully Stella-donna was right, and I'd get a warmer reception in Emerald City. I was really doubting her motives right about now, but what else was I going to do? I didn't know jack squat about this place, really.

So, I plodded down the bright yellow brick-looking road, *away* from Moonkin City.

I walked and *walked*, over the hilly landscape, past brightly colored fields of flowers and what I thought might be fruit or vegetables. This wasn't Kansas, for sure, but maybe not all *that* different when it came to the miles of rolling fields. My home state was once known for its farms. It had evolved into an overpopulated place, just like the rest of old Earth. But in Kansas, every roof and available flat surface was covered in bot-run farms that grew the latest genetically modified corn. Some things never *really* changed. They just…evolved.

Eventually, I crested a hill covered in rolling, endless acres of something that looked like a cross between sweetcorn and sunflowers—tall green stalks with oblong bunches of something orange growing on them.

I was ravenous by then. I only had a couple of ration packets left from the space pod, and the villagers hadn't seen fit to provide me with food—other than the rotten stuff they used as ammunition when I left. I only had a very rudimentary knowledge of what was edible, and Toto's database wasn't limitless. I'd have to start testing things eventually. Might as well start now.

I stepped over a knee-high wooden fence that belonged to some farmer I was about to steal from, and reached up to grasp a tall green stalk. Pulling the plant down to eye-level, I thought I recognized the orange thing on top as something I'd been served in the Moonkin village. I broke off the fruit and started pulling off the little protective layers around it to get at the edible bit so I could run it by Toto.

A blood-curdling shriek startled me so badly that I dropped the fruit and nearly tripped over the fence behind me. The sound rang out again, somewhere between human and the shrieking of some sort of big bird of prey. It was terrifying. But on further hearing…it sounded like a creature in pain.

I sighed at my stupid impulses. "Girl," I muttered to myself, digging around in my pack to get out the small jackknife I always had on me—a leftover habit from my time as a traveler. "You just don't know when to walk *away* from the drama."

Then I headed further into the field.

A cluster of dark orange birds about the size of Earth crows was gathered around one of the plant stalks, milling and whirling in the air before diving in to attack something. Another one of those inhuman shrieks had my hackles standing on end. Then a burst of what I can only describe as…black light…burst from the middle of the melee. The birds took off, a couple falling from the sky dead as the rest flew for safer altitudes.

What they left behind was…a surprise.

A person had been tied to a pole, staked out in the middle of the field. Their head flopped forward, chin-length black hair sticking up in spikes and falling in clumps around a blood-streaked face as they half-panted, half sobbed.

The hands weren't human…bumpy textured black skin that ended in…bird talons? Their ragged clothes were torn and faded. I crept closer. "Are you okay?"

Dumb question. But what else do you say in situations like this?

A harsh, startled sound escaped the creature's throat and their head lifted. Yellow eyes met mine, keen and bird-like in a masculine-looking face. They had feathers in their hair, iridescent black feathers that fanned out from their temples, framing a lean face. And wow. *Okay.* Their mouth was like some combination between human lips and a bird beak. Their skin was a rich golden-brown color, but it looked bruised.

"Who?" they managed, the voice deep and rich, but the word sounding weird and a bit mangled coming from that half human, half bird face.

I crept closer. "A traveler," I said, somehow staying in character despite the stressful turn of events. Playing Dotty was second nature to me at this point. I could keep up the act all day. "Just a girl down on her luck, on her way to the Emerald City."

I stopped a couple feet from the bird person. "You…who the hell did this to you? Why are you up there?"

Was he some sort of criminal? Given recent events, I wouldn't be surprised to find out the locals had a nasty sense of justice. But was this guy being punished for some really horrible crime? Or was he like me—just in the wrong place at the wrong time?

He huffed a tired sigh, opened and closed that weird mouth, then finally managed, "scarecrow," in that resonant voice.

I blinked at him. "You're…a scarecrow?"

He closed his bright yellow eyes, sagging further on his post. "Made. To scare. Crow people...." The translator lagged over whatever he was saying. "Bird people." He opened his eyes and gave me a sad smile. "Cursed."

Ah. Yes. Okay. Curses. Magic. Not in Kansas. Got it.

"Are you a good witch, or a bad witch?" I asked the bird guy dryly, one hand on my hip. "Cause, let me tell you, my fine feathered friend, I am a little confused by the definition of 'good' and 'bad' in this place. I don't think those words mean the same thing here as they did back home."

The *scarecrow* huffed again. It looked like he tried to shrug, but couldn't, thanks to his current position. Had to be painful. "Down?" he asked hopefully.

I shrugged. Why the fuck not? "Just…don't try to eat me or something. I *am* just a poor, defenseless lady."

He arched a black brow at that, then snorted.

I huffed a laugh and circled around behind him, looking for a good way to get him down. "Yeah, everyone's a critic. Hang tight, sugar. Pun intended. I'll get you down."

It took a few tries. But eventually, I just cut through the thick ropes holding the scarecrow, and he went crashing to the ground. Not the most graceful or gentle rescue in the world. But effective, all the same.

When he didn't do much more than groan and hug his knees, I decided he probably wasn't about to attack me. I tucked my knife away and bent, getting my arm around his skinny waist and his arm over my shoulders. Then I heaved him to his feet. "How long you been up there?" I asked, politely ignoring how bad the poor thing smelled. The diva in me was really hoping my dress didn't get stained. Some habits are hard to break, even when you're not on stage.

"Two?" he panted as I steered him over the low fence and got him sitting on the gentle slope beside the road.

"You were stuck up there fighting off birds for *two days?*" I said, appalled.

He shook his head and ran a hand over his face, pushing the long, lank hair back out of those yellow eyes. "Weeks," he said, his speech still sounding odd with his weird mouth. I could sense my translator nanodes struggling.

I blinked at the scarecrow in surprise. "How the fuck are you even alive after two weeks?"

He shrugged and lifted a hand, letting out a tired, faded puff of that dark purple-black light. "Magic?"

I rubbed my forehead. "Okay. Magic." Who knew what this person's alien physiology was like? He was probably just really hardy.

I retrieved the fruit I had dropped earlier, then got another and returned to sit beside the…scarecrow. I offered him one of the fruits and he took it, awkwardly munching on it with his weird mouth.

"Safe for humans, do you think?" I asked, gesturing at the fruit. At the scarecrow's nod, I dug into my own food, enjoying the sweet-sour bursts of juice on my tongue. "My name's Dotty," I said between bites of fruit. "Is there something I should call you, other than 'scarecrow?'"

He tried several times before he managed to get out words that the translator could parse, thanks to his rough voice and his weird beak mouth. But eventually I got "Singing Crow."

Probably not his actual name, but an approximation based on words I would recognize. I smiled at him. "That's a pretty name. I like it."

He huffed. As if the idea of his name being pretty was ridiculous. "Dotty," he mumbled, frowning when he completely mangled the word.

I laughed and patted him on the back. "Close enough."

When we finished, I glanced at my new friend. "Are you safe here? Will whoever did this to you catch you and put you back up there?" I gestured back at the post behind us.

He hunched his skinny shoulders and sighed. "Leave."

I nodded. "Probably a great idea." I have no idea why I offered, but I found myself opening my big fat mouth. "I'm headed to the Emerald City. I hear there might be more humans like me there. Less angry Moonkins."

He snorted a laugh. "Smiley, smileys."

I nodded in agreement. “You’ve got that right. No place for a refined girl like me.”

He shook his head, but those yellow eyes seemed amused. “Wizard?”

I frowned at them. “Wizard?”

He frowned back and waved his oddly graceful bird hands. “Wizard. Of. Oz.”

Some bit of information floated up from the recesses of my mind. “Oh! Maybe? I’m not sure if he’ll be able to help either of us, but it’s worth a try?”

The Wizard of Oz was the fifth player it the political landscape. But one I’d almost forgotten about. He supposedly represented the interests of the planet itself. Some weird native belief system that I didn’t really understand. Most of the info I’d read glossed over his role as inconsequential. But one source claimed he was a powerful magic worker who was able to answer any question or provide for any need—for a price.

Hell, if anyone could get me answers and possibly lift a curse? Probably that guy. Maybe. Who the hell knew? If nothing else, he sounded like someone who knew who to deal with and how to get what you wanted on this backward little planet. Probably a good person to get to know, if you were a banished ex-Earth citizen looking to make a name for yourself and solve the riddle of why you were banished.

Curses? Who knew? But the crow…scarecrow…person could probably do with a change of scenery.

“Do you want to go with me?” I asked, standing and looking off toward the forest that loomed along the distant reaches of the yellow brick road. I had no idea how far away the Emerald City was. It might be a good thing to have a native along to alert me to the dangers of this place.

Singing Crow swallowed, the long column of his graceful throat working. Then he nodded once and held out a hand… talon…thing. I grasped it, feeling the rough skin and the way the claws curled around my own fingers. I tugged the bird person to his feet. He was wobbly. To be expected after hanging from a fucking pole for *two damned weeks.* So we went slow. I supported him when he needed it, and his steps grew steadily stronger, much faster than I had expected.

“You really are magic,” I teased him once he was walking along at a good clip under his own steam. “I would be dead if I was hung out there like that for so long.”

He cocked his head in that birdlike way of his, probably trying to interpret what I was saying. “Yes,” he said simply, then he turned and led me into the forest.

Chapter 5

The forest seemed to stretch on forever. Eventually, what little light filtered down through the canopy of trees over the road began to fade. My freaking legs were fading too. I have some fabulous gams, don't get me wrong. This body was sculpted to perfection with frequent gym days. But I was *not* used to long-distance treks fueled only by one measly piece of toast, some fruit, and half a space ration.

I was done in.

Singing Crow drew to a halt as the light began to fade. "Water," he said, pointing off the path toward what appeared to be glimpses of a little stream.

I smiled and stepped off the path, but the scarecrow caught my upper arm in a firm grip, his yellow eyes searching my face. "Careful."

I nodded, giving him a serious look to let him know I understood, that I wasn't as ditzy as I often sounded to the unsuspecting. "Got it. I'm staying with you. And we're keeping the road in sight. Any dangerous flora or fauna I should know about?"

Singing Crow scrunched up his birdish face, thinking. Then he shrugged. "Not here. Probably."

I guess that was as good as I was gonna get. I followed the scarecrow into the woods. He pushed aside some tall bluish-green reeds and I sighed in pleasure. The steam was deeper than I had thought—about knee high—and the water was clear. I fished my empty canteen out of my pack and filled it, then shook it to activate the cleansing device inside. I watched in amusement as Singing Crow started enthusiastically stripping out of his old rags.

He was skinny, but I couldn't deny that he was nicely put together…for a bird…guy…person, with long limbs and ropey muscles. I turned away like a *lady*, before I could ogle any other bits.

I stripped off my own dress, bustier, and the clingy shorts I wore underneath. Thank the stars I'd had the shorts on when they snatched me from Earth. Otherwise, I'd be stuck trekking cross-country in lace and bows. Cute, but not exactly practical.

I piled my stuff to the side, wound my shoulder-length hair up into a knot on top of my head, then turned back to the water. I froze when a clawed hand touched my chest. The scarecrow was standing right there in my space, his head cocked the side, frowning in confusion as he petted my now flat pecs. "Male?"

Oh. I tilted my head back and laughed, letting myself slip out of character and into my own skin, my voice deeper and my stance a bit more masculine. "Uh…yeah. That was just…a costume?"

"Disguise?" he asked, those yellow eyes raking over my naked body.

I licked my lips. Awkward. And weirdly erotic. No. Just awkward. "Hmm…sort of? I mean, I was a performer, back home. And when the EARTH goons took me, they just grabbed me off the stage." I shrugged. "I figured it was easier to keep playing the part."

That was *way* oversimplifying things. I was well aware that this person's inability to form big, long sentences didn't mean he was an idiot. In fact, I was pretty sure the speech impediment hid a razor sharpness.

He narrowed his eyes at me. "Disguise."

I sighed. "Yeah. Disguise." I wasn't sure how much it was safe to share with this alien stranger. But I highly doubted he was involved in anything concerning my EARTH drama. "I don't know why they took me and dumped me here," I admitted. "So, it's probably better if I just keep pretending to be Dotty—uh, female." I shrugged. "And it's not like it's a hardship. I enjoy playing dress up."

He smiled, an odd expression, pinched as it was by his beak. "Yes."

I arched a brow, letting myself look at him in return, since he'd already ogled me. "And you? Are you male as well? I mean, do your people assign genders and such?"

Thankfully, he didn't seem offended by my less than smooth inquiry. "Yes." He patted his skinny chest with a bird hand. "Male."

He turned away, giving me one more side-long glance before he bent and started splashing handfuls of water over his face and body. I followed suit. The water was cold, but it felt good on my sweaty, overheated skin.

When he cupped his hands and went to drink straight from the stream, I reached out and stopped him. "You might get a parasite or something." I pointed back at my canteen. "That's self-cleaning, so we can share."

He shrugged. "Magic." Then he slurped up his protozoa-filled water like it was the finest wine.

Well, each to his own, I supposed. And besides, he lived here. He probably knew what he could and couldn't ingest.

I stood and headed back to the road. We both awkwardly drip-dried for a few minutes, and I gave in to my curiosity. We had talked about our genders. So I could ask about his body, right?

"That's not how you've always looked, is it?" I said, gesturing at his face and his hands. He even had a couple ridges of black feathers on his back along his shoulder blades, reminiscent of wings.

He frowned, looked down at his hands, then shook his head. "Curse. To scare crows."

I tried to look at the words from different angles. Finally, it clicked. "Someone did this to you to scare…someone *called* the crows. Your people? To scare people you call the crow people?"

He nodded, his yellow eyes on mine. "Too much talk. Didn't…rules."

I had a feeling I knew where he was going with this. Though a lot of it was just supposition on my part. "You spoke out against someone you shouldn't have." This man was meant to be a warning to others. Of what would happen if you spoke up.

He looked up at me from under his long black lashes, his yellow gaze full of hatred. "Witch."

Ah. Yep. Colonial oppression. I could totally see that.

"Well," I said as I started dragging my clothes back on. "Full disclosure. I may have pissed off the wicked witch myself. I might, possibly, maybe, have *accidentally*…murdered her sister."

Stepsister, if I remembered my facts correctly. East and West represented different interplanetary interests. But I think they shared a father.

Singing Crow paused, his pants pulled halfway up his legs, a beautifully made, almost human-looking cock and small ball sack on full display. "What?"

I may have taken just a beat too long to answer, to figure out what he was asking me, since I was busy staring at his dick. He pulled his pants the rest of the way up and I got my brain back online.

"Oh. The witch? My pod landed on the witch of the east. Totally random accident. But the witch of the west seemed just a *tad* bit upset about that. And…the witch of the north seemed just a little too pleased."

He huffed and pulled on his dusty old shirt, hiding his lean torso. And man did I need to get laid. Might help with the stress. And the newfound penchant for ogling weird alien crow dudes.

He grumbled something under his breath, but words seemed to fail him and eventually he just shook his head and waved away my questions. Something about the situation with the witches bothered him. But really, what about the situation with the colonial heads *wasn't* bothersome?

We managed to gather up enough dry branches to make a fire near the road, since I had a feeling that would be safer than being out in the woods at night. The scarecrow didn't seem pleased about the fire, glancing to the sky occasionally and frowning.

I put a hand on his arm, drawing his attention back to me. "You think someone will see the smoke and come looking for us? Someone witchy and unpleasant?"

He sighed, shrugged, then gestured at the woods around us. "Better than dark."

I grimaced. "So, I was right about potentially dangerous animals."

His eyebrows rose and he let out a short, unsettling, bird-like laugh. “Yes. No. Spooks.”

I rolled my eyes. Honestly? The guy was afraid of ghosts?

I managed to find a reasonably lump-free patch of ground near the fire and curled up, my jackknife near my head, just in case.

I dozed for a while, but woke to the realization that my head was resting on a hard, dusty lap. I didn’t have much time to ponder why I was sleeping on the scarecrow before I heard the voices.

Eerie shit, let me tell you. They whispered, and moaned, and flittered at the edges of my awareness, whispering a cacophony of accusations and suggestions. I heard snatches of “not good enough,” “not smart enough,” “no brains in that head of yours,” and “deserve to be cursed,” on the heavy night air.

A flicker of pale shapes appeared at the edges of the circle of firelight before Singing Crow moved above me, stretching out a long arm to toss another piece of wood on the fire. The fire flared, and whatever was out there faded back. But the voices continued, worming their way into my head.

“Turn back,” they whispered. “Leave what you took from the witch.” Then, they dug deeper. “You’ll die alone here on this alien planet. No one wants you around. No one really cares what you have to say.”

The whispering voices plucked at my fears and insecurities, worming their way into my brain like icy fingers. And…that was about enough of that bullshit.

I sat up, making the scarecrow lean back on his hands so I didn’t knock him in the chin on the way up. His yellow eyes glowed in the darkness.

“What the fuck?” I asked succinctly.

His cheeks looked flushed in the firelight, and his eyes darted away. “Spooks.”

I sighed. “So I heard. What are they? Surely they’re not ghosts.”

“Worthless,” the voices continued to whisper, “ugly. Deformed. Monster.” The scarecrow flinched and I grabbed his hand, the bird-like talons immediately curling around my own.

“No.” He whispered, his voice ragged. “Not ghosts. Ghosts are…dead? These live. Witch’s people.”

“Oh.” I ignored the whispers that were clearly directed at all my own fears and insecurities. “You’re not really an ugly monster, if it helps. And I’m sure you’re quite intelligent.” I said weakly.

He snorted and squeezed my hand again. I thought I understood how my head had ended up pillowed in his lap. The connection with another living, breathing, tangible person helped drown out the taunting voices.

“You’re not…unwanted,” He replied in return, clearly having heard my own insecurities whispered on the breeze.

And yeah, didn’t that sound pathetic, knowing the deep inner fear the spooks had latched onto in my case was just a stupid need for belonging? Although, there was quite a bit of muttering about leaving whatever I’d taken from the witch of the east behind. What did the wicked witch want with a pair of ratty old hiking boots?

“Thanks,” I muttered.

Singing Crow lifted his free hand to shyly stroke my head, drawing his claws through my long, tangled brown hair. “Who….” He swallowed hard, scowled at his inability to express his thoughts, probably, then heaved a sigh. “Who?”

I cocked my head, and maybe leaned into the petting just a little bit. I did like having my hair combed. It felt nice. Not being *alone* felt nice. I had the stunning talent of feeling alone even when surrounded by a whole meeting room or performance venue full of people.

"Who?" I echoed him, bringing my mind back to the conversation. "Oh, you mean who doesn't want me?" I laughed. "Um. Pretty much everyone? I have skills," I said, knowing it sounded arrogant, but that it was true. "Strengths that people have always wanted to use. But…in the end I'm always just 'too much.' Whatever that means."

I had never had any patience for the little, microscopic gains one often made in politics and diplomatic endeavors. I wasn't happy to settle for baby steps when people's lives and happiness were at stake. My brashness and pushiness often upset the political players. But I also made enough of a splash to bring about rapid reform where needed.

It was the same with the drag gig. I was amazing at giving a performance. But people were always telling me I needed to learn to turn off the persona when I stepped off the stage.

The crow man huffed indignantly, spreading his arms and puffing up his chest. "Not made…to be…quiet."

I stared at him for a beat before I burst out in honest, heartfelt laughter. "No, my friend. We certainly were not!"

He and I might seem different on the surface. But he had apparently been cursed for opening his mouth one too many times, speaking out against some injustice or other, and *I* was stranded here on an alien planet because I had no doubt spouted off to the wrong person or advocated too strongly for the wrong thing at some point in my past. We were both in the situation we were in because we were *too much,* and people were trying to shut us up.

I tilted my head back and howled my laughter, startling some little forest dwelling creatures into a scurry and drowning out the whispers of the spooks. "You hear that?" I shouted to the treetops. "You can try. But you will never shut us up!"

Singing Crow grinned at me, then tilted his head back and let out a loud, piercing trill that made my ears ring.

I grinned back at him as his cry faded off and his laughing eyes met mine. "Listen," I said, nudging his shoulder with my own. "Hear that?"

Silence. No whispers. Only the slow return of the song of the night insects and the crackling of our cheery fire.

"Cowards," the scarecrow said with a haughty lift of his angular chin.

"Of course they are," I said with a nod. "The ones set on silencing the voices of others are always cowards at heart."

He patted my head fondly. "Good…girl? Boy?"

I rolled my eyes. "Sweetie. When I'm wearing a dress, it's 'bad girl.'" I waggled my eyebrows at him. "But when the dress comes off, it's 'good boy.'"

His lips curled up in that pinched smile of his, his riveting yellow eyes sparkling as he glanced at my dress. He patted my head again. "Good bad girl."

I gave him a fierce, queenly look. "Oh, I am."

He tilted his head, glancing down as if gathering his courage, then back up again. He ran one claw along the hem of my dress, his eyes never leaving mine, the question clear. He was wondering if that part about the dress coming off was an offer.

Was it?

I really hadn't consciously meant to flirt. I was just lost in the moment, and as usual I took it too far.

But…those dark lashes lowered, and his cheeks flushed as he drew back, clearly regretting his life choices and feeling the sting of oncoming rejection. And you know what? Fuck it. This guy was kind, I was lonely, and despite his strange bits, he *was* attractive in his own weird way. Who knew what fresh hell would greet us tomorrow? Might as well enjoy today.

I leaned toward him, glancing up for permission before pressing my lips to his exposed collar bone.

He shuddered at the touch of my lips on his golden skin. One hand wrapped around my hip, while the other slid through my hair to cup the back of my head, to keep me close.

I chuckled against his warm skin, moving to straddle him. "I'm not sure how any of this works," I said with a coy look his way. "I mean…obviously I know how sex works. But…I've never fucked a…well, whatever you are."

He rolled his eyes, settling those strange hands on my hips and pressing me closer, grinding his hardness against my own through our clothes. "Similar," he huffed out.

I tilted my head back and laughed. Apparently, I wasn't his first human. My laugh cut off on a husky sound as he leaned in and ran his nose up the side of my throat. I knew he would be trailing kisses there, if he didn't have half a beak. I thought, *stars, I'm about to have sex with someone who's half bird.* Then he nipped at my shoulder, little bites that were a teasing combination of teeth and the sharp prick of his beak. *Aw, fuck it. Bird or not, that's amazing.*

"Dress?" he said, pulling back. He ran a claw down the front of my dress, over the glittery rhinestone buttons. "Boy?" He twisted his lower lip about, managing to sink his teeth into the side of it. Maybe afraid he'd offend me.

I smiled at him, running my hand through his silky black hair, fingers trailing over the small feathers there. "You prefer men?"

He met my eyes, gave a little shrug, then nodded.

I leaned in and kissed the tip of his nose. "That's good. Because I'm not a woman, and I don't think of myself that way. Like I said, this is just a costume. An act."

I unbuttoned my dress, enjoying the way his keen eyes watched me, even though he'd already seen it all earlier when we washed up. Once I tossed the dress and the bustier aside, he ran the flat of his palms up my sides, careful to keep his claws from touching me, his eyes drinking me in like a thirsty man in the desert presented with a tall glass of ice water.

I shuddered at the strange sensation of his slightly rough, wrinkled hands on my skin. It wasn't unpleasant, just…different. My achingly hard dick had no objections, but Singing Crow drew back, his expression concerned, taking those wonderfully strange hands off me. "Sorry."

He had clearly misinterpreted that shudder. I grabbed his wrists and put his hands back on my waist. Then I cupped his face in my own hands, forcing him to look into my eyes as I rocked against him, rubbing my trapped erection against this own. "Does it *feel* like that bothered me, sweetheart?"

He huffed. "No." Then his mouth quirked. "Maybe."

I pressed my forehead to his and chuckled. "Okay, bothered. Definitely hot and bothered. But not *bothered,* bothered."

He slid his hands to my hips, those glowing yellow eyes full of pain. "You…please. Take what you want. I don't…want you hurt." He squeezed his eyes closed and swallowed hard.

I pushed my hands up under his ragged shirt, palms skimming over smooth golden skin and lean muscle, feeling the quiver in his abs as he tensed. “You’re afraid? Scared you’ll hurt me?”

He nodded furiously and I took pity on the poor man—and on my rock-hard dick, which was screaming for attention. “Okay,” I said, tugging his shirt up then off as he obligingly raised his arms. “I’ll take care of us both, babe, don’t you worry.”

He laughed as I pushed him backward, making him sprawl on the questionable comfort of his shirt and my dress over the mossy ground. I got rid of his pants and shoes, then made quick work of my own shorts and ridiculous hiking boots.

Sprawled out naked under me, the crow man was a long, lean work of art, the firelight dancing over him, painting him in orange, and gold, and shadows, picking up the occasional glint of his iridescent feathers. Sure, he could stand to eat a few burgers, but he was still one of the hottest guys I’d ever seen—curse and all.

I sat over him, straddling him as I ran my hands over all that golden skin, pausing to tease his small, dark nipples, loving his little hiss of surprise and the buck of his hips. I was too keyed up and too desperate to take my time the way I’d like, but I forced myself to slow down a *little* bit. The poor man was drinking in every touch like he was starved for it, and I had to wonder how long it had been since someone touched him without the intention to wound or belittle him.

Hell, how long had it been since I’d given myself permission to express genuine affection for a partner like this? Too damned long. Most of my encounters of late had been casual fucks between shows. No one I particularly *liked*, just someone to scratch the itch. And before that…well, no one in my military career circle wanted to be caught fucking the troublemaker. Might jeopardize their own climb up the ranks.

For some reason, this complete stranger felt precious somehow. I could tell he needed me to show him he was worth more than that. Maybe we both needed it. So I slowed down.

I leaned in and nibbled at the corner of his lips, kissing him as best I could with his beak in the way. Then I pressed lingering, teasing, open-mouthed kisses to his jaw and throat, working my way down with lips and tongue, fingers and teeth, worshipping every bit of his skinny frame.

I could be a bit of a drama queen when it came to grooming. But weirdly, I didn't even mind the lingering hint of sweat and musk that clung to him after our hasty creek bath. He was delicious. Addictive.

I rubbed my swollen length against his own twitching cock as I worked my way down his body. He caressed me as well as he could with the bird hands in the way, smoothing his palms over my back and ass, pressing me close and arching up into me with little breathy sounds that went right to my balls.

I slid lower, wiggling between his thighs, licking a teasing, exploratory swipe up his hard length. His equipment was noticeably different from mine, but like he'd said, things seemed to function in similar ways. No foreskin, and no noticeable flare at the head of his dark cock. Just one long, smooth rod. His sack was smaller, tighter, and completely smooth. Otherwise, the differences were negligible.

Hopefully he didn't have poison cum or something. Always a risk with unknown alien species. But earlier, it had sounded like he'd been with a human before. And I was fully inoculated against most things he might give me. I gripped his cock, giving him a long, firm stroke from root to tip as I looked up at him, meeting his intense yellow stare. “This okay? No toxins or… barbs or something I should know about?”

He laughed and dropped his head back onto the ground with a strangled laugh, his hands coming to my head to carefully comb through my hair. “Not. Poison,” he managed in a choked voice. “Not…barbs. No…danger dick.”

I snorted and licked the tip of his cock, which was leaking a pearly drop. “Did you just make a *joke?*”

He huffed and lifted his hips. “Might. Kill. *Me* though.”

I rolled my eyes. “So much drama. I thought *I* was supposed to be the queen here.”

Then I winked at him and swallowed him down like the cock-sucking master I am. His claws raked through my hair and pricked my scalp, the little hint of danger and the evidence of my effect on him making my own dick twitch with need. I hollowed my cheeks and sucked, pulling off slow before diving back down, using my hands and mouth together to bring him right to the brink of release, tension humming through his body.

He curled his long fingers in my hair and pulled harder, panting as he dragged me off his glistening cock and yanked me up into his arms. “Together,” he pleaded, carefully cupping my cock in his palm.

I grinned and pressed another kiss to the corner of his mouth. “Absolutely,” I promised, reaching down to grip both of us in one hand, loving the press and glide of his hard dick against my own, the added friction from my hand.

He wrapped his long fingers around my hand, as if he wanted the illusion that he was the one jacking us off. My spine tingled and my freaking body was on *fire* as orgasm rocketed through me out of nowhere. My forehead pressed into the crook of his neck and shoulder as I spasmed against him, his own hot release joining my own.

I went limp and breathless against him, but he kept his hand wrapped around my own, stroking us both slow and sweet, wringing out every last drop of pleasure until I couldn't stand it anymore.

When he let go, I pressed even closer, gluing us together, not willing to give up the perfect warmth of his body against mine.

He didn't seem to mind my clinginess, nuzzling his face into my hair and letting out a long, contented sigh.

Absurd. Absolutely ridiculous that the most satisfying sex in my life had just been had in the middle of an alien woods with some cursed bird-man. But, well, that was how these things went, I supposed.

The cool breeze tickled my bare skin, and I resolutely dismissed the sensation of eyes on me. I hoped the damned spooks enjoyed the show.

Chapter 6

Morning came way too soon for my liking. Not that I'd actually gotten much in the way of quality sleep, what with napping mostly naked on the hard ground—and on the intermittently hard crow man.

We got up, worked out the kinks and stiffness—and not in that fun sort of way—and rinsed off in the stream again. Then we ate a paltry breakfast made from the few edibles Singing Crow had managed to scrounge up in the woods and one of my two remaining ration bars, split between us to make it last.

I pulled Toto out and tried again to connect to the IMAD station—or hell, even a passing ship at this point. But no luck. I had to admit to myself that whatever was blocking the signal wasn't just storm interference, since today was bright and clear.

I wasn't generally prone to bouts of rage. Diplomacy had been hammered into me from a young age. I was smart enough to know that giving in to anger put you at a disadvantage. But I was hungry, stiff, and tired, and I could feel a tinge of grumpiness creeping in on the periphery as we resumed our trek.

Singing Crow seemed to sense my plummeting mood. He kept giving me sidelong looks from under those long, dark lashes. Finally, I snapped.

"What?" I demanded.

He paused in the middle of the road, startled by my reaction, then hurried after me, his longer legs eating up the distance between us. “I’ve…made. You angry? Regret?”

It was my turn to stop in my tracks. *Honestly. Good going, Dotty.* I was supposed to be good at reading a room. And here I was, oblivious to the fact that of *course* he’d assume my newfound grumpiness was because of him. He was clearly sensitive about his cursed state. If the whispers from the spooks last night were anything to go by, he thought himself a hideous monster who deserved his fate for being too dumb to keep his mouth shut.

I sighed and waited for him to turn back to look at me. “I’m not mad because of you,” I said, walking fast to catch up to him. “I’m mad because I’m tired, and hungry, and I don’t know why I’m even here!” I threw my hands up in frustration. “Last night was….”

What? Last night was what? Weird. Wonderful. Just sex. I mean, it wasn’t like crow boy was suddenly my soul mate because we’d rubbed our dicks together. It was fun. Enjoyable. Comforting? But it wasn’t like we were dating, or engaged to be life mates, or something.

And yet…could I honestly, truthfully say it was nothing but a quick fuck in the woods?

I sighed. “Last night was nice. I’m not sure what it means to you. Or to me. But I’m not *mad* about it. No regrets here.”

His shoulders dropped, releasing a tension I hadn’t noticed until he let it go. “Oh.”

Yeah. Oh. Sometimes the best words were no words at all.

“Do you know how far we have to go before we get to the Emerald City?” I said, dismissing the discussion about our little nighttime encounter.

He ambled along easily at my side. Lawd, wouldn't it be nice to be that leggy without the need for six-inch heels? "Unsure," he said with a frown. "Sixteen? Twenty?"

I sighed. "Hours? Days? Weeks? Months? *Years*?" Nothing would surprise me at this point.

He tentatively reached out and patted my shoulder, his expression full of weary understanding at my snarkiness. "Days."

Great. So, two weeks…maybe three, of walking. Then maybe, *possibly,* we'd get some answers.

I guess it was better than twenty years. Have I mentioned that patience and small degrees of progress toward one's goals were *not* among my strengths?

The forest around us only seemed to get denser as we went, closing in so much that at times, hardly any light filtered through. I was beginning to think maybe there *was* no Emerald City, and we were the victims of an epic prank. We'd walk forever, circumnavigate the damned planet, and end up right back here. In the woods.

Clearly, Dotty the queen had taken over my brain and we would be melodramatic for the rest of our lives.

We walked until darkness closed in, foraging as we went, Singing Crow teaching me what was edible and what was not, which animals were harmless and which to avoid at all costs. Luckily, there didn't seem to be many of the latter category nearby at the moment.

At night, we would curl up by the fire, wrapped in each other's arms as we slept. It was comfortable in a way I just *knew* I'd probably regret once we reached civilization and reality intruded. But for now, I took what happiness I could get.

Our fifth day out, we were just cresting a rise, Singing Crow doing his best to explain to me the difference between the dark red apple in his right hand—edible—and the slightly-more-orange-if-you-squinted-just-right apple in his left—likely to cause explosive diarrhea. The things were the same damned shape and color until they were ripe. And the trees they grew on looked the same to me. So…no apples unless you were absolutely sure they were dark red. Or, you know, just no damned apples at all, just to be safe, thank you very much.

I did *not* envy the first military folk who were down in the rough of it before military grade TOTOs and other fancy tech to do analysis. I wouldn't want to be the one exploring new planets and finding out the hard way that red was *not* the same as slightly red when it came to edible fruits.

Singing Crow insisted the apples were two completely different colors. I paused mid-rant about the nuances of color receptors in the eye and how much they varied between different species, my own gaze drawn by a glint of something in the distance, like sunlight bouncing off metal. "Do you see that?"

He peered ahead. We had established that his vision was much better than mine, after an awkward conversation about how *no I hadn't seen the deadly yellow snake in the middle of the fucking yellow brick road before I almost stepped on it, thanks.*

Singing Crow tilted his head this way and that, like a curious bird. Then he shrugged. "Metal."

I rolled my eyes. "Helpful."

He smirked.

I was beginning to catch on to the fact that not all his smart-assed replies were accidental. Sometimes he played dumb just to get a rise out of me. We continued walking, on the lookout for anything suspicious. But what we found didn't seem dangerous, just…weird.

"Metal man," the scarecrow said with a helpful shrug.

I snorted. "I can *see* that, Mr. Obvious," I said, hands on hips. "But what is it? Is it alive? Dead? Inanimate?"

He sighed. "Witch."

Of course. I paced in a circle around the…statue? The man was taller than Singing Crow, which put my nose at about the level of his upper chest. I wasn't short—I was just so fabulous that a little went a long way, thank you very much. The statue's long, not-metal silver-blonde hair whipped around in the breeze, and he was dressed in real clothes that looked like some sort of lightweight, utilitarian uniform in a light gray color.

He was almost lifelike. Except for the whole being metal thing. Most of his face and one hand were white marble, smooth and flawless. One half of his jaw, cheek, ear, and neck, apparently extending on down to the hand on that side were shiny, sleek metal. The metal hand held a wicked-looking axe, and the way he was posed, silver eyes narrowed, and arms and legs arranged just so, it looked like he was caught in forward motion, an angry automaton frozen mid-lunge.

"Who builds a statue out here in the middle of nowhere?" I muttered. I knew better, really. But I was just not willing to acknowledge what I was seeing.

"Not. Statue." Singing Crow said softly, grabbing the back of my dress and pulling me a little further away from the metal man. "Weapon."

I huffed. I knew I was going to regret asking this. "Is it alive?"

He gave me a sad look, then lifted his hand, letting loose a little flicker of that dark, purple-black energy I'd seen him use when we first met. The metal man…*groaned.*

"Frozen." The scarecrow said tiredly, as if either the state of the world or the use of his magic had drained him. I was guessing it was a little of both.

Okay. Cool. I glanced around me. So, there was a person. Frozen. Out here in the middle of nowhere. And who the fuck knew how long he had been out here? Singing Crow had been tied out on his post for two *weeks* when I found him. This thing might be a weapon, but it was still a living thing. Probably.

"Oh, for fuck's sake," I said, pulling at my own hair. I needed to just keep walking. Get to Emerald City alive. Not go poking at frozen cyborg weapons in the middle of the forest.

"How do we unfreeze him?" I said on an exhale.

Singing Crow sighed, then nodded, as if to say, "Yeah, we're both utter morons, but what are you gonna do?" Then he beckoned me around the back of the metal guy, gathered the thing's long, silver hair, and pulled it out of the way to reveal a little slot in the back of the guy's neck, like a keyhole or a data port. "Switched. Off."

I sighed. "So, someone just came along and what? Pulled his plug?"

He shrugged. "Tech." The look he gave me said, "Fuck if I know."

Luckily, I had at least a bare minimum of knowledge about this stuff. At least enough to know which data ports were universal and which ones needed to be handled with more care.

I hadn't stripped the pod of components for nothing.

I opened my knapsack and turned Toto on, patting his shiny metal dog head when he barked at me. "Okay boy, I'm gonna need you to assist with some soldering. And to double check I'm not about to electrocute myself." His side opened up and the little portable welding iron dropped down.

I dug around in my bag, pulling out several different data cords, an e-pack, and some wire cutters. Examining the guy's neck port again just to be sure, I crouched down in the middle of the road and got to work.

About ten minutes later I stood, grinning like a maniac. This was either going to work, or I was about to fry my *own* circuits. "Better stand back," I told the scarecrow.

He glanced at the manic look on my face, then at the cobbled-together device I held. Then he took a couple of slow steps backward. Smart man.

"Toto," I said, holding the device up to my rotund floating pufferdog. "What do you think? Will this fit that port?"

He barked happily. "It should work sir," his prim voice informed me. "Unless you've botched the seam or there's a hidden security measure inside the AI."

"Well," I said with all the false bravado I could muster, accompanied by a lurid eyebrow wiggle. "Let's see if the big guy likes being on the receiving end!" Then I plugged in the device and waited for the pain.

Nothing happened, and I let out a breath. Cool. Glancing down at the screen of my handheld scanner, I watched as the tech did all the heavy lifting, neatly breaking through any and all security safeguards and giving me full access to some sort of code. I'd learned this little trick on a diplomatic mission gone wrong, when I had to gain access to the controls of a hastily obtained Ultorian escape pod. I frowned at the unit until I was able to decipher which choice was the equivalent of "unlock" and touched the appropriate light sequence on the screen.

I could have hooked the thing to Toto, but there was no way I was going to risk my little pufferdog if it all went sideways. I needed him to talk to the bigwigs at the space station, if we ever managed to get a connection.

The statue in front of me came to life with startling speed and a groan of protesting metal, whirling around so violently he yanked the device from his neck port and sent it tumbling from my hands. See? Good thing that wasn't my dog going for a tumble.

An axe blade hovered at my throat, and *intense* silver eyes flicked from side to side, studying my face while taking in everything around him. "State your purpose."

I sighed, happy to realize that I had *not* just peed myself. "Just passing by," I said with my best eyelash batting and breathy girl voice.

He narrowed those silver eyes at me and pressed closer, kicking the device I'd cobbled together farther away with a toe without even looking down. "You broke into my command port."

I shrugged. "You looked bored out here all by your little lonesome, sugar."

He snorted and whirled away, then stumbled, going to one knee with a clang, that pretty silver-blond hair swirling around him like a cloak.

Singing Crow stepped closer, taking my arm and pulling me back toward the yellow brick road. But of course, I resisted. "Are you okay?" I asked, watching the metal guy struggle to stand.

He didn't reply, just pushed awkwardly to his feet and stood there, rubbing his knee with his non-metal hand and muttering to himself. I crossed my arms and patiently waited until he turned and took a stiff step toward us. I was well used to the stoic soldier type, if that was what this was. Best to just wait them out.

They'd only accept help when they were damned good and ready.

"Knee hurt?" I asked in a bored voice.

He ignored me, making his way to the road, then looking right and left, brow creased in thought. He absently rolled his metal shoulder, the motions stiff and slow.

"Seized," Singing Crow provided helpfully.

I nodded. I supposed being stuck in one position out in the weather for who-knows-how-long might cause some mechanical issues, even if the metal parts looked to be made of a weather resistant material.

"Would mech oil help?" I asked, swinging my pack around again to find the small thumb ring of miracle grease that was used on starships.

The metal man slowly turned his head toward me, his silver eyes still narrowed. "Why?"

His voice was nice. Smooth, but bitchy. My imaginary lady parts agreed that he did bitchy real well. I ignored that little thought and rolled my eyes at the metal man. "Because we were *trying* to help you, sweetheart. Do we *look* like whatever enemy you're supposed to be soldiering against?"

His gaze landed on the scarecrow, and he arched a pale brow. Singing Crow bristled, his mouth twisting into a sneer.

Okay, wrong question, apparently. I held up a hand. "Okay. Stop. I'm not from here. I didn't mean to cause an interspecies incident. How about this?" I crouched and set the mech oil on a nearby rotting log. "I'll just leave this here and we'll be on our way, Captain Shine-and-Growl."

I stood, snatched up my equipment, and joined Singing Crow, taking his arm as we both silently agreed to continue walking. The last thing I wanted to do was get the cursed guy killed by some sort of cyborg soldier with a grudge against bird people. I didn't need any more accidental alien deaths on my conscience.

I didn't look back, but I definitely heard the distinctive little clinks of the thumb pump on the mech oil dispenser.

After we'd put some distance between us, I looked up at Singing Crow, his arm still tucked through mine. "This wizard in Emerald City," I said softly. "How hard is it going to be to get him to meet with us?"

I'd had years of experience cracking the tough nuts, but that was back when I had some political clout myself, and a diplomat's title to wave around. Now I was just little old Dotty West, drag artists and bundle of awesome.

Singing Crow frowned. "Don't. Know."

I sighed. I wished I could talk with him more easily. I felt bad that I was always having to draw conclusions. I could be wrong. And he wasn't really able to explain the gray areas in between absolutely correct and only sort of a little bit right. "Do you mean you don't know anything about the wizard? Or you don't know anything about Emerald City?"

He rubbed the back of his head. "Rumors."

I nodded. He only knew what he'd heard. Which could be completely inaccurate. "Do you think if we—"

"The wizard of Oz is a charlatan." The metal man's voice spoke from *right* behind me, making me jump. "Most likely a fake."

I turned to find him following us. "Um. Hello. Can I help you?"

He held out the little mech oil dispenser, his motions smoother and more fluid than before. I eyed the wicked-looking axe that was now tucked into a little strap at his belt. Then I took the oil.

"The crow people are primitive. They don't often leave their lands," the uptight silver guy said flatly. "This creature can't give you the information you seek."

Singing Crow frowned but didn't comment. We all walked along in silence.

I finally stopped and turned, nearly colliding with a broad, gray-clad chest. "Are you following us now?"

The metal man looked down his perfect alabaster nose at me. "I am walking this way." He pointed up the road in the direction we are headed. "You are in my way."

I huffed. "Oh, cut the crap, honeybunch. If you wanted company, all you had to do was *ask*." I looped an arm through his non-metallic one, drawing him up beside me and the scarecrow.

My boldness earned me a raised silver brow and a frown, but he didn't jerk his arm free or remove my head from my body with his axe, so I counted it as a win. I could feel Singing Crow scowling his disapproval at me from my other side. But I ignored it. I enjoyed the bird-man's company. Absolutely. And he had been quite helpful. But a girl had to grab onto the opportunities presented to her. And this silver opportunity was able to form full sentences and answer all my questions. Even if I had a feeling it was going to take a good bit of prodding on my part.

I needed to learn more about the political mess I had a feeling was brewing on this damned planet, and where the fuck I fit into it all, so I could go the fuck home to Earth.

That was going to require more info than I currently had.

"Now," I said, clinging to the taller man, even as he tried to unobtrusively pull his arm free. "Tell me all about Oz."

Chapter 7

You know how they say to be careful what you wish for? Unfortunately, I had often found that little saying proved true.

I had pinned all my girlish hopes and dreams on learning about Oz. Well, I was learning alright. I just wasn't really liking the picture that was forming in my mind.

The stoic, indifferent metal man—whose name turned out to be Tin'amen —had eventually told us that since he wasn't under anyone's control anymore thanks to my tampering, he figured his best bet was to head to the Emerald City. Apparently, the place was a mixing bowl for the varied people of Oz. It was a place where people went to lose themselves—or to lose the people hunting them. Or to just get lost.

I frowned at him. "I wondered about that," I said, hands dancing as I finally spoke my suspicions out loud. "The stuff I read on my flight down to the planet all talked about this unique governing system with the four colonies and the natives co-existing on the planet. It sounded like this perfect system. Which I *know* is impossible. No set up, no matter how well-intentioned, ever runs that smoothly." In fact, in my experience it was often the most utopian-seeming ones that were the most corrupt.

The metal man's expression didn't change. It was flat and heartless as he described the state of things on his planet. "The witch of the north controls the poppies. She uses the pollen to control the people there. The moonkins." He said 'moonkins' with a cold dismissiveness, just like when he was talking about the crow people. The natives of Oz were definitely divided. And what the hell did poppies have to do with anything?

At my blank look, Singing Crow nudged my shoulder. "Drugs."

I frowned. There *had* been the whole thing with all those blue flower petals in my food….

"I think the words are losing something in translation," I said slowly. "Poppies back on Earth were once used for medicines and intoxicants…but it was an ancient drug. *Really* mild compared to the stuff on the market these days. How could the witch control people with something like that?"

Tin'amen shrugged, as if it wasn't a big deal at all. "Poppy pollen causes euphoria and a feeling of wellbeing. Pollen junkies are perpetually happy. It is how she keeps her citizens content. And they are so lost in mindless bliss that they find no issue with this arrangement."

Ha! I *knew* no one could be that creepily happy all the time. I tucked that away to think about later.

"No one else on Oz has taken issue with one of the colonial leaders drugging the natives for her own gain?" I asked.

The metal man waited for me and Singing Crow to clamber over a fallen tree that blocked the road before continuing on. "The witch of the south also benefits from the north's drug trade. She uses it in tonics and spells to help with her metal magic, and to keep her own people calm. The drug has a disproportionate effect on the native populations—my people, the moonkins, the crow people, and the winvies to the west. It has become… pervasive."

I nodded, but my mind was stuck on what he'd said about the south. I swept my eyes over the metal man's body. "Metal magic? So…you're not unique, then. I mean, you're not the only one with cybernetics like this?"

Tin'amen's silver eyes flicked away from my face, avoiding my gaze, but his expression remained as impassive as ever. "No. I am not the only stalker to be physically altered."

"Stalker?" I glanced between the two men.

Singing Crow shrugged. "His people."

Ah. I nodded. I think I recalled something in my reading about Oz previously taking in a couple of other alien species over the years and integrating them into their culture. That would explain the variations between the people I'd met so far, and possibly their penchant for separating into different areas…though I had a feeling that was more political, than the natural evolution of things.

The metal man gathered his long silver hair up and wound it into a knot at the base of his neck as he walked, carefully tugging at the mass to ensure his neck—and its conspicuous neuro access port—were covered. "The witch of the south offers the stalkers extended life with her metal magic. And some have the honor of serving in the southern guard."

I narrowed my eyes, reaching out to touch the metal hand that hung at his side nearest me. I was surprised to find the smooth, hard material warm to the touch. He looked down at me, face as impassive as ever.

"What kind of metal is this?" I studied his face, the way the metal on one side of his jaw and face melded so seamlessly with his flawless white skin. It was like no other cybernetics I'd seen. And I'd seen some good tech on my interplanetary travels.

His brow pinched slightly, a faint flicker of some emotion flitting over his features before the flat expression returned. "Mage metal. It is…living metal. Created by the witch of the south."

I stopped, dragging him to a halt along with me. Singing Crow turned and regarded us with a curious look.

The metal man didn't resist as I grabbed his hand and picked it up. "Can I look? Does it bother you?"

He blinked at me. "Why should it?"

Okay…that didn't sound like an actual answer. But I was *really* curious, so I let it slide. I gently pushed up the sleeve of his lightweight shirt, exposing his forearm, where the smooth metal extended. The shape of it echoed a flesh and blood appendage perfectly. No obvious seams or rivets. It was all smooth and warm to the touch. I drew a finger up the inside of his arm and his hand twitched, the mechanism so responsive that yes, it really *did* seem alive. Living metal was a good description.

Pulling his sleeve back down, I reluctantly let go of Tin'amen's hand, the human in me knowing I was being rude, even though the knowledge hound in me wanted to know all there was to know about this new bit of technology. "Thank you," I said, clearing my throat.

Then we resumed walking. My mind was whirling with questions, ideas, and suppositions as I tried to ferret out the larger web of connections that must be running beneath the surface of Oz.

It was midafternoon the next day when our suspicious bit of good luck ran out. We reached an open area between stretches of forest. A field of tall purple and orange grasses stretched out over the rolling hills on either side of the yellow road. It was nice to be out from under the stifling cover of the trees, even if it *was* incrementally hotter out here in the full sun. And me without my sunscreen or my parasol.

Singing Crow was telling me a story about flying over an open plain like this one, back before he was cursed. I didn't get the finer points, but that was okay. I understood his remembered joy well enough as he pantomimed gliding with his wings spread wide.

"Wait," I said at one point. "Do you mean you were *actually* a bird? Are the crow people *literal* crows?" My head hurt.

Tin'amen had drawn ahead of us while the scarecrow carried out his antics. But he paused to look back at my question, his brow furrowed. "Crow people are…." My translator seemed to be struggling with whatever he was saying. Then it caught up. "Shapeshifters."

I felt my eyebrows climb into my hairline and knew I had a look of full-on diva shock on my face. "Shapeshifters?"

I'd heard rumors, of course. Stories about alien races that could change their forms. But they tended to be a bit withdrawn from intergalactic politics, more nature based and less concerned with trade and power plays. I had never met a shapeshifter in person.

Singing Crow tilted his head, then dropped his arms back to his sides, his shoulders slumping a bit. "Yes."

I looked between the two men. "Explain."

Tin'amen looked impatient to get going, but he sighed and came back to join us, his arms crossed over his broad chest. "Everyone in this area knows the story about the scarecrow."

I crossed my arms over my own bustier-enhanced chest and glared up at him. "Well, I'm not *from* here, in case you didn't notice. Enlighten me."

He stared down impassively at me. "The crow people are a wild people. They aren't as civilized as the rest of Oz."

Singing Crow made a clucking noise at that, but the metal man ignored it. "They don't get involved in power struggles between the witches," he said evenly. "But a group of them decided they should. That they would speak up against colonization. Their mouthpiece was a particularly charismatic young man who could shift into a glorious black bird. The color was rare among the bird people. The crow people thought this was a good omen. He spoke when he should have kept silent, and was cursed by the witch, stuck in an ugly half-and-half form as a warning to any shifter who thought about sowing dissent in the future."

I gaped at him. Then I turned to look at Singing Crow, who suddenly sat down in the middle of the road, as if his long legs just couldn't hold him anymore.

I glared up at the metal man. "Couldn't have been a bit more sensitive, could you?"

Tin'amen just shrugged and looked down at the dejected scarecrow. "I only relayed the story you requested."

I shook my head and went to crouch down beside the scarecrow. "Heartless bastard," I muttered. Then, to the traumatized shifter, "I'm sorry. I shouldn't have asked. Shouldn't have let him ramble on like that."

He waved me off, giving me a sad look with those yellow eyes, a wry twist to his half-man, half-bird lips. "Not. Wrong." He said tiredly. "Stupid."

I shook my head adamantly. "You are *not* stupid. It isn't stupid to speak up when you see a wrong. It's—"

I stopped and we all looked around. "What the hell is that noise?"

An ominous hum had started, rising to skin-tingling levels.

"*Bees,*" the metal man said, looking past us, up over the nearby canopy of trees we had emerged from earlier. He bent and grabbed me and the scarecrow, each by our upper arm, dragging us to our feet and shoving us toward the distant cover of the woods.

I swallowed the irrational fear that was clawing its way up my throat. "Dangerous, then?"

Singing Crow gripped my wrist and yanked, tugging me into a run toward the woods in answer to my question. We had been nearly in the middle distance between the two bits of shady forest. Right out in the open. A perfect target.

I stopped asking questions and *ran*, my luscious legs pumping as fast as they could in my clunky borrowed hiking boots. My lungs were burning before we'd made it halfway. I definitely needed to add more conditioning workouts to my routine if I was going to go traipsing around alien planets for funsies.

My boots thudded against the yellow brick road. Singing Crow had pulled ahead, but he slowed to reach back for me and help drag me along.

"Venom," he managed, yanking me forward so hard I nearly tripped.

I risked a glance back to see a fucking *massive* cloud of fist-sized green insects descending on us, wicked stingers glinting in the afternoon sun. They were so fast. There was no way we were going to make it to the questionable shelter of the trees. And even then…even if weaving through the trees slowed them down, we were still fucked.

A metallic clang sounded, followed by some wild, hair-raising, ululating battle cry. I glanced over my shoulder again as Singing Crow and I reached the edge of the forest. *Fuck. A. Duck.*

Tin'amen had stopped out there on the exposed road, sunlight glinting on metal, his arms extended as he taunted the murderous insects.

They dove on him like a crashing wave of green death, some pinging off his metal appendages, others lodging in his perfect white skin. He slashed with his axe, cutting a few in half. But most simply fell down stunned after they flew into him.

"What is happening?" I panted between ragged sips of air, bent over, my lungs burning.

Singing Crow draped a long arm over my back and pulled me into his side as he heaved in air along with me. "Sting. Die."

I shook my head, my brain not fully functioning. The metal asshole was going to get himself killed. I had to do something. But fuck if I knew what.

It was over faster than I would have imagined, the swarm of oblong green insects lying in a twitching heap at the metal man's feet.

He swayed. Went to his knees.

I glanced at the sky, but I was already moving, the scarecrow shouting something unintelligible at me as I jogged back down the yellow brick road to the metal man's side.

"You idiot!" I said, picking my way over dead bug bodies. His perfect skin was covered in welts, one eye swollen almost closed as he swayed on his knees, using his axe to prop himself up. "What were you thinking?"

Tin'amen looked up at me, surprise registering on his face before his usual bland expression covered it up. "I was… neutralizing the threat."

I got an arm around his waist and pulled one of his arms around my shoulders, relieved when the scarecrow joined me, taking the guy's heavy axe and helping me heave him up.

Okay. Tin'amen was fucking heavy. Sure, he was big and metallic. But he always moved with such grace and ease. Now, he barely helped by moving his legs as we dragged him into the woods, and I got a good dose of appreciation for just how damned strong he must be.

"Bees. Sting. Once." Singing Crow panted as we hauled our weird companion into the shelter of the trees, well within the canopy of the woods. The light was fading, and it wasn't like the metal man was in any condition for a hike. It looked like we were making camp here tonight.

I helped lower the metal man to the ground, where he sat propped up against a tree trunk, his eyes closed, and his breathing labored.

"Oh!" I said stupidly. Like Earth bees. Once they attacked, their stingers were pulled out, effectively killing the bee.

"You said they were poison?" I asked the scarecrow, my fingers moving to undo the buttons along Tin'amen's shirt front.

Singing Crow nodded, getting an arm around the other guy's shoulders to help pull him forward so I could strip off the shirt. Yep. The skin parts were covered in welts. And some of the exposed bits on his face, neck, and arm still had nasty looking stingers the length of my pinky finger embedded in the flesh.

I worried my lower lip between my teeth as I studied the stingers. I had to pull them out, but would that just get *me* poisoned in the process?

Singing Crow stood and pulled off his own shirt, then handed it to me, gesturing at the stingers. "Can't. Don't have fingers."

He gestured helplessly with his bird claws. I nodded and took his shirt, tearing off a few squares from the bottom and folding them up into a thick pad that I then used to grip one of the stingers protruding from Tin'amen's arm. Using the fabric as a barrier, I gently pulled the stinger out and set it aside, then moved on to the next one.

The metal man's one non-swollen silver eye opened, and he focused on my face, watching without a word or a single sign of emotion as I yanked stingers out of his flesh.

When I was done, I gathered up the stingers and took them off into the woods to dump them, where we wouldn't accidentally step on one while out taking a piss in the night or something.

When I returned, I used what was left of the water in my canteen to rinse off the stings I could get to while Singing Crow built a little fire in the middle of the road. The scarecrow helped me drag the Tin'amen over closer to fire, then we all collapsed.

"What now?" I asked, my eyes glued to our pale sliver friend. "What do we do about the poison? I have an antimicrobial and a pain cream in my bag. And a couple different antivenoms I took from the pod's first aid kit. That stuff's safe for humans, but I don't know if it's safe to use on him."

The silver guy was reclining against my knapsack. He lifted a hand and waved away my concern. "No need." His smooth voice had gone all deep and husky, and he sounded slightly drunk, as whatever was in those stingers affected him.

I knee-walked closer to him and took his cold, flesh hand in my own. "I'm sorry I can't do more."

He grunted. "I am altered," he murmured, sounding a bit dreamy before he started shivering. "Can't die that easily."

Then he passed out.

I looked over at Singing Crow to find him frowning. “Magic,” he said with a nod.

I certainly fucking hoped so. The metal man might be a bit stand-offish. But I wouldn’t wish *anyone* death by green murder hornet.

Chapter 8

Singing Crow and I watched over Tin'amen in shifts, sharing the bits of food we'd managed to forage during the day, and talking quietly. I tried to pull up information about the bees *and* stalker physiology on Toto, but of course he had limited saved files and no connection to the starnet.

From what I'd managed to glean from Toto and from Singing Crow's short answers, the bees were fairly rare. They were most common in the west, and they usually only attacked in a swarm like that when they'd been threatened or provoked. I mean, no insect wants to go commit suicide by having their butt yanked out if it doesn't have to, right?

So…I was pretty sure the wicked witch of the west hadn't gotten over the whole accidentally murdering her stepsister thing. The spooks were probably hers too, though it seemed like a lot of trouble just to get back a dead woman's shoes.

I felt a little ill when I realized that we'd been targeted by the killer insect swarm because of me. Singing Crow could have died. The metal man looked like he was at death's door even now. All because they chose to walk down the freaking street with me.

I knew it wasn't really my fault. I tried to talk myself out of the guilt. But I couldn't fully chase it away.

I stared at the metal man's pale skin in the flickering firelight. Already, the welts were less swollen, his breathing easier. So, he hadn't been engaging in heroic dramatics there before he passed out. He knew he'd be okay.

Didn't make it right. Didn't make his suffering easy to witness.

We took turns dozing and keeping watch, but at some point, we must have fallen asleep together. I woke in the middle of the night, the scarecrow's silky black head in my lap as I leaned back against a boulder at the roadside, not far from the fire.

While I was trying to figure out how to squirm out from under Singing Crow without waking him, so I could put more wood on the fire and check on our companion, the fire flared brighter.

I blinked at the sudden light, then sat back, taking in the sight of the metal man, shirtless and gleaming in the firelight. He was sitting up, cross-legged and conscious across the fire from us.

"You're okay," I said on a little sigh of relief. Sure, he had *looked* like he was getting better. But you never knew.

He nodded his head. "I am alive."

I let my eyes drift over his naked torso. It was all smooth, marble-white perfection. He was broad-shouldered and the chest currently on display had the sculpted look of marble, like the statue I'd accused him of being when we first found him. Living metal, he'd called his prosthetics. And there was magic involved, energy manipulation. It probably affected his whole body. Either that, or there was some nanode involvement. Whatever the reason, you'd never know that just hours ago he'd been covered in swollen wounds and filled with bee venom.

"Thank you," I blurted.

I was pretty sure if he hadn't taken the stingers for us, me and Singing Crow would both be dead. I gently ran my fingers through the sleeping man's hair in a soft caress, relief making my fingers shake. I wasn't sure what we were to each other. But I had to admit to myself in this moment, I was more than fond of the guy. I would have been gutted if he'd died. I would miss him when we parted.

I looked up to find shining silver eyes studying me from across the fire. "He is your…lover?"

I felt myself blush like the sweet little midwestern girl I was dressed up to be. "Something like that, I suppose."

He nodded. "That seems…desirable."

What a weird thing to say. Maybe the translator was struggling with some local slang or something. "Uh. Yeah. It's nice. To not be alone."

He nodded, his face as unreadable as ever.

The fire crackled as we sat in silence. He looked around and found his shirt—which was somewhat worse for wear—and dragged it on, his lean muscles flexing and rippling in the firelight. I noticed the smooth way the metal at the top of his pec and shoulder on the one side flexed and moved in concert with the normal skin before the shirt slid down, hiding his body from view.

"How did you get your prosthetics? Um. Alterations? I'm not sure what you call them in your case." Because I apparently just had no tact these days. "I mean, if it's okay to ask. You don't have to tell me. I just…I've traveled a lot over the years, and I've never seen anything like them. They really are remarkable."

He shrugged, the motion rippling and graceful, at odds with the knowledge that he had a lot of heavy metal parts. "I lost my foot in a farming accident," he said in an emotionless voice. "My family was not part of the stalker elite. We couldn't afford to have the limb repaired. But living with such an obvious defect in a city known for its living metal tech…was considered crass. We risked being shunned."

I opened my mouth to bitch, but clamped it shut again before my objections could find voice. I wanted to hear the rest of his story. It wouldn't be right to start in criticizing his people the second he shared something with me.

He stared into the fire, lost in memory. The flames reflected in his eyes, making them look almost warm. "I enlisted in the city guard in exchange for free treatment. My foot was replaced, and I became community property, in the usual way of things."

I gritted my teeth together at his wording, but again, kept my mouth shut. *Community property? The* usual *way of things?*

He smoothed his normal hand up his metal leg, petting the limb almost unconsciously through the fabric of his pants. "I was a quick learner. And I wanted to bring honor to my family, help them rise above the station of common farmer. So, I worked hard to become a good soldier. I gained promotions and worked my way up to the honored among the witch's personal guard. I lost my leg protecting the border from West's beasts." He patted his opposite arm with the soft thud of metal. "I lost my arm in a fight with a militant clan of eastern savages."

I swallowed hard. I had never heard about all this infighting between colonies. "And…your face?"

He stroked his own cheek absently, fingers trailing over the seam where metal met alabaster flesh. "Blast injury while working as an assassin."

I blinked at him. "Assassin?"

He nodded, his silver eyes becoming more present, meeting mine with a purposeful coldness. "That was my final promotion. I was the witch's most prized assassin. I was on a mission when someone hacked my neural controls mid-kill. The next thing I remember is you and your friend, with your code-cracking device."

What the hell do you say to something like *that*? I blinked at him. "You're an *assassin*?" For the witch of the south. One of the supposed *good* witches.

He cocked his head to the side, a waterfall of silver hair falling over his shoulder as he regarded me. "Not anymore. You freed me when you unlocked my neural controls."

Oh. Well. Yay me! "Good," I said stupidly. "So, she can't control you anymore?"

He scowled. "She could try. Using my alterations and her magic. But my mind is now my own. I was cajoled into giving up my free will for the sake of my people's 'honor' once before. It was a lie. My people have no honor. It will not happen again."

Wow. That was not okay. Gee willakers, nothing on this fucking planet was okay. This was *not* dear old Kansas, for damned sure.

"What will you do now?" I asked, curious and suddenly invested in the man's happiness. Fuck knew he deserved a little joy after that shit-tastic tale.

"I will go to the Emerald City and disappear, lessen my chances of being reclaimed."

This situation definitely needed a little levity. I arched my brows and put on my best fierce diva voice. "And then? What will you do now that your life's your own?" I leaned in, pitching my voice in a conspiratorial whisper, as if this was some sappy motivational movie on the fem-power station back home. "What's your deepest desire, bitch? Your burning heart's yearning?"

He just stared at me in confusion for a beat, then his face finally expressed some emotion. Too bad it was a bitter, twisted thing, rather than the humor I'd hoped for. "My heart's desire? I have no idea. That useless organ was lost to me the moment the first bit of metal was fused to my flesh."

God. My own heart ached for him. He sounded so damned cold and jaded.

"Honey," I said softly. "Tell me that's a bad metaphor." The witch hadn't really taken out his heart, had she? Was that even possible? Who the fuck knew?

He closed his eyes and pressed a fist to his chest. "It still beats. But it is absent all the same." His eyes opened and he glanced between me and my sleeping lover. "If I had a heart, I think I'd want…this. To know what it is to be loved. Not by parents who see you as just one more able body to work the fields or a way to improve their lot in life, not by a power-drunk woman who sees you as a prized possession to be ripped apart and put back together over and over again just to serve her. But something else." His silver eyes studied me intently. "I've heard others speak of it…love without condition. Does something like that exist? I wish I still had a functioning heart, so I could find out."

I swallowed hard. Something in my eye. Maybe some alien allergen. That must be what had my nose all snuffy and my eyes overflowing.

"Allergies," I hiccupped.

Tin'amen watched me cry with no expression on his face. "Working hearts are painful things to carry."

I nodded in agreement. "They sure as fuck are, sugar," I managed. "But I'm still proud to have one."

He was silent for a long time.

Chapter 9

Another couple of days on the road had me sick to death of walking. I was sure glad I had been practical enough to get over my squeamishness and steal the dead witch's shoes when I crash-landed on Oz. No way would I have made it this far barefoot or in six-inch silver stilettos. Even though I would have looked *fabulous* the whole way.

It was weird how infrequently we saw anyone else on the road. Occasionally, an Ozonian would trundle by with a farm wagon or one of those round, pod-like cars they favored. But no one made eye contact with our odd group, and they zipped away as quickly as possible.

When I commented on it, my companions seemed to think this behavior was nothing out of the ordinary. "Keep away," Singing Crow had replied, giving my hand a squeeze. "Better."

I looked to Tin'amen for a more detailed answer. And…lord, did his stiff, metal-wearing self just *have* to be so damned hot? The boredom of travel must really be setting in, since all I seemed to be able to focus on today was looking forward to cuddling up with the lean crow-man at night and ogling the tall, silvery god at my side all day long.

As if the universe was mocking me, a little breeze danced around us, lifting stray strands of Tin'amen's long silver hair, fanning it about his face and shoulders like something from the cover of a romance book. *Eesh, Dotty, get it together girl!*

For his part, the stoic silver angel seemed completely oblivious to my drooling. He shrugged and answered my question. "The people of Oz are divided. They know it's safer to stick to their own kind and they rarely socialize or interact with people from other regions." He slanted a silver glance toward me and Singing Crow. "Most people have heard some version of the scarecrow story. It serves as a warning. And rumors of the alien who killed the witch of the east and aided the witch of the north will be spreading as well."

I gaped at him. "I did *what* now?"

He arched one pale brow. "You killed the witch of the east and aided the witch of the north in cementing her claim over the moonkins."

Singing Crow patted my shoulder with one clawed hand. "Not. On purpose?"

I blinked at him. "Did I purposefully crash-land my pod on top of one of the rulers of the planet? Uh, no. Not even remotely. I thought I was gonna die myself, honestly. Little ol' Dotty was far too busy having herself a heart attack to be aiming her propulsionless hunk of space metal at unsuspecting witches!"

I spun my hand, gesturing for him to back up a bit. "Let's rewind the conversation to the part where you said I *helped* the witch of the south takeover the moonkins."

He sighed. "The moonkins were originally under the rule of the witch of the east. But north's pollen has spread over the years, becoming a pervasive issue. A lot of the moonkins are addicted. It's nearly impossible to get clean, since they can't stop chasing the perpetual state of bliss the drug induces. And north controls the supply. It will take some time to communicate news of the witch's death to the appropriate authorities and establish the new eastern ruler. In the meantime, north will be able to use the delay to bring the addicted moonkins fully under her control."

He spoke so evenly. As if he were relaying news about the weather. As if he wasn't talking about a colonial emissary manipulating a native population by use of mind-altering substances.

"You really *are* heartless, aren't you?" I muttered.

He didn't reply, just kept his gaze pointed forward as he trucked along with that distance-eating stride. Now I knew why his people were called stalkers. He didn't walk, or amble, or stride anywhere, he *stalked.* Like those long legs weren't capable of any other pace.

Singing Crow tilted his head and studied me, then the metal man, frowning. "Not. Kind."

I sighed. "Yeah." The scarecrow was right. I had spoken without thinking. "I'm sorry, Tin'amen," I said, pushing my own legs to keep up. "I shouldn't have said that. You're not heartless."

He looked down at me as we walked. "You only spoke the truth. I learned long ago that it's not worth it to care about others. It puts you at risk. Makes it difficult to do your job."

I shook my head. The poor, cold, damaged bastard. "You know, pretending you don't care won't stop it from hurting."

Something flickered behind his cool gaze and his perfect lips twisted into a faint grimace. "Guilt is not for soldiers or assassins who wish to continue being useful."

Okay. *Ouch.* That was like a punch to the gut. It sounded like a lot of soldiers and doctors I'd met in my time with the EARTH military—like the words of someone who'd seen too much to let himself feel. I reached out and gripped his arm, the metal smooth and hard under my fingertips. "Whoa. Stop."

When he halted, I went up on tiptoes to cup the normal side of his face and make him look me in the eyes. "I'm sorry for what the witch did to you. What your own people did to you. I'm sorry your heart is so broken. I didn't mean to make it worse by running my mouth."

He stared down at me, as immovable as ever. Then a little crack appeared in his stoic expression, a teeny, *tiny* softening around the corners of his eyes and mouth. "You cannot help it. You seem to care overly much for anyone who might suffer."

I lowered from my tiptoes to stand flat on my feet, putting a bit more distance between us. "Yeah. You're right. I tend to put my nose where it doesn't belong." I huffed, pulling my hand away from his face. "That's probably how I ended up here, alone on an alien planet."

I froze when his soft, flesh-and-blood hand reached out, sliding along my jaw to cup my face the way I had just done to him seconds before. "You are not alone." His eyes locked on mine and for one insane moment I swore he was going to kiss me.

A girl could get lost in those not-so-cold-as-he-wanted-to-pretend silver eyes.

Then he glanced over my shoulder, at the scarecrow. "You have found connection here," he reminded me. He pulled his hand away, his expression desolate once again. "You will undoubtedly gather more people to your side when we reach Emerald City. It is in your nature. Your warm, fiercely beating heart calls to the hearts of others."

He turned and continued walking, like he hadn't just spouted poetic compliments at me. I just stood there, breathless and tingly in my not-so-girly parts. Oh, man. I was so stupid.

I startled when Singing Crow gripped my shoulder. His yellow eyes met mine, and he cocked his head, something like a smirk lifting one corner of his half-bird mouth. “Okay?”

I snorted. “No, not really.”

He kept pace at my side as I started slowly following after our weird half-metal companion. “Wounded. But…attractive?” he commented in a low voice.

I glanced at him in surprise, only to find him eyeing the ramrod straight back in front of us, with its long silver braid and the perfect ass that wasn’t even remotely disguised by the thin fabric of the metal man’s pants.

“Oh. My. God.” I breathed, giving the scarecrow a girly swat on his shoulder as if I was scandalized. “You *degenerate*.”

He just chuckled his strange, endearingly bird-like chuckle and picked up the pace so we could catch up.

That night, I checked in with Toto again, not really surprised when he still couldn’t connect with the starnet. We made camp under the trees once again. My companions said we would come to the end of the forested area in another day or two. I wasn’t sure how I felt about that. On one hand, that probably meant being closer to civilization and away from the threat of alien beasts, but on the other hand, being out in the open would leave us vulnerable to things like attack by giant swarms of poisonous bees.

I felt antsy. I had always had a tendency to take comfort in sensual things. If I was worn out, nervous, scared, or sad I soothed myself with physical comforts. It was one of the perks of being a high-ranking diplomat, and later of being a spoiled diva. But since I couldn’t exactly draw up a big ol’ bubble bath, or order a hot stone massage or a triple-layer chocolate delight, all that was left was the need to curl up in Singing Crow's arms and lose myself to *other* pleasures for a while.

But that was kind of impossible with an audience. So, I did a lot of pacing and fidgeting, trying to focus my mind on politics and plans instead.

It was hard to form any sort of plan when I barely knew the lay of the land. "So," I said once we were all settled around the fire for the night, sharing some sort of sweet nuts that we had roasted over the flames. "In all the EARTH files I read about Ozma-4, North and South were portrayed as beneficent and kind. They were supposed to be the ones who are most loved by the natives. East was supposed to be neutral. And I got the impression West was just a thorn in everyone's side, but mostly kept her bad attitude to herself if you stayed out of her territory."

I sighed. "Clearly, that's complete bullshit. I get here and find out that North is running a drug trade to control the populace, South is benefitting from the trade so she can make metal slaves of the natives in her own area while pretending to be some magical benefactor. And I haven't gone anywhere *near* West's territory and yet she's giving me death threats and sending spooks and murderous insects after me." I threw my hands up in a helpless gesture. "What can you tell me about the Wizard? Is the 'emerald' in Emerald City code for some other bit of fuckery?"

Singing Crow snorted and handed me the last roasted nut. "Coin."

"Right," I muttered. Currency on the planet was unified, with most people using the global emerald coin. It was made from a somewhat rare, nearly indestructible gem similar in color to Earth's emeralds, but structurally different. I assumed the Emerald City name was a play on this. "All the sources I read said that the Emerald City was the richest place on Oz." Was it really just that obvious? Couldn't be. This was my life we were talking about, nothing was ever that simple.

Tin'amen came over and settled beside me, so we weren't speaking across the fire. He folded his long legs and sank down gracefully, not a clink or clank of metal to be detected. "The wizard controls the money. Emerald City is orderly. Cleanliness and shine. Polish. But it hides an edge of darkness. The wizard knows everything. He has a cure for every ailment, a solution to every problem—for a price. His magical power is knowing what people most need and what they are willing to pay for it."

I sighed. It didn't sound like Emerald City was going to be the upright, welcoming place I had hoped. But then, I guess I knew that all along. I was just clinging to my optimism out of habit. Nothing was ever as simple as it seemed on the surface. *You know this, Dotty, girl.*

"That might make things difficult," I said tiredly. I mean, what little cash I had stowed away in my bag didn't amount to much, and it was all in EARTH dollars. "But nothing's impossible." I shrugged. "There's always a way with that type. There's always something other than money that you can offer, if you get a good read on them."

My companions didn't comment. We all stared into the flickering fire for a while, huddling close to escape the slight chill of the night air. It was still nice enough during the day, but it was starting to get colder at night. I thought maybe the seasons were starting to change on Oz. A short cotton dress and sheer thigh-high tights wasn't the warmest ensemble one could choose to trek around in. And I wasn't sure what season came next or how extreme the weather could get. I should see if Toto knew, when I started him up to check for a signal tomorrow morning.

Maybe I could barter for or steal some pants, if we ever came near civilization. But that was a worry for another time. I was currently busy wracking my brain to figure out what I could offer the infamous Wizard of Oz for a trip to an IMAD station.

Of course, I couldn't really go anywhere until I figured out why I'd been banished in the first place. Unless I wanted to live the rest of my life trying to hide from the EARTH military, I needed to have evidence to build a case to present to IMAD and get myself cleared.

Tin'amen's smooth, deep voice brought me out of my musings. "I wonder how much a new heart would cost?" the metal man at my side said, his voice flat.

I huffed. "If only it worked that way. Do you really believe the wizard has magic?"

Silver eyes met mine for a moment, then he shrugged, holding out his metal arm, turning the hand over as he studied it, the light glinting off the metal in warm sparks of red and gold. "If magic such as this exists in the world, then surely there is magic to heal a damaged heart."

I sighed. "Sure. Who needs therapy when you've got mind magic or whatever, right?"

Singing Crow patted my knee and I glanced over at him. He gestured at his own body, at his beak and his creature hands. "Magic. Did. This."

And he did have a point. When was I going to just admit that it wasn't all advanced science and tricks? Magic—or something damned close to it—was real. How else could I explain everything I'd seen on Oz? I considered myself a pretty open-minded guy, but this one thing was a sticking point for my biased, logical mind.

"Well, when we ask for Tin'amen's heart, we'll put in a request for curse removal for you, yeah?"

Singing Crow nodded, looking down, to where his bird-like hands were curled in his lap. "Yeah."

I sighed. "Don't worry. We'll figure it all out eventually." Pasting on a grin I added a flamboyant, "That's what I *do* after all, dahlings. I negotiate with powerful people and come up with solutions—whether they like it or not!"

Though that usually required a completely different costume, and was way less fun than being Dotty West.

Singing Crow wrapped a long arm around my waist, drawing me against his side. "Not. By…yourself." He nuzzled the side of my neck, giving me goosebumps.

It was a weird thought, that I might not have to fight this particular battle alone. I had always felt alone in the political arena, even when surrounded by "likeminded" individuals from all over the galaxy.

A big, warm hand landed on my opposite knee and Tin'amen's smooth voice surprised me. "I will assist as well. Just as you assisted me. Were it not for you, I would still be frozen in the forest, good for nothing but a roost for the birds until the witch got around to finding me and reinstating me."

I put my hand over his, surprised as always at the warmth of the metal. He was stiff at my side, but he turned his hand over, fitting his palm to mine as our fingers laced together. It was a big hand, made for holding weapons. My own absolutely average human male hand looked small in comparison.

Singing Crow's hand at my waist moved up and down in a soothing rhythm, and he made an inquisitive, curious sound in his throat that was half man, half bird.

I agreed with his sentiment. What was going on here?

Turning my head, I looked up at the metal man. His silver eyes studied my face and I thought he must be crazy to think he didn't have a heart. Right now, it was right there on his face for all the world to see.

From that look on his face and the way it took my breath away, it was obvious that Tin'amen had more feeling in his heart than he knew what to do with—longing, pain, *loneliness.* And I thought maybe, for a little while, I could do something about that last one.

I leaned toward him, my chin tilted up in question and invitation.

He only hesitated a heartbeat before dipping his head in answer, his soft lips sliding over my own, hesitant at first, then hungry.

I knew that feeling. The desperate need to *feel* after so long being numb. I'd been there, done that. After I was discharged and thrown away by EARTH the first time, I lost my boyfriend in the process. Back when I felt like my only worth was my title, and that with that gone I was nothing. No one.

I arched upward, deepening the kiss, my tongue tangling with his, as if I could breathe my thoughts into his aching heart. *You're not worthless. You're not broken. You're more than a tool or an object to be cast aside by your maker.*

I came up for air, panting and dizzy, then jolted when I remembered the man at my other side. The scarecrow had pulled away while I kissed the ever-loving *fuck* out of the metal man. Oopsies.

I glanced at Singing Crow, prepared for his wrath, even though he *had* been checking the other guy out with me earlier. "I'm sorry?"

Somehow it came out as a question. Because I really wasn't sorry at all. Because maybe…I didn't need to say sorry?

Singing Crow's eyes were heavy-lidded with lust, the silky chaos of his black hair falling forward around his high cheekbones as he tilted his head in confusion. "Sorry? Why?"

I let out the breath I'd been holding. "I wasn't sure if you would be angry? Some cultures frown on multiple partners."

He shook his head, letting out a low chuckling sound. "Not. Mine."

I nodded. "Oh, thank fuck." Because I would have honored his needs for his new partner to *not* fuck other guys…but my dick and I would no longer be on speaking terms.

I leaned in and trailed sucking, nipping kisses along the scarecrow's throat and jaw before pulling away, turning back to Tin'amen.

Our stoic companion watched with heat in his curious silver eyes. Then he lifted his metal hand to brush back the strands of hair that had escaped my Dotty braids. "Does this mean I can kiss you again?"

I nodded emphatically. "You'd damned well better!"

Then we were falling, my arms around his neck, his hand cushioning the back of my head as we hit the ground. His warm mouth plundered mine with all the command of the deadly thing he was, my front pressed to the big, strong metal soldier, while Singing Crow's warm, lean body pressed against my back.

Sure, politics or alien bugs might kill me tomorrow. But tonight…I was going to thoroughly get to know the natives. Cultural research, right?

Chapter 10

Usually, I'm not the kind of girl to roll around in the dirt. I swear. But *you* get yourself pinned between two hot guys in the middle of nowhere and see how many of *your* sensibilities get tossed out the window!

I pushed myself up on my elbows and flipped over, setting to work on the scarecrow's clothes, since he struggled to undo his fly with the bird hands and all. He let out an impatient huff and flopped back onto the ground as I undid the buttons on his trousers. His clothes were pretty much rags at this point. Maybe he should just go naked from now on. Easier that way.

I grinned an evil grin.

He arched his black brows at me, clearly wondering what the source of my smile was. "Oh, just you wait," I told him, dipping a hand inside his fly for a teasing squeeze. "I have so many ideas. Marvelous ideas. Genius, even."

He just chuckled.

Once I let him go, he moved to kneel, leaning in to nip at my shoulder in his half-beaked version of a kiss. His luminous yellow eyes were full of want and his cock hard as steel when I gripped it and gave a few more slow, teasing strokes. And speaking of steel....

Tin'amen knelt behind me, his longer legs bracketing the outside of my thighs, big hands on my hips as a truly impressive hardness pressed against my ass through our clothes. He planted hungry kisses to the other side of my neck and shoulder and I shuddered, twisting to get a handful of his pretty hair and give it a tug.

He lifted his head, and I met his eyes. "Have you been with a human or a…um, crow person before? Is there anything we should know about your body?" I smirked and waggled my brows. "You don't have, like, a hydraulic penis or something, do you?"

He froze, pulling back slightly, an odd expression on his face as he frowned, considering my words. "I…don't think hydraulic is the correct word."

I pulled away from Singing Crow so I could turn all the way around, both of us staring at the metal man. "That was a *joke*," I whispered, not sure if I was horrified, or aroused. My dick pulsed, letting me know that yeah, we were definitely aroused. Because we were unapologetic degenerates, the both of us.

But…. "You can't be serious."

Tin'amen glanced between me and Scarecrow, some of that stoic mask dropping over his handsome face again. I lurched forward, getting a hand behind his head and pulling him into another of those amazing kisses, feeling him slowly unthaw again as his lips caressed mine.

Pulling back, I studied his face. "I'm sorry. Talking out my ass again. I didn't mean to insult you. Please don't go all heartless on me."

He huffed. "I didn't really consider that my anatomy may be…off-putting to others. The witch of the south seemed to be quite amused by her work."

I swallowed hard, some of my arousal fleeing at his words. "Okay, time out. Do you need to talk about this? Are you okay? I didn't mean to push you to do anything you're not comfortable with." I paused as a horrible thought occurred to me. "Oh, my *stars*. You don't think you *have* to have sex with us just because we're all traveling together and me and the scarecrow are a thing, do you?"

He startled me by placing his smooth metal hand over my mouth to stop the verbal flood. "Please, stop worrying over me," he said calmly. "I am a tool, and my heart may be damaged, but I find my other needs are still intact. Maybe a bit more so since meeting you."

I blinked at him. He slowly removed his hand from my mouth, watching me suspiciously for any more signs of imminent verbal outpouring.

Singing Crow shuffled closer to Tin'amen, laying a tentative bird hand on the other guy's arm. "Are you. Different? Needs?"

Ah, if only the poor bird guy could really express himself. I was kind of feeling sappy over the concern in his yellow eyes. No one seemed to care that we had just paused our orgy for a mental health check-in. This was way too much caring for a bunch of random guys who'd only known each other for a few days and were about to screw in the woods. But the weirdness and slight discomfort felt...*comfortable,* if that made any sense.

Tin'amen pulled his shirt off over his head and tossed it aside, where it might make someone a sad excuse for a cushion against the hard ground. He lifted his hands to the front of my dress, fingers deftly undoing the rhinestone buttons. "I function just like either of you," he said calmly, as if this conversation wasn't strange in the least. "My maker made sure of that."

And see…that was the part that was causing my dick to wilt. "She abused you?" I whispered, my eyes glued to his face, even as he parted my dress and pushed it aside to run those big hands over my satin bustier and the illusion of small breasts it gave, fingers trailing along my ribs, exploring. "She…forced you?"

His silver eyes met mine and he shrugged. "It was long ago. I was a servant. At the time I merely saw it as part of my service, neither pleasant nor unpleasant. Please let me pleasure you, strange little Dotty West. Do not let your soft heart be an unnecessary obstacle between us."

I sighed. "It's only Dotty when the dress is on, sweetheart. Once it comes off…I'm just plain old Daniel."

I held my breath as he untied the ribbon at the top of the bustier, undoing the laces and doing away with the illusion of breasts as he freed my chest and tossed the garment aside. Unlike the scarecrow, he didn't seem at all confused about my gender. Or maybe he just didn't care either way.

"What if the dress is only partially on?" he said, one corner of his mouth lifting in the bare hint of a smile. "Should I call you Dotty or Daniel, then?" Oh, my stars and nebulas, now he was making *jokes*? What was even happening right now?

I planted a hand in the center of his chiseled chest and slid it upward, over defined pecs, his skin smooth and flawless. "I don't really care *what* you call me at the moment. And…it's not an obstacle," I insisted. "My heart. You said you wanted your heart back. Well, let me tell you, you'd sure as shit care if it was one of us who had been wronged."

I couldn't help swiping a thumb over one of his small pink nipples, so sweet against all that snow-white skin and warrior's body. He sucked in a breath and kissed me again, then pulled back to unbutton his pants.

I left the dress on, unbuttoned and open at the front. I suspected the metal man liked the combination of feminine and masculine. Plus, it was a bit chilly for rolling around completely naked in the woods. I slipped a hand down across my stomach, pushing down the waistband of my clingy shorts, but I found myself pressed between two eager male bodies before I could take myself in hand.

Glancing down, I smiled. Tin'amen's package looked a lot like mine or the scarecrow's. The shape was vaguely different—smaller at the head and thicker at the base—but the idea was the same. No gleaming metal, though it *was* quite a bit larger than my cock, and had some girth on scarecrow as well. Proportional to his bigger body, I suppose.

I slid my hand down his chest and across his lean abs, enjoying the contrast between my body, his, and Singing Crow's. Where I had the light muscle of a pretty boy gym user, the scarecrow was thin and wiry. The metal man was bigger than both of us, not bulky in that body builder kind of way, but with layers of muscle that had been defined through actual use. Through work and battle, rather than my sit-ups and weight machines or Singing Crow's starvation-induced leanness.

The scarecrow looped his arm around my waist and rested his chin on my shoulder, watching from behind as I drew my fingers down Tin'amen's abdomen, through a faint, shimmery happy trail the same color as his silvery-blonde hair. My fingers wrapped around Tin'amen's hard shaft, and I let out a little moan. Okay…that was a little strange. "How are you so *hard*?"

I mean, there was hard, and then there was absolutely, inhumanly *rigid.*

Duh, Daniel. Metal man. Modifications. But still.

His big hands did some exploring of their own, even as he answered my stupid question. He wrapped his surprisingly warm metal hand around my hip while the other hand fondled my sack before gripping me and matching the pace of my slow strokes. "The metal shaft is under the skin," he said softly, pausing to lean in and kiss his way from my jaw to my ear before whispering. "I'm always hard, Daniel, to some degree."

Oh. Wow. Even as he said this, the flesh on the outside of his dick became even more engorged, throbbing against my hand. So…maybe he wasn't always quite *this* hard. Sweet Kansas, that would be uncomfortable.

I reached behind me with my free hand, brushing Singing Crow's fly open and gripping his own long member, stroking both men at the same time. I felt like I was living every gay boy's dream.

"God, I wish I had supplies so I could have one of you in my ass right now," I muttered. "Maybe *both* of you." *Geesh Daniel, slut it up*. Hadn't really meant to say that out loud, but oh well. A queen wants what a queen wants.

Singing Crow huffed a deep, birdy cackle against my shoulder, his odd hands sliding lower, flipping up the ruffled skirt of my dress and sliding down to grip my thighs suggestively, conveying his agreement. Tin'amen growled against my lips.

Yeah. There were hotels in the Emerald City, right? Surely, I could garner enough sympathy as an ex-diplomat get us one night in a damned hotel with a bed. And amenities. Like lube.

"Circle," the scarecrow breathed against my skin as he thrust into my hand. "Please?" He rubbed a hand over his deformed mouth with its beaky middle. "Careful. I promise."

"Circle?" It took me a second, my lust-addled brain not quite keeping up with words. But when Tin'amen removed his hand from my cock, the cogs started turning again. "Oh! Circle. Yes, please."

They were both laughing at me, silent smirks that said they thought the way I lost the ability to think during sex was just adorable.

Of course, I *am* adorable. But not right then. Right then, I was *hot* damn it. Not cute. I turned to Singing Crow and pushed him down, arranging him on the ferns beside the road as best I could. I don't think any of us were all that concerned with comfort at the moment. At least…not that sort of comfort. The energy between us was intense. I was pretty sure we could end up fucking on a bed of nails and not give a damn.

A little shifting and shuffling, and we formed Singing Crow's circle by the fire. Yeah, I was really starting to believe in this whole magic thing. *Something* certainly jolted down my spine like lighting when I sucked the scarecrow's long, hard cock into my mouth and felt Tin'amen's perfect lips envelop my own aching dick.

I lifted my head long enough to get a good look at the scarecrow as he carefully leaned in, not using his clawed hands, one palm braced on the ground and the other laid flat on Tin'amen's thigh as he licked a stripe up Tin'amen's unnaturally hard shaft.

Okay, so they were apparently past all the politics that had made them glare daggers at each other when they first met. I said a prayer to the gods of lust. Because the sight of Singing Crow's silky black head dipping in to swallow down that long, thick cock was going to be burned into my memory for the rest of my life.

I bent my head to the pretty dick in front of me, groaning against Singing Crow's satiny skin when Tin'amen slipped a finger behind my balls, teasing around my hole as my dick hit the back of his throat and he *swallowed* around it. Holy fuck!

He hummed against my skin, his motions becoming rough and desperate as he no doubt chased his own release. I didn't think any of us were going to last, and that was fine by me. Because I needed to fly, to shut my mind off for five fucking seconds and just exist in this total bliss, to lose myself in the warmth of another person. Or two.

One of Singing Crow's hands reached for me, claws tangling in my hair as he pushed deeper into my mouth and shuddered, his hot cum flooding my throat. I swallowed, even as I wanted to shout, my own dick exploding inside the wet, velvety heat of Tin'amen's mouth.

The metal man milked me for every last bit of pleasure, then released my softening dick, sitting up to curl himself around scarecrow, threading his long fingers through the other man's jet-black hair and tensing, every perfectly defined muscle thrown into stark relief as he silently came apart with a harsh breath. Apparently, the beak hadn't been an issue. Careful indeed.

Singing Crow sat back on his heels, wiping the back of his hand across his mouth and grinning like he'd won some sort of prize. He saw me watching and shrugged. "No worries."

Tin'amen looked at him with an unguarded fondness that made my absolutely *not* nonexistent heart overflow with feeling. "No worries," he echoed, pulling the scarecrow in and pressing a kiss to the corner of his mouth, undeterred by the beak part.

I wormed my way in between them, earning laughter and fond smiles as I stole my own kisses and cuddles like the greedy thing I am.

My heart felt light, alive. Full.

But later, once we were all clothed again, curled up by the fire with me playing the middle spoon, my arm around Singing Crow, and Tin'amen's arm around me…the sadness started creeping in.

This felt too good. Too easy. Too right. But once we reached the Emerald City, it would all be over. They had their own lives to live, and I had an escape and revenge to plan. I wasn't meant to be on Oz.

This was just sex. Just comfort. I wasn't meant to care for them.

Chapter 11

By the time the sun rose the next morning, I was in a better mood—stiff, achy from sleeping on the ground, footsore from walking, but happy, nonetheless. The only thing really nagging at me was my continued inability to reach the station. I also hadn't received anything else from Freddie. And I had been certain he would try to keep me informed about what he saw at EARTH. It *could* all just be due to atmospheric interference, something to do with the planet's fields, any number of reasonable explanations. But my intuition insisted that communications were being blocked.

And if the person doing the blocking could keep Freddie from finding a way through, then they had to be powerful or well financed…say, like an elite allied republic or something….

I would feel a lot better if I knew what was going on out there in the universe beyond Oz. What games and machinations were playing out? How did my little drama fit into the greater scheme of things? It had to, somehow, for me to have ended up suddenly banished here.

Singing Crow nudged me with a bony shoulder as we walked along, and I tucked Toto away for the time being. "Not. Much. Further," the scarecrow said slowly, pointing out past where the forest petered out and rolling hills covered in flowers took over.

On the distant horizon, I could just barely see a few tall, gleaming green spires that must be part of the Emerald City. I grinned. "About damned time."

The yellow brick road curved around a bend, then dipped down to a last little wooded area. The trees here were sparser than the wood behind us, their trunks silvery white, with small, round leaves that danced in the breeze—kind of like white birch trees back on Earth. "We can stop here and rest," Tin'amen said, gesturing at the small grove. A sparkling pool was visible through the trees. "Spring-fed, likely," he commented, leading the way under the trees. "It will be cool. A nice opportunity to bathe."

I nearly clapped my hands together and bounced up and down at the chance to get clean, even if it was in a little pond. We were all looking—and smelling—a bit worse for wear after all the hiking and sleeping on the ground. By the time we reached the Emerald City, we'd look like straight-up vagrants. It wouldn't hurt to try to preserve whatever appearance and dignity we could. People tended to be more likely to listen to you if you looked put together and sane. That was why I had always maintained such an immaculate appearance when I was a diplomat. God, what I wouldn't give for those stuffy old threads now. I was getting a bit sick of the dress and thigh-highs. Not that I'd *ever* admit that out loud!

As we approached the little pool of sparkling water, a low, rumbling growl erupted from off to the side. I turned, gripping Singing Crow's arm as a massive, golden-furred beast slowly emerged from the shadows.

"Mine," the thing rumbled in a rough voice that was part beast, part man. "Leave."

We slowly backed away, toward the road behind us. “Okay,” I said, holding a hand up to plead for peace. “We didn’t mean any harm. Just wanted a place to rest.”

We reached the even surface of the yellow brick road and Tin’amen positioned himself in front of me and Singing Crow, shielding us from the threat. His metal hand rested on the axe in the belt at his waist.

The beast growled, pacing around us on huge paws, reminding me of some sort of giant, shaggy lion. It was covered in long, curly gold hair, the feline head sporting big green eyes and long, wicked teeth.

“Leave us, beast!” Tin’amen warned, his voice even.

The lion-thing growled again. “This is my territory. No men allowed here.”

“What?” Singing Crow said, tilting his head and looking back over his shoulder. Clearly, he wasn’t talking about what the lion-thing had just said.

I followed his gaze, slow to tear my own eyes away from the beast that prowled around us, sizing us up for lunch. What I saw was confusing. Birds? A flock flew toward us, glinting in the afternoon sun.

Tin’amen didn’t take his eyes off the lion.

“Uh,” I said, reaching out to grip the back of the metal man’s shirt. “We might have a problem? Maybe?”

“Oh, we have no problem,” he said in a cold voice, clearly intending on gutting the golden beast before him.

Then several things all happened at once.

Tin’amen drew his axe in a quick, fluid movement, lunging for the lion…who *screamed* and tripped over his own big feet in his rush to get away. Then the birds reached us and started diving, all sharp talons and wicked beaks—and they were made of metal.

I shrieked like the girl I currently resembled, shielding my face with my arms and running for the meager cover of the nearby grove of trees. The birds were tearing at me, plucking at my hair and clothes, slashing my exposed forearms. I felt a jerk and realized that they had grabbed onto my knapsack and were attempting to rip it off my back.

What the actual hell? Were the birds…*stealing my stuff?*

The lion was making ridiculous little high-pitched keening sounds as he swiped at the metal birds with his big paws. He looked absolutely terrified, but somehow managed to battle the demon birds right alongside Tin'amen, even as he sobbed in fear.

The metal man was a terrifying cyclone of flashing metal death. Whatever that axe was made of was more than up to the task of slicing through metal, cutting birds in half like a hot knife through butter.

It can't have lasted long. It felt like the barrage of beaks and claws and feathers would never end, and yet, the silence that closed in after their attack was sudden and deafening.

We panted loudly in the aftermath. I darted a glance around, finding Tin'amen uninjured. Singing Crow and myself were a bit scratched up, but nothing major. The birds had managed to yank my knapsack off my back, and my stuff had spilled out. One silver stiletto was clutched in a dead birdy beak. I mean, sure, my shoes were royally shiny, but still, what would a bird want with a shoe?

The lion-beast cowered against a tree trunk, shivering, and I wondered if maybe he had some wound that I couldn't see. Was the creature going into shock?

I didn't want to get too close. But then, he *had* helped us fight off the birds. And he seemed to have human intelligence. He wasn't just an animal. I couldn't just leave him there to die of some unseen wound, right? I edged closer, ignoring the scarecrow's grab for me and Tin'amen's resigned sigh.

So I had a mushy heart. It was just how it was. They should really be used to it by now.

"Are you okay?" I cooed in my best soft, high, Dotty voice. "Poor thing. Where'd they hurt you?"

I reached out a hand, trying not to show the fear that trembled through me, the shudders fueled by fading adrenaline and the very real chance that I was about to get my hand ripped off by a wild animal.

I froze in shock when the lion's wide, wild green eyes met mine and he…shimmered. My mouth was probably hanging open like an idiot when the fierce, injured creature melted away, shifting into a big, stocky, *naked* blonde man. Then those big green eyes rolled back in his head, and he fainted.

"Well," I said, my voice nothing more than a breath of air. "That was unexpected. Do you think he's hurt?"

Singing Crow came to crouch by the unconscious man, head tilted to the side curiously. I reached out and did my best to feel for a pulse in one of the beast-man's thick wrists. It was *probably* somewhere in the same vicinity as other humanoid-looking species, right? My basic training classes had said biology, while wildly varied, did tend to follow patterns. The thumping proof of life was a bit to the left of where I'd expected to find it, and I had no idea what was normal for a lion-man. But it was at least present, strong and steady against my fingertips.

I glanced up at Tin'amen as he approached. "Well?"

He snorted and reached out a foot to nudge the poor guy in the leg with his boot. “Coward,” he muttered dismissively. Then he turned away, heading back toward the pool with his usual cool indifference. “Best bathe and refill your canteen before it wakes up and starts caterwauling again.”

Chapter 12

And that was how I ended up walking into the Emerald City with a giant lion-beast prowling at my side. Okay, so *prowling*, wasn't really an apt description. The giant monster—who said his name was Lio, of all things—cowered behind me or kept himself glued to my side, his curly gold self plastered along my leg and hip in a way that made it difficult to walk.

But somehow, I couldn't quite find it in myself to push him away. He was clearly traumatized. His deep voice had tremored and stuttered the previous night as he perched naked by the fire and spoke in halting, broken words about the death of his entire clan and family unit at the hands of South's metal abominations. His green eyes had continuously watched Tin'amen in darting, fearful glances, as if he expected to be murdered at any moment.

He had clearly *wanted* to scare us away from his lonely sanctuary in the little grove, but it was all bluster. The appearance of the metal birds had pushed him over the edge, showing his true colors.

He had fought alongside us, so I knew he was no coward—no matter what Tin'amen said. But once the threat was gone, all that was left of the lion was a quaking mass of anxiety.

Poor guy. I'd seen it countless times before. Some soldiers, when presented with horrible experiences, went all cold and quiet like Tin'amen. But others reacted more like the lion—with constant fear and hypervigilance. PTSD, we'd called it back on Earth. And it had taken centuries for humans to wise up and figure out effective treatments.

My two other companions had just stared at me last night when I put my arm around the quaking mass of manliness and suggested that maybe he could find help in Emerald City.

Once the sky lightened, we had walked at a fast pace, making quick work of the distance. The spooks, the killer bees, and the metal death birds—none of that had been random. And I shuddered to think what nastiness would be sent after us next.

I hefted my knapsack higher, gripping the shoulder straps in my hand. I wasn't stupid. The birds had been trying to steal my knapsack. The spooks had told me to leave behind whatever I'd stolen. Everyone seemed to know I had taken something from the witch of the east, but no one seemed to know what. The wicked witch probably assumed I was carrying whatever I'd stolen in my bag.

I looked down at my worn hiking boots as we trudged the last few yards to the massive green city gates. What the hell was so great about a clunky old pair of boots? They weren't even attractive, with thick, almost platform-like soles and sturdy, utilitarian laces. They'd been scuffed and well-used even before I took them. Nothing special.

I shook my head. Clearly, I was missing something here.

We stopped at the city gates, and I glanced at my companions. "Uh. What now?"

Singing Crow shrugged. "No. Idea."

Tin'amen frowned at the giant doors. "I've never been here in person, but I don't think the gates are usually closed." He stepped forward and planted the palm of his metal hand in the center of the door, frowning as if he were conferring with the barrier. “No,” he said finally, withdrawing his hand. “They were closed for a reason. The city is locked against casual entry.”

Singing Crow gripped my hand and pulled me over to what looked like a windowless guard booth. He pointed and I saw the smooth, dark screen embedded in the glittering green metal. “Scan?” he asked with a bird-like tilt of his head.

I shrugged. “One way to find out.”

I planted my hand on the screen. A glowing green line appeared, rapidly scanning across my palm. Then a weird green holo face appeared above the device, a voice echoing from a speaker somewhere nearby. “Human. Genetic male. Trace magical energy. State your name, affiliation, and business.”

I arched a brow. “Dotty West, no affiliation, refugee. I am seeking sanctuary and an appointment to speak with the Wizard of Oz. My traveling companions have requests for him as well.”

I felt stupid saying the name. But “witch” and “wizard” and “magic” were the closest words my language had for these things.

The disembodied voice flowed from the speakers, all business. “Scan all members of your party.”

Each of them took turns, Tin’amen looking wary and the lion slapping a big old paw on the device. But their species and genetics were identified accurately. The device even detected the stalker’s metal alterations and the scarecrow’s cursed status.

“You may enter and seek sanctuary,” the stuffy voice informed us. “However, the wizard is not taking appointments at this time. Laser weapons, weaponized nanotech, and any personal protection devices over level two are prohibited in Emerald City. All stun weapons must be powered down. Violators will be severely and publicly punished as a warning to others. Enjoy your stay in the Emerald City! Please proceed."

I huffed, but decided to take whatever victory I could at this point. "We will also need accommodations," I informed the device. "We have little in the way of money."

The voice didn't respond.

The big doors swung open with a groan, revealing a bustling city filled with people of all shapes, sizes, and colors. One of the weirdly round Oz vehicles glided past with a hum, the exterior changing color on some sort of schedule.

I blinked, trying to sort through everything my eyes were seeing. After so long out in the unpopulated open spaces, this degree of busy civilization and technology was disorienting. *This* was what I had expected when I first landed in Oz. I had no idea that the planet's population was so divided and so strangely clumped together into enclaves and clans.

Taking a deep breath—and getting a good handful of the lion's curly pelt to tug him along with me and quell his nervous shaking—I stepped through the gates of Emerald City, and into chaos.

First things first. "We need to find lodging. Somewhere to stay until I figure out how to get the wizard's attention and get us an audience with him."

Tin'amen, who was at least a head taller than me and had several inches on Singing Crow, glanced around over the heads of most of the crowd, then pointed down the sidewalk. We followed him as he cut a swath through the bustle, gaining quite a few curious looks from the citizens going about their day. Thankfully, they weren't all grinning.

Finally, I caught sight of where Tin'amen was directing us. It was a tidy-looking row building with an old-fashioned façade made to look like a green cottage with cheery white trim. It was at odds with the modern city, but at the same time, it seemed to fit right in, since everything here was so eclectic. I paused by the bright sign out front long enough for my translator nanodes to inform me it welcomed visitors in need.

I was suddenly very conscious of how dirty and worn we all looked. And how little money we had—only my bit of EARTH currency, which they probably wouldn't accept, and a little Emerald coin Tin'amen had in his pockets from before he was abandoned in the woods. A little bell above the door rang when we entered, and a tall, sleek woman with pale green skin and a dark emerald suit dress popped up from behind a shiny wooden counter.

Her professional smile didn't waver at the sight of us. But if this place really was a mecca for travelers and the melting pot of the planet, she'd probably seen weirder. "Hello. Welcome to the Emerald City. How may I help you?"

It took me a second to figure out what was off about her. Then it clicked. Android. Well, that explained the complete lack of judgment. "Hello," I said, straightening my spine and approaching the counter. "I am a refugee. My companions are all natives of Oz. We have had some difficulties in our travels. We seek sanctuary. And an audience with the wizard."

The woman pulled up a hover screen and flipped through options with little flicks of her eyes. "We have one vacancy for public assistance cases at this time," she said in her even voice. "It will be cramped for so many people. However, if you would like, I can book the room for you for a maximum of one standard Oz week before additional lodging will need to be procured, per Emerald city code."

She glanced up at me for verification. “I will need handprint scans of all guests for security and identification purposes. Unfortunately, I cannot address your other request, as the Wizard of Oz is not accepting appointments with visitors to our fair city at this time.”

I sighed. I was sensing a pattern here. “We will take the room, thank you. We don’t have much in the way of money, though.”

She kept her eyes on me like a real person would as she talked, but at the same time, she was busy flicking her fingers from side to side as she input information in the tablet through gesture. “No payment is necessary at this time. The appropriate compensation will be determined at the end of your stay.”

Huh. Okay. The suspicious political schemer in me insisted that was a bad idea. What kind of compensation would be demanded? Who got to determine what we owed? But I was tired, dirty, and in need of a little time to think without the threat of attack or worrying about how to forage for food.

“Thank you,” I said evenly. Then I mustered up what I could of my Dotty persona. “And please, sugar, tell me a hot bath and some chocolate is included with the room.”

The AI smiled and flipped the tablet around to let us scan our hands. “The room includes luxury bathing amenities and full room service.”

Great. All that as part of a “free” public assistance program for people in need? I smelled a very large rat. But what choice did I really have? I planted my hand on the tablet and gave the AI, whose mechanical eyes probably doubled as security cameras, a sweet smile.

All-in, I supposed. I moved aside and let the others scan themselves. No one voiced what we were all thinking. This place was just as weird as the rest of Oz.

"I will need the shapeshifter who is not spelled to shift back to person-form," the AI requested calmly. "Beast form is prohibited in the Emerald City except for emergencies. This helps to ensure the safety of our citizens."

The lion-beast pushed harder against my side, as if he could crawl inside me and hide. "He's more comfortable in this form," I informed the AI.

She frowned. A clear indication that I was being rebuked, since AI didn't have emotions of their own. "I'm afraid I must insist. It is for the safety of our citizens. If he does not assume person-form, I cannot provide room and board, and the creature will be contained by the city guard. We must follow the rules. Order for the good of all, you know!"

I sighed and looked down at the lion. "Come on, big guy. Let's get this over with so we can get to our room, get cleaned up, and get something to eat."

He let out a mewling sound that was really weird coming from such a massive monster. Then he shifted back to his massive, dark-skinned man shape, stepping behind me and pressing up close as he scanned in, not seeming to realize that his being *naked* might make that position vaguely inappropriate right now.

I smiled sweetly at the AI, as if I wasn't standing smack dab in the middle of a pack of weirdoes. As if I wasn't the *ringleader* of the pack of weirdoes. "Can we go to our room now?"

She clipped a little wristband on each of us that would allow us to unlock the room, then pointed us toward a second-story room at the end of a narrow hall.

It didn't escape me that we'd been identified, signed up for some future mystery payment to be collected in a few days, *and* tagged with bracelets that only the AI could remove.

Welcome to Emerald City.

Chapter 13

Thank the stars, there was an *actual* bed waiting for us. And a beautiful little bathroom with hot running water and lovely herbal soap that smelled almost like Earth lemons and sage.

The room was small, just like the AI had warned us. But at this point, it really didn't matter. Tin'amen read through a little pamphlet that we'd found on the nightstand, informing us with what was almost a *grin* that we could obtain meals downstairs in the dining area.

Apparently, the diva in me was programmed to expect luxury anytime I left Earth. During my time as diplomat, most places I'd visited had offered me the best accommodations and food. Even when dealing with more primitive cultures, I had still been granted their version of the best they had to offer. Roughing it in the wilderness in the same set of clothes and foraging for my meals wasn't really my cup of tea. I could do it. I could survive just about anything, if I *had* to. But I was damned happy to have a soft pillow to lay my head on at night, let me tell you.

By the time we all got cleaned up, enlisted the front desk to get Lio some clothes, and got our bellies full, it was starting to get dark. There would be plenty of time for exploring the city and figuring out how to get an audience with the elusive wizard tomorrow. Tonight, I just wanted Tin'amen and Singing Crow in an actual bed.

I eyed the little replicator on the wall and let out a wistful sigh. It could produce necessities like toothpaste, lotion, soap… *lube*. But I had a feeling my dreams of sexy times were going to remain just that…dreams.

I stepped over the massive, shaggy golden beast who had flopped down on the rug beside the bed. There was no way we were going to fit *four* people on the bed, even if we wanted to. And Lio was more comfortable in his beast form anyway. He said he felt a bit less afraid when he had claws and fangs.

I clambered into bed between Singing Crow and Tin'amen, all of us stripped down to just our underwear. It was *heaven*, lying there sandwiched between the two men, cushioned on something other than the hard ground and covered with a light, fluffy comforter. Bliss.

Lio flopped over and started snoring loud enough to wake the dead.

Okay, so…maybe there were a few things that could be improved upon. Stars and nebulas, he sure passed out fast. Being terrified all the time must be exhausting.

I snuggled into the covers and ignored the noise coming from the floor, grinning when a warm, slightly calloused hand slid up my thigh. I turned my head to kiss Tin'amen as that hand trailed higher and started stroking my cock through my underwear.

Singing Crow pressed tight to my other side, nuzzling into my hair. Shifting around, I managed to get a hand down each guy's pants. It was awkward, and half my mind was worried Lio was about to wake up and catch us. But I got over that fear pretty quick, arching my back and letting out a little helpless hiss when Singing Crow bit down on my shoulder with his beak.

I froze when Lio snorted. A curly gold lion head appeared in the dim light that illuminated the bathroom threshold. Crap. I felt like a teenager caught jacking off.

Lio huffed, turned, and trotted over to the bathroom. The soft sound of the door sliding open and closed seemed loud in the bedroom. We all just lay there for a few minutes, waiting. Eventually, muffled snoring drifted through the bathroom door.

I snorted. Singing Crow vibrated with suppressed laughter as he buried his face in the crook of my shoulder. But Tin'amen, ever the practical one, slipped out of bed and immediately went to replicate some lubricant.

Thank the stars for sympathetic lion shifters.

In the blink of an eye, I found myself on my hands and knees, doing my best to swallow Singing Crow's cock and fighting back a moan as Tin'amen slowly worked his inhumanly hard cock into my ass. I shuddered and talons curled into my hair, keeping me where I was, preventing me from pulling off Crow's cock so my voice was muffled.

I'm sure we weren't quiet. At the moment, I couldn't care less. Tin'amen filled me up with long, powerful strokes, shifting his hips to peg my prostate on every thrust. I gripped the bedsheets with one hand, trying not to come. Then Tin'amen leaned forward, folding over my back so he could reach a long arm around me to grip my cock. His smooth metal hand squeezed and stroked in time with his slow, deep thrusts, and I lost my mind.

Holy exploding red dwarfs! I started to shout as pleasure wracked my body, but Singing Crow thrust his hips upward, still holding my head in place with his clawed hands. I came hard, literally choking on Crow's long dick when he came too, not even caring if I was about to die.

Death by dick would sure be one hell of a way to go.

Tin'amen released my spent cock to wrap his arm around my waist and pull me upright, positioning me so I sat back on his lap, my legs on either side of his as we knelt. I let my head fall back to rest on his metal shoulder, eyes closed as he thrust up into me with a soft growl. The sound cut off as he sank his teeth into my shoulder to hold back the noise, his cock pulsing inside my ass as he came.

Singing Crow's yellow eyes glowed in the dark as he helped me untangle myself from Tin'amen. "Beautiful," he murmured, his voice rougher than usual.

I laughed when I realized we couldn't really clean up with Lio sleeping in the bathroom. I mean, sure, it wasn't like he didn't know what we were up to when he purposefully gave us privacy. But I wasn't sure what the big, scary beast's tipping point was, you know? Maybe being rudely woken up a *second* time by horny idiots would be the straw that broke the lionbeast's back. I had come too far in my journey to risk being eaten by an angry shifter now. I unapologetically yanked the bedsheet off and used it as a rag, thoroughly sullying the poor thing before we all piled back into bed in a contented heap.

My head was pillowed on Crow's skinny shoulder, my hand on his chest as Tin'amen tenderly stroked my hip, curled around me from behind in big spoon position.

I wavered between utter happiness and anxiety. It was dangerous to let myself get attached to these men when we were in the middle of getting me home and curing them so they could go their separate ways. All it could ever be was a brief moment of pleasure. Just shallow sex and a bit of companionship during hard times. That was all.

But as I drifted off to sleep, wrapped up in the alien men I'd just made love to…it didn't feel shallow at all.

Chapter 14

Lio didn't say anything about our nighttime escapades the next morning when I shooed him out of the bathroom so I could use the facilities. He simply shifted back to man-form, pulled on his new clothes over miles of brown muscles, and went with the others to get us some breakfast. I got cleaned up and dressed, then pulled Toto out and fired him up for yet another attempt at contacting someone outside the Oz atmosphere.

My attempts had failed so many times, it surprised me when Toto gave a happy little bark and said, "Incoming message."

I quickly answered the call from an untraceable source. Only a few people knew where I was, and I was betting it wasn't an EARTH higher-up calling me to chat. I grinned when a patchy, pixelated image of Freddie's face appeared on Toto's screen.

"…aniel!" He said through the crackling static. "Hot…amn! You *are* alive!"

I huffed at him. "Like I couldn't survive a little bit of exile."

The connection cut out, then came back online again. "Not sure how long I have," Freddie said urgently. "Found a thin spot in the blocking net someone put…planet."

I frowned. I wasn't really surprised. I had suspected for a while now that my inability to get a message off planet wasn't a coincidence. "Any idea what's going on?" I asked my old friend, hoping he had answers, but also hoping he wasn't risking more than his career to help me.

"I'll give you the short story. Commander Ashburn has a brother who is on Sumborto. He's looking to invalidate an inheritance contract you helped draft. Ringing any bells?"

I swore. "The mining rights."

Freddie cut out, then came back into focus. "Gotta jet. I'm about to get busted. Don't get dead, Danny."

The call cut off, and I stared at Toto's blank screen.

Fuck my life.

"No good deed goes unpunished, huh, Toto?"

The metallic pufferdog yipped. "We have fifty-seven available closed files on the Bule family negotiations on Sumborto, sir. Should I compile them for your viewing?"

I sighed. "No. I remember all the details." Which was probably why I was here. It wouldn't do to try to take away a child's inheritance and strip-mine an allied planet with the diplomat who had protected them strolling around free.

"Can you get through the blockage to reach IMAD now?" I asked, clinging to a thread of hope.

"No, sir. All coms are down again. Mr. Freddie was running hacking programs that allowed a limited breech directly to his com unit only."

I turned Toto off and tucked him away as the others came into the room with breakfast trays. Nothing had changed, really. I knew why I was here now, but that didn't change the fact that I still needed to get an audience with the wizard and find a way to contact IMAD with my suspicions about one of EARTH's most prized military commanders.

"Well, guys," I said, once we were all done eating. "Time to figure out how to deal with a wizard."

Emerald City was a strange place. But that was nothing new to me. I had learned over the years that every city had a rhythm to it, a pulse that kept it alive. While places might look and feel different, when you got right down to it, they were all sustained in only a handful of ways. At its shiny, busy, *orderly* root, the green city ran on a simple principle. Trade. It was one of the most basic ways for a system to operate. And trade here had a lot in common with some primitive cultures back on Earth, in that the trade didn't have to involve money. People here seemed to be open to accepting items, services, information, you name it. It was just a normal, accepted part of the bartering process for two individuals to spend some time assessing what one might provide for another in exchange for a desired good or service.

It was fascinating to my sequined little diplomat's heart. Seeing what made people and cultures tick got me all fired up. But in a more practical sense, this was also excellent news for a group of misfits with no money.

However, I wasn't starry-eyed enough to think this was some sort of utopia where you could bargain for anything you needed with ease. Nope. I could easily see why the person running the place was called the "wizard." He was supposed to be a famous healer. But from everything I gathered—both from my research before I landed here and from what I'd seen and heard from the people on this planet—the guy who ran Emerald City and represented the planet's interests was first and foremost, a savvy businessman.

He knew all the right things to trade, all the right things to offer up to work his way to the information, goods, or services he needed to keep him in power and keep this city running like the glimmering utopia it presented to the world.

I was instantly suspicious.

It made me nervous that we already owed this place an undefined favor to be collected at a future date. Now the debt worsened with every little necessity we attempted to barter for.

We all needed clothes. Legally allowed personal protection weapons of some sort wouldn't be a bad idea, if we could get our hands on them. We'd need housing of some sort after our three days of charity was up. Information about Emerald City. Therapy or medical services for at least two of our group. Employment for those of us who wished to stay here. Transportation. Some means of communicating off-planet. The list went on and on. None of it was going to be free. And what did we have to trade? Virtually nothing but our time and knowledge.

I offered up labor, styling services, and knowledge about other people and places in exchange for some really basic clothing for all of us. Tin'amen provided personal defense lessons in a corner of the busy town square in exchange for emerald coin. I was shocked when scarecrow started doing oddly mesmerizing acrobatics on the other side of the thoroughfare as a street performer, collecting coin, cards offering services, and random bits of donated clothing and accessories.

It was a bizarre, but oddly refreshing, way to provide for ourselves. Lio followed in my shadow, shy and shrinking as always, jumping at any loud noise or unexpected movement around him. I had taken a job working a few hours for a clothier today, and I was currently hanging up a display of handwoven scarves and dresses, a shift in the store bartered in exchange for a few more necessary items of clothing.

Lio passed by, hauling in boxes of fabric and thread that had just been delivered on a hovercart from somewhere else in the city. He looked remarkably tasty—and *normal*—in a plain pair of blue work trousers and a loose white shirt rolled up to show off his muscular forearms. When he wasn't cowering, he was tall and wide, with all of Tin'amen's muscle, but a lot more bulk. He wasn't bodybuilder ripped, but more like farmboy strong—work-hardened but with a nice layer of padding.

I stopped ogling the guy as he went inside to drop off the last of the boxes. *Golly gee, Dotty.* Clearly, I was in need of more mental stimulation than hanging up pretty clothing required.

A part of me was forced to admit there were times when I really missed my diplomat gig, even before all this exile bullshit. I missed having to think things through and puzzle out all the million moving pieces behind every single person's motivations and political decisions. *Holy heck, what a masochist.*

What I *needed* to do, I reminded myself, was focus on figuring out a way to unravel my own twisted situation. Lio came back outside to plop down on the edge of a nearby urn of flowers, wiping sweat from his forehead with the edge of his shirt.

"That is no way to treat new clothing," I said mildly, deftly folding a scarf over a hanger while my poor brain tried to figure out a way to get an audience with the wizard of Oz.

Lio snorted. "It's just a shirt." Then he hunched his shoulders a bit, running a hand through his tangled blond curls. "Sorry. I know you spent a lot of time bargaining to get us clothes."

I shrugged. I had given myself a headache bartering for something other than rags for us to wear. I had even gotten some of our old stuff fixed up enough to be serviceable, which was no small feat. But that was the least of my worries at the moment.

"Do you have any special skills?" I mused, trying to figure out a way to get us an audience with the reclusive wizard. Maybe if we had something he wanted, we'd stand a chance of wheedling our way in.

We had all trekked across the city this morning, to the massive dome-shaped building where he apparently held court. But we hadn't been able to get past the gilded front gate.

Lio sighed. "Nah. Nothing special about me. Unless you're looking to start up a circus." He shuddered.

I paused to stare at him. "Pardon?"

He had been really guarded about his past, refusing to talk about whatever had traumatized him so badly and ended with him living alone in the middle of a small grove of trees.

He looked down at his big hands. "It was a bad joke. Sorry. But that's all I was good for, before you found me."

I hung up the last scarf on the outside display rack and went to perch on the stool the proprietor used to supervise the area for theft. This job really was the most boring thing in the world. Not suitable at all for a lady of my astounding talents. I had decided to stay in drag, since I had used Dotty's name to gain entry to the city. Probably safer that way.

"Wanna talk about it?" I asked softly, wanting to know more about the guy, but afraid of pushing for too much.

He heaved a gusty sigh. "No."

I thought that was the end of discussion, but he shifted on the planter, poking at a trailing leaf from the purple vine that grew there, then said, "They're illegal, the circuses. Or supposed to be. But no one really polices the areas in between the main cities."

I nodded. I could see that. The wide stretches of planet between the seat of each colonial ruler were largely unpopulated.

It would be a great place to get up to some shit. Maybe start some sort of shady traveling side-show and hit up all the smaller burgs, staying under the radar of the rulers. And also, I was pretty sure at least two or three of the rulers didn't give a flying fuck about the populous of Oz anyway. They probably encouraged the behavior.

"They kept you as a sideshow freak?" I ventured, afraid of setting him off.

He shrugged. "A few shifters. Some magic users. A few people with deformities and stuff. I was strong enough to leave. But I was just too scared of their electric whips and taser-prods. Afraid I'd get caught again and they'd treat me even worse because I'd escaped the first time." He swallowed. "Always afraid. Such a coward."

I frowned. What the actual fuck? Crossing my legs and putting my elbow on my knee, chin in my hand, I bent to meet his eyes. "Hey. You're not a coward for being afraid of torture." I was pretty sure whoever kept him had probably been good at using psychology to convince him that staying was less painful than trying to escape. I knew the type. I had lobbied against them and put them in EARTH prisons often enough.

Lio nodded. "I know. But it feels that way sometimes." His golden-brown eyes met mine, open and pleading. So full of emotion. "Especially now. I'm not a prisoner or a captive anymore. But I'm still so weak. Scared of everything. It's like a spell that I can't break."

I sighed. More magic talk. But hell, maybe he was right. It could just be plain old PTSD. But this was Oz, a place ripe with powerful energy manipulators. He very well *could* have some magic laid on him. Something that made him so fearful he'd be easy to imprison and manipulate into behaving however the ringmaster, or whatever they called themselves, desired.

I opened my mouth to offer comfort, to tell him maybe the wizard would have an answer to anything magical that might be ailing him, but my mouth snapped shut when a thought occurred to me. The witch of the north hadn't seemed to know me, or to know of an exile being transported here. I knew it wasn't just my flawless drag, and my amazing acting abilities. I knew EARTH hadn't even bothered to follow the regulations for exile. Probably on purpose. By Terran law, they were required to provide *some* explanation for why an Earthling was dropped off on another planet. It was part of a ruling that was made by IMAD after EARTH had plopped one too many difficult people in the wrong place and they'd staged a planet-wide uprising. Oops. Our bad. Earth people really did suck sometimes.

Anyway, if no one had been informed of my exile, that meant I had yet one more potentially valuable piece of information I could use to bargain with the wizard—an accusation to be levied at EARTH by the planet itself, rather than just on my behalf. That, combined with what I'd seen so far on Oz, and Lio's story just now…I could cause a ruckus. I just had to decide the right way to go about it. So many options, really.

If I lived long enough, that is. The wizard kind of sounded like a mob boss. And he might have a stake in what the witches of the north and south were up to. If that was the case, he'd just have me eliminated for threatening his little empire. No one would know, since I was probably an unregistered exile. No one knew I was here.

Only one way to find out, I supposed. I needed to get a message to the wizard. And if he wasn't going to let me make an appointment the old-fashioned way, well, I was Dotty West, diva queen extraordinaire. If anyone could make a spectacle, it was me.

We set up our stage on the public street right outside the wizard's…house? Office? Compound? Whatever the big green domed structure qualified as, I had it on good authority that it was where the reclusive ruler of Emerald City spent most of his time, running his empire and doling out healing and favors when he saw fit. We didn't have much in the way of resources. But if there is one thing I know how to do, it's put on a show—no matter the venue.

It all went faster than I had anticipated. I expected to have to spend a long time annoying the guy. In the end, it only took two days and a voice amplification device I bartered off a woman who ran auctions. Polished to a high shine, Dotty West paraded up and down the street, spewing conspiracy theories as loudly and in as profane a manner as possible.

I started with the claim that I had evidence the wizard of Oz didn't even exist. He was so reclusive, and he was refusing to see people. Maybe he wasn't even real. Maybe the town was being run by AI bots built by the witch of the south. The AI bots were clearly in league with the witch of the north, which was why there were so many pollen users in Emerald City.

It hadn't escaped my notice that there were a ton of other people in the city wearing bracelets similar to the ones we'd had slapped on us when we arrived. The locals hadn't wanted to give me any information, but chatting people up for their secrets was kind of my specialty. In the end, I had discovered that the people wearing bracelets were all pollen addicts. So…maybe some of my conspiracy theories were a bit more true than others.

I must have gotten something right, since barely two hours into our second day of loud and proud accusations about everything from the wizard himself, to drug cartels, to secret spy implants in their food, the gates to the wizard's abode opened up and a disgruntled employee came striding out.

"Miss West?" he ground out.

I smiled and patted my hair. "Why yes, yes I am. You can call me Dotty. Did you *need* something, sugar? I'm kind of busy here."

I pressed the button on the voice amplifier that was stuck to my Adam's apple, causing my voice to blast him point blank. "I have to inform the uneducated masses about the corruption in this fair city."

His eyelid may have started twitching.

"The great and benevolent wizard of Oz requests an audience," he ground out.

I grinned at the constipated expression on his purplish face. His coloring was completely different than my metal man, but from his build and his sharp features, I'd wager he had some stalker blood. His black suit was suitably stuffy.

"Why…me?" I said with feigned shock. I turned to look at my companions, who had prowled the street with me the last couple days. "Did you hear that, boys? The big old wizard wants to talk to little old me. Whyever for, I wonder?"

I'm pretty sure our escort was grinding his teeth at this point. "Would you mind turning off the amplification device, Miss West?"

"Oh?" I said, louder than necessary, causing a squeal of reverb when the sound bounced off a nearby building. "Is this thing still on?"

Look, *someone* had to pay for making me beg for a meeting. It just happened to be this poor schmo's lucky day. I slipped my arm through his and strutted down the walkway like it was a catwalk, dragging him along like a needless accessory.

Chapter 15

We were led through the glistening entryway, all smooth white and sparkling green, with accents of gold and silver. It looked like the temple of a healer who was good at what they did—airy, warm, and lacking the antiseptic feel some places of healing had.

I was both surprised and yet not at all surprised, when we were led past the welcoming front of the building and to a staircase. It went down, of course, into the bowels of the evil lair.

I tried not to show my disdain on my face. Something about the wizard and his setup had me suspicious already, I didn't need to be dragged to a dark dungeon or underground laboratory to have my fears confirmed.

I shared a wary glance with my companions. Everyone seemed hesitant. Except Tin'amen. He just looked as stoic as always, though I could tell his jaw was clenched from the way his cheek muscle flexed. His silver eyes were watchful. Great. If the ex-soldier was just as uneasy as I was…that didn't bode well.

When we reached the bottom of the stairs, we were led even deeper into the building. There was no way the original dome was this wide. We must truly be below the city streets now. The décor changed as we descended. The windows and skylights were gone, of course. But the colors made a subtle shift too, until by the time we were standing outside a set of dark, polished wood doors, the healer vibe had become that of some decadent den of iniquity.

The white floors had been replaced by shiny black stone. The green walls were replaced with red, with occasional green gems set in the leaves of the vines that were painted on the wallpaper. The gold accents were still there, but their glow was dimmed without all the natural light.

Sleek recessed sconces lit the place in a warm glow that felt close, like being in a womb lit from the outside.

Sure, it was creepy. But it also looked just as expensive as the upstairs. The doors opened and we were ushered inside by the employee who had brought us in. The room turned out to be a study, the walls covered in miles of bookshelves that held not only books, but glass and crockery jars containing all sorts of liquids, and powders, and lumpy things suspended in fluid that I didn't examine too closely.

A dark green rug with gold poppies stamped on the edges led from the doorway of the long room all the way to a big, gleaming black desk. It reminded me of the royal carpet that was used in some empires, and I swallowed hard. I sure as hell felt like we were suddenly approaching royalty. The doors closed behind us with a soft thud, and we slowly walked the length of that plush runner.

At the desk sat a chestnut-haired man with sharp, exaggerated humanoid features, his skin a pale green, eyes black as night. A pair of short, nubby horns protruded from his hairline. Sensuous lips curved upward in a slight, patient smile as he rested his chin on his folded hands, a dark overlord awaiting the approach of his lowly subjects.

Well, screw that. I drew my shoulders back and walked tall in my silver spiked heels. He might be king of this weird city, but I was a damned *queen.*

I stopped in front of the desk, raking my eyes over his black suit with the red pinstripes. It looked vaguely vintage Earth in style. But this guy wasn't human. Nor was he native to Oz. I was raking my memory for the specifics, but I'd met his kind before. Far, far away from here, in a place that called to mind more earthy farmer vibes, and less gangster.

The wizard was supposed to represent the interests of the planet itself. I had assumed—or been led to believe—that he was native. Clearly that was an outright lie.

I tucked the information away for future pondering. It probably had some bearing on his interests in this weird game the colonists were all playing.

"Welcome to Oz," the man said in a voice so deep it shivered over my skin and resonated in my bones. His smile became a smirk as he sat back in his posh office chair, a deep dimple appearing in one cheek as one corner of his mouth lifted.

I huffed. "Thanks." Extending one hand, I tried to play it cool and not let my tiredness and frustration show. Suddenly, I wasn't sure I was up to the level of game playing he was about to do. "I'm Dotty West." I nodded to my companions. "These are—"

"The cursed scarecrow, the heartless metal man, and the cowardly lionbeast," he said, interrupting me in that same smooth, congenial, yet dangerous voice. His smirk deepened. "The wizard knows everything, isn't that the word on the street? Though…apparently someone recently claimed that I don't exist."

I crossed my arms over my chest, pretending to be a hard-ass, but really wondering about my life choices. Stars and comets, this guy was intense. Maybe provoking him like a child hadn't been the best idea I'd ever had. I was *so* not in Kansas.

"If you know it all, then you know I'm here as an illegal exile and that we've come to bargain with you. I need to get to Interstellar. Singing Crow needs his curse lifted. Tin'amen and Lio need…whatever magic you have that can help them, but probably also a good therapist or whatever equivalent you have here."

He watched me with nothing showing on his face. Just this small almost smile that seemed to convey bland disinterest. "A tall order," he said in that low voice, reaching out to pick up the round tumbler on his desk and take a sip. "And you believe you have something valuable enough to buy all that magic? After you attacked my citizens and threatened my rehabilitation program?"

I rolled my eyes. Rehab. Right. *That* was totally why there were a bunch of marked pollen users in this town, and not so he could track their movements and manipulate them somehow—probably with the promise of more drugs.

"You're right," I snarked in response to his question. "Why would anyone ever just help someone because it was the decent thing to do? You left me no choice but to get weird in order to get in here, dude. All I wanted was a chat. Was that so much to ask?"

His smile grew a fraction, but his eyes narrowed, watching me like a predator. "I used to give away my services for a pittance," he said easily. "Back when I was nothing but a young boy orphaned on a strange alien planet, pedaling my miracle tonics out of the back of a beat-up old traveling cart."

He arched one dark brow. "I believed everyone should have access to what they needed, regardless of their social status or their ability to pay. So, I bartered. I traded—sometimes money, sometimes food or clothing, sometimes something as worthless as a button or a pebble found on the side of the road—in exchange for my healing magic." He spread his hands in a magnanimous gesture. "Why do you think Emerald City operates on trade, my dear…girl? It is the foundation of my empire—I only want every citizen to have a fair chance at happiness and wellbeing."

I somehow managed to strangle back the laugh that wanted to escape at that. Right. *This* guy was a humanitarian.

"Seems to have turned out well for you," I said easily, shooting a meaningful glance at all his expensive decor. "But in answer to your question, I have information to barter. I could use that information to destroy Oz and throw everything it is into chaos. I could play the kidnapping victim. I could spread lies and half-truths. I could reveal how you are all exploiting the natives and violating at least half a dozen interstellar laws and treaties."

I arched a brow at him, imitating his earlier expression. "*Or* I could use this information to help you set yourself up to avoid the destruction when it all falls apart. I could ensure you get some sort of immunity."

I wouldn't. I mean, I probably *could* negotiate some twisted backroom deal with my skills. But nope. He was as dirty as the rest, I was sure of it. And he was going to go down with them.

He huffed a soft laugh. "So, you offer to trade…blackmail."

I shrugged. This was probably where he had me murdered to shut me up. But wouldn't it be better to turn me loose and look like a helpful benefactor in the eyes of Interstellar?

He stood. And fuck, he was every bit as tall as Tin'amen, shoulders broad and straight, tapering down to a trim waist. Not a man who sat around doing nothing all day and getting nice and weak. Nope. He'd probably fight his own fights. Maybe murder me with his own two hands. Great.

"Fine," he said with another of those smile-smirks. "I'll trade you blackmail for blackmail."

I blinked at him. What? "Uh. No, that's not what—"

But once again, he kept talking right over the top of me. "I will grant all of your requests. But first, you will run a little errand for me. Call it a…test of your integrity, shall we?"

I gritted my teeth together. "What do you want?"

His smile grew, bright and easy. And I felt the temperature in the room drop and my heartbeat slow. There was a chill in that smile. Like, so much ice it made me shiver.

"I want you to visit a friend of mine in the west and bring back something that belongs to her. Something she values. I will send you to Interstellar with a bow round your neck…Dotty. I'll heal your companions. I'll even throw in a free gift and get the witches of north and south to stop bothering you the way they have on your little trip." He arched a dark brow. "See? I do know things."

Then his expression went serious. "But first, I need you to bring me the crystal ball West uses to spy on us all and cast her spells. She is a mixed blood, you see? Only someone with human blood can touch the crystal."

I blinked at him. "What?" That sure as hell sounded like a death trap.

He raised his brows at me. "In order to prove my abilities, I will heal one of your companions before you set out. The others will be healed, and you will be sent on your way to Interstellar, just as soon as you return here and place that crystal in my hands."

I closed my eyes. This was some kind of weird trap. I wasn't a secret agent or an assassin. I was going to end up dead. But then again…I did *know* an assassin. And a guy who could do acrobatics and a little magic. And a dude who could turn into a scary (if he managed not to cower) beast. Maybe I wasn't completely helpless?

No. That was just stupidity mixed with a little dash of my own hopeless optimism.

"That's the dumbest thing I've ever heard," I said flatly. "First of all, the woman hates me. There's this little thing that happened where I accidentally squashed her half-sister under my landing pod…. Just, no. She's been trying to get to me the entire way here. She sent spooks, and bees, and killer birds…."

He tilted his head, sharp black eyes examining me. "Did she?"

There was something there, some implication in that question. But he moved on before the puzzle piece could slot into place.

"One of your traveling companions will remain behind. Call it insurance. Wouldn't want you deciding to give up along the way."

The three men around me shifted restlessly at his words, and I knew they were dying to speak up, to refuse to be left behind.

I scowled. But honestly, it wasn't just *my* wishes at stake here. If I could pull this off, all three of my new friends would get their lives back.

"Fine," I said on a sigh. "I'll do it. And you can keep one traveling companion here."

His dark eyes downright *sparkled.* "It is a bargain then." He held out a hand and I took it, surprised at how cold his skin was. Energy sparked between us, sealing the promise. Magic workers were some scary shit.

"Choose which companion I will heal," the wizard said, crossing to the bookshelves to run a finger along a row of labeled jars.

I took a deep breath, turning to look at the three silent men at my side. Tin'amen gestured at the other two with his metallic hand. "One of them. If we go to fight, a heart—the ability to feel—would only be a liability."

I didn't really agree. But I respected his request. I watched Lio as he worked on getting words out past his fear. "The crow," he said softly. "I'm a coward. Not cursed. His thing is more important."

Again, I didn't really agree with him, but I knew I wasn't going to convince him otherwise.

And he *was* kind of right. The most physically impaired was certainly the scarecrow. I glanced at Singing Crow. He shook his head and gestured a taloned bird hand at the others. "Them."

I smiled. "You're all so selfless. I don't know how you do it."

I turned back to the patiently waiting wizard. "Remove Singing Crow's curse, please."

He nodded and pulled down one of the jars, a small wooden box, and a dark purple gemstone. We all watched as he took the stone, rolled it in some glittery dust inside the box, then dipped it into whatever liquid the jar held. He then chanted something in his native language that even my translator couldn't parse. Energy flowed from him in a visible wave, infusing the stone and doing…something. All I knew was I could feel the energy in the air, like a palpable snap as he activated the magic.

Then he beckoned to Singing Crow. When the lanky guy approached the desk, the wizard held out the stone. "Swallow it, and the curse will dissolve over the course of a day or two."

Singing Crow reached out to take the stone, but the wizard pulled his hand back at the last moment. Leaning close, he gripped the back of the scarecrow's head and leaned in to whisper something into his ear.

The scarecrow froze. When the wizard pulled back, they stared at each other for a couple of drawn-out heartbeats as I wondered what the hell the wierdo wiz had just said to my crow. Then Singing Crow lifted his hand and tossed the gemstone in his mouth, closing his eyes, lips moving as he chanted something to himself and swallowed. I thought I heard the phrase "I believe."

What the hell? Had the wizard just given Singing Crow a *mantra?* He was a complete charlatan. But what other choice did we have?

The wizard smiled. "One down, three to go." Then he looked at me like he was some sort of beneficent angel bestowing favors on the masses, rather than a psychopath sending me out on a hopeless death quest. "I will keep the metal soldier."

I blinked at him. *Ha.* "Nope."

He gave me a patient look. "That was part of the bargain, sealed with magic. I get to keep one of your traveling companions here as insurance."

I smiled at him, my own voice syrupy sweet. "But you never said *you* got to choose who stayed."

He narrowed his eyes at me. "Then you may choose. I suppose it doesn't matter." He flicked a glance at Tin'amen, though, that said he had *really* wanted my metal man. I shuddered to think why. Experiments, maybe?

I grinned. "Okay. I choose Toto."

I took off my knapsack and opened it, awkwardly pulling out the pufferdog and handing it to a confused wizard.

He looked at the dog. Then at me.

I winked. "That model *is* marketed as an excellent traveling companion." Then I frowned. "But be careful with him, please. I've had that old guy for a long time. I'm kind of attached to his pretty face."

The wizard's expression was priceless as he looked down into the ugly face of my weird TOTO.

Then he lifted his black eyes to meet mine. And he *laughed.* The sound was like melted chocolate pouring from a spoon. I think I got half a stiffy. Scared horny. For fuck's sake.

"I *like* you, Dotty West," the wizard said when the laughter subsided. "I do hope you make it back here in one piece."

I shook my head. So did I, dude. So did I.

Chapter 16

So, I guess we didn't have to worry about what to do when our temporary charity housing arrangement expired. That was a plus. Although, the service we were rendering the wizard seemed less desirable than doing a little house hunting. The AI at the inn informed us we were allowed one extra night, per the wizard's request. And the stupid bracelets stayed on.

I glared at the hateful thing attached to my wrist as I packed away the last of my stuff. I suspected they were tracking devices. That way anyone who decided to use the temporary housing and then skip out without paying the city back could be easily located and dragged back here for forced labor.

Now, they served as a convenient way for the Wizard of Oz to keep track of us at all times. There would be no "accidentally" getting lost when we decided to give up on the quest.

Glancing around the room, I braced myself before joining the others downstairs. I really wasn't much of a rough and tumble guy. But here I was, about to embark on yet another foray into the Ozma-4 wilderness.

We had to make our way to the wicked witch of the west on foot. Apparently, she had some sort of enchantments or security tech that kept people from approaching or using machinery in her territory. Paranoid of her. But smart, I supposed, given the state of affairs between the colonial rulers and all.

On the up side, we wouldn't be roughing it quite so much this time around. I hefted my heavy pack. It seemed like the wizard really did want us to be successful in this little snatch and dash endeavor. A bunch of equipment and supplies were delivered to our room the night before we left. Sleeping rolls. Food rations. Small personal tasers. A map. Even a com on a private channel that we could use to communicate with the wizard until we lost signal.

Golly gee, how nice of him to outfit us properly for marching to our doom.

Why he didn't just send his own people, the world may never know. He *said* he thought the witch might believe we were coming to her for assistance because the rest of the colony rulers had it in for us. I was willing to play that up. Hell, I *did* kind of want to escape them all. North was a creepy drug lord, South ripped people apart and brainwashed them into thinking they were only valuable as cyborgs, and the wizard was a manipulative mafia boss. How much worse could West really be?

Don't answer that, please, sweetheart. Geeze, I'd spent so long in character that even my *thoughts* were starting to take on a decidedly "Dotty" tone.

The Wizard of Oz knew who I was now, and traveling in drag *was* a bit of a…drag. *Ha, ha.* So, I left our borrowed room in trousers, a men's pull-over shirt, and a light, utilitarian jacket. It was weird being myself after so long in costume. I kept my stolen boots. I'd broken them in, so they hugged my feet by this point. I wasn't about to start the process over again with a new pair of shoes.

My mind played over our last interaction with the wizard the previous evening. He had nonchalantly asked me how I walked all the way to the Emerald city from Moonkin City in heels. His dark eyes said he knew I had stolen the boots. And for fuck's sake, what was it with the damned dead witch's hiking boots that got everyone so hot to trot?

"They're reliable footwear," the weirdo wiz had said, slapping me on the shoulder and leaning in to whisper the words like they were a threat. "Don't lose them."

While I really didn't want to follow the creep's instructions, clearly there was something weird going on here. So, I clunked down the stairs this morning wearing my battered, *reclaimed* boots.

As we left the Emerald City—following the yellow brick road once again, since apparently it connected all the major colony cities—I could sense the tension in my companions. None of us liked this one bit.

"Well," I said with a big grin, hoisting up my backpack straps and puffing up my chest. "Everyone ready for an adventure? Some sightseeing? Take in all the colorful scenery Oz has to offer?"

Tin'amen just looked at me, his face impassive. "Being Daniel doesn't seem to have any effect on your mouth."

I arched my brows at him as Lio huffed a beastly snort from my other side. "*Excuse* you?"

I got a maybe, teeny, *almost* there smirk before Tin'amen turned and started off down the road.

I looked to Singing Crow for help, my eyes wide. "Did…did he just make a *joke*? Was he *teasing* me?"

The scarecrow laughed and nuzzled my neck affectionately. And I thought the sound seemed more human, less bird. "Must.

Really. Like you."

I rolled my eyes. "Stars forbid."

I couldn't stop the doofy grin that was probably on my face as we left Emerald City. Sure, we might be about to die horrible deaths. But the shiny guy liked me. So, everything was fine, right?

We made good time as we traveled the yellow brick road through fields with actual people and bots working in them. It was the most life I'd seen on Oz so far, outside of a city. The farmers watched us from a distance with a bored sort of interest, rather than the hostile wariness I'd noticed from the few people we'd passed on the way *to* the Emerald City from the north.

Interesting. How was it, exactly, that the people living between the territory of a slick manipulator and a demented force of evil looked…content …while everywhere else the natives were either stoned out of their minds, fighting amongst each other, or treating their fellow natives with suspicion?

Lio bumped against my thigh as we walked, and I threaded my hand loosely into his curly pelt for reassurance. Honestly, I'm not sure who needed it the most, the constantly frightened shifter, or me. I hated that I had gotten them all tangled up in my drama and was even now leading them into danger with me.

Singing Crow paced at my side, his yellow eyes raking over me, perceptive as always. "We will survive."

I glanced at him, arching my brows. "Hold up. Did you just… you spoke a full sentence! And it sounded so easy, and human. Or…you know, not human, but not a bird." I flapped my hand lamely to dismiss my faux pass of calling another humanoid-looking being "human." It was elitist and ignorant to regard humans as the only form of higher life that mattered.

His lips quirked up in a half smile. "Feels different."

I studied him critically, noting the slight shrinking of his beak and bird hands. "Holy shit, I think the wizard's magic is *actually* working!"

I didn't try to hide my disbelief. I assumed the vaguely sinister wiz was just a special kind of snake oil salesman. Sure, I *hoped* his powers were real—but I didn't actually believe he could fix people or magically solve all of our problems.

And yet…I was sure the scarecrow was looking less cursed as the day progressed.

Tin'amen had drawn ahead of us, but he slowed and waited for us to catch up. His facial expression didn't change, but he tilted his head and lifted his flesh-and-blood hand to touch Singing Crow's face. "Daniel is correct. You are changing."

His fingertips lingered, and the two men stared at each other in the most adorably awkward way. Then Tin'amen dropped his hand and turned away with a muttered, "I'm sure you'll look just like every other crow in no time."

The big softie.

Singing Crow just shook his head, and we all continued walking, the yellow brick road taking us over more hills and valleys and toward a forest. I eyed the distant trees warily. The forest we had traveled through on our trip between Moonkin City and Emerald City had been fine. A bit dark, but it offered shelter. And no horrible native beasts had emerged from it to devour passing travelers. But this….

We paused on the rise of a hill with a good view of an endless stretch of dark trees. From a distance, they resembled the conifers back on Earth. But the whole of the forest looked… gloomy. And a low fog clung to the ground where the rolling Ozma fields gave way to the encroaching forest.

Some sort of large birds soared over the tops of the trees, gliding along like vultures on the updrafts.

"Does anyone else suddenly feel like running for no logical reason?" I said asked dryly.

Lio pushed up against my thigh again in agreement. Singing Crow nodded. Even Tin'amen paused to give the question real thought. "It is just a forest," our metal companion said, resuming his stalking toward the evil wood of darkness.

I mean, if I was going to finally admit that magic existed, then I was going all in. If magic existed, then so did evil witches who lived in dark forests and ate human flesh….

Tin'amen didn't even look back as he spoke, still headed toward danger. "This is why a weapon has no heart. Are we completing our mission now? Or would you rather turn back?"

I rolled my eyes and pushed myself into motion, jogging to catch up with his long-legged stride. "Well *excuse* me for having a healthy sense of self-preservation."

He glanced at me from the corner of his silver eyes, a faint smirk lifting one corner of his perfect, snarky mouth. "Don't worry, Daniel. I will hold you in my arms at night to keep you safe."

I'm not an innocent guy, but I admit I blushed. "Damn right you will. But despite the dress wearing and the archaic Earth gender stereotypes, I'm not *actually* a damsel in distress, you know."

He just shrugged. "You are not a soldier."

I huffed. "Technically, still military, even if they shoved me off into the far reaches of space. They never discharged me. Just retired me."

He laughed then, the sound rich and wonderful. But irritating. "You were a wordsmith. A *cajoler*. Information and a quick wit were your weapons. You know what I meant. I can survive physical altercation much easier than you. And I am well aware you are no damsel."

Again with that sideways look that made my whole body heat up by a few degrees. "Well. Good. Just so we're on the same page then," I muttered.

He laughed silently at my side.

We reached the dark, scary woods before I even realized how much ground we'd crossed. Tin'amen's banter had distracted me from the fact that we were approaching the border between the wizard's territory and the land claimed by the wicked witch of the west. Which, yeah, was probably his intention the whole time. Sneaky silver snake.

"Into the woods," I sang out, not really expecting my companions to understand the reference to an ancient Earth musical production. I wasn't disappointed. Crow just shook his head fondly at my antics, but Tin'amen startled and looked at me like he was concerned for my wellbeing.

"Oh, I'm fine," I said, waving away the silver guy's concern. "One day, I'm gonna expose you to so much Earth culture your little brain will explode."

He just sighed. Singing Crow patted my shoulder in passing. "I'm lucky to be so brainless, then."

We all froze at the soft, lilting sound of his voice. "Holy shit," I breathed.

He glanced back at us, one black brow quirked in question. "What?"

I shook my head. "You sound like…*magic*."

He ducked his head and turned away. "I sound like me. Finally. It's…strange."

Tin'amen licked his lips and took a deep breath. Clearly, he *also* enjoyed that rich, sexy new voice. Then he ruined the moment by saying, "Stay close to each other and be watchful. This place is overrun by the witch's beasts."

And on that note, we entered the wicked witch's forest.

Chapter 17

This woods and the woods we'd traveled through before were two completely different creatures. The darkness under the canopy of trees was oppressive, as if something filtered out the natural ambient light that would usually exist. And the moment we stepped under the shade of the first tree, I was wracked with a deep sense of foreboding. I got a chill down my spine, and goosebumps stood up on my arms. It was the strangest thing I'd ever felt—and I immediately knew it wasn't natural. I was *not* that much of a fainting flower, thank you very much.

Clearly there was magic at work here. Maybe something to repel trespassers or enemies of the wicked witch of the west.

It nearly worked. Everything in me wanted to turn around and run back to the Emerald City as fast as my legs could carry me. But there was more at stake here than just my own freedom from exile. Tinman and Lio needed me to keep going so they could receive their magic cure-all from the wizard. And I suspected Singing Crow would need help reintegrating with his people, since they'd essentially shunned him when he was cursed. So, I squared my shoulders and soldiered on.

There was a clear path to follow. The yellow brick road would lead us right to our destination. *You're brave enough to walk down a damned road*, I remined myself firmly.

But Lio wasn't so lucky. He had shifted back to his person-form, and the big guy clung to my hand like a lifeline, his entire body shuddering with poorly suppressed fear. I squeezed his hand in silent reassurance, wishing I could do something to ease his terror.

"It's just a forest," I told him quietly as the others walked ahead of us. "Just trees and the occasional squirrel…or whatever you have here that's similarly small, and furry, and harmless."

He swallowed with an audible click, his bright green eyes darting from side to side, scanning the trees. "I was in the deep forest when they grabbed me," he said in a voice that was one step removed from a whisper. "It just…I feel like they'll jump out of the trees at any moment with their electric prods and their restraining magic and I won't be able to fight them off." He shook his head. "I *know* I'm being a coward. But I just keep seeing the bars of my old cage. I can almost feel the burn of being zapped."

Oh. Well, that rather explained the fear of the woods. I pointed up ahead of us, where Tin'amen was telling Singing Crow some story about when he was younger. Before all the soldiering had hardened his heart.

"You see that big shiny guy up there?" I whispered to Lio. "The one with the axe and the bad attitude? I'm pretty sure nothing's getting past him."

At Lio's snort, I continued. "We've all got tasers, and I'm not afraid to use mine with *extreme* prejudice against anything that could possibly try to harm you. And the scarecrow… well, I'm pretty sure his magic is returning as his curse fades. I'm not sure what all he can do, but I know he'll fight with us. You're not alone. You're not an easy target this time." I squeezed his hand again. "And you're *not* a coward!"

He looked skeptical, but at least he slowly stopped shaking.

"Tell me about your people," I said, hoping to calm him further, but also just curious to know more about shapeshifters. "Are they all like you?"

He licked his lips and gave me a shy look. "You really want to know? You're not just asking to distract me? I don't want to bore you."

I rolled my eyes. "Do I strike you as the sort of person to purposefully ask for boredom?" I nudged my shoulder against his side. "Tell me about lion people."

So he did. I smiled to myself, feeling this warm little glow in my belly as the big, golden-haired guy unwound. I could tell that he loved his people. His voice was full of joy as he told me all about the village where he had grown up and spent most of his life. He eventually let go of my hand to gesture wildly as he told me about rambling through the fields and forests with his pride of fellow lion shifters.

This was the real Lio. Big and warm, and taking up space with his exuberant presence. I watched with awe as the cowering beast was replaced by one of those people you just gravitated toward. Someone whose very presence invited you to bask in its comfort.

I wanted to murder the people who had hurt him, who had tried to break him and rob the world of *this*. I would steal a million valuable objects from dangerous witches if that was what it took to heal his fear and trauma.

Tin'amen was right. My soft heart was a liability. I was coming to care about my companions far too deeply. But I couldn't find it in myself to stop. It was like I was running downhill, picking up momentum as I went, until I was left grasping at anything I passed in a futile attempt to slow my descent.

We walked as long as we could, making the most of the fading light. But eventually, the darkness started to close in.

"This place looks good," Tin'amen said, he and Singing Crow stopping to let us catch up.

I glanced around. It was fairly flat here, the trees a bit further from the road than they were in some places, and we'd be on top of a gentle rise, where theoretically Tin'amen and Singing Crow —and probably Lio too—could see danger approaching in the night with their superior vision. "Looks good," I said agreed.

Singing Crow gestured at the trees. "Should we risk gathering firewood?"

I smiled reflexively at the sound of his beautiful voice and his perfectly easy words. He caught me staring and smiled back, and I realized he barely possessed a little hint of his beak.

Tin'amen watched this little exchange impassively. As if he wasn't also waiting with bated breath to see what our crow looked and acted like when he was fully himself again. The big liar pants. He was fooling no one. I knew full well that he was getting closer to the crow man with every passing day.

"I will go with the scarecrow to collect wood," the metal man said evenly. "You two stay here. I don't think it's safe to be alone. We should stay in pairs at all times."

I nodded. I wasn't really keen on wandering the creepy black woods by myself. And besides, it wasn't like I was just going to up and abandon Lio, when the place clearly triggered all his old fears. "We'll stay put," I promised. "Maybe check in with our generous and caring benefactor." That last part? Heavy on the sarcasm. Cause the wizard was definitely not my favorite person right now.

With a curt nod, Tin'amen headed into the woods. Singing Crow trailed behind him, studying his own hands as he went. *Yeah, buddy, I really want to see what you can do with functional hands too….*

I shook myself out of a really nice fantasy about hand jobs and fingering. Seriously, my ability to focus on the important things had really gone to shit since I arrived on Oz.

Sighing, I took my heavy backpack off my back and dropped it on the ground, then rummaged around until I found the little com device the wizard had given us.

Plopping down to sit cross-legged in the middle of the road, I flipped open the screen, opened a link and waited for it to connect. Lio sank down beside me, dropping his own pack and leaning back against it like the backrest of a chair.

Static crackled from the com, and a holo-image flared to life, seeming too bright in the gathering darkness. The wizard of Oz smiled indulgently at us, too put together and perfect, even for a holo image. "Good evening, my new friends. I'm happy to see you're in one piece."

I didn't roll my eyes or call bullshit, but it was a close thing. If he was *so* concerned for our welfare, he wouldn't have demanded that we go on this suicide quest in order to earn his assistance. "Yep," I said in a flat voice. "Reached the creepy-assed woods. Setting up camp for the night, boss." I gave a sarcastic salute.

A soft, happy bark sounded, and Toto appeared in the viewing area. His adorably ugly holo image warmed my heart.

Then the wizard ruined it by tapping *my* pet on the nose with one elegant finger and grinning like a happy child. "I must say," he cooed. "I find the companion you left behind even more delightful than the one I wanted. Such a fascinating little creature!"

I refrained from gagging and lifted my chin a notch instead. "Stop being cute with my Toto. It's disgusting. Really ruins your mafia boss image."

He chuckled, the sound dark and full of devious promise. "Did you know I'm a wiz at electronics? Your TOTO companion's security codes were decent. But I managed to get around them. Now we're *best* friends, he and I."

Those devious eyes stared right into my own. I growled at him. "What? Stay the hell out of my files! That's personal information!"

He just chuckled. "Stay safe, Danny boy. Be vigilant. Good luck."

Then the bastard cut the connection. I just stared at the comm device for a few seconds, fuming. That slimy snake was rooting around in my private files! The stars only knew what kind of information he was getting his grubby hands on, or how he would decide to use it against me later. He called me Danny. That wasn't a coincidence. The only person who ever dared to call me that was my mother. Was it a threat? Was he planning on going after my family to extort some other service from me if we survived this trip?

Lio patted my knee with one big hand. "You okay?"

I sighed and stuffed the com back into my backpack, then I aped Lio's posture, leaning back against my lumpy backrest. "Oh, I'll live. Just annoyed. I've never wanted to punch someone in the face quite so badly as I'd like to clock that asshole. It's irritating. I don't usually let people get to me like that."

He smiled fondly at me as twilight fell around us. "I think he just knows exactly what buttons to push." He gestured at my pack and the hidden com. "He threatened something important to you?"

I sighed. "Yeah. My family. I think."

He nodded. "That makes sense. You're such a solid, calm guy. But you get riled up when people you care about are being mistreated."

Okay, yeah. He had a point. I was willing to be passive to a fault. Up to a point. But give me an injustice or a wrong to right and all bets were off. I may have been called ruthless a few times in my diplomat career.

I let out a breath and tried to focus on the here and now, rather than thoughts of what potential evil the wizard could possibly get up to at some point in the future. "I'm sorry," I muttered. "How are you doing?" I turned toward him to study his face, to look him over for any signs of tension. "No more shakes?"

He shook his head and reached for me, sliding one big, warm hand along my jaw to cup my face. "I'm okay. But I feel bad that you have to worry about me on top of everything else."

I licked my lips and tried not to get all hot and bothered staring into those bright green eyes, entirely too conscious of his touch on my skin. "It's not a problem. I promise."

His gaze flicked downward, toward my lips, then back up to meet my eyes. "Thank you. For putting up with me. For trying to save me from myself."

I swallowed as heat flooded my face. "Not a hardship. Trust me." My heart was suddenly thudding away in my chest like high heels down a runway.

Then Lio leaned in, pulling me closer with his grip on my jaw, tilting my head up and pressing his lips to mine.

All I could think of was how *warm* he felt. How golden his energy was. How I could just sink into the big, fluffy shifter, wrap him around me like a comfy blanket. I kissed him back like I was starving. I should be thinking of comforting *him*, but instead, all I could think was how much he felt like shelter in a storm. Like a cozy fire on a cold day. Like—

"You'll get a crick in your neck if you keep sitting like that," Tin'amen said dryly.

I jolted, pulling away from Lio as the scarecrow and the metal man dropped their armloads of wood. Great timing. "Of all the fucking—"

"Do you know where your auto flint is?" Singing Crow interrupted, holding out his nearly human-looking hand. "I think mine is buried in my pack somewhere."

I narrowed my eyes at the soft smile on his face. They had both just caught me kissing another guy and they couldn't care less. Sure, I was relieved that there wasn't more screaming and throwing things. But a guy could develop a complex with that lack of reaction. Like…shouldn't they care just a *little bit.*

I rooted around in my pack and handed over the auto flint. Then I started pulling out some soup rations to reconstitute with hot water. We were well supplied, but we were really still roughing it here. No self-heating camp kettle. No fancy food. It was a disgrace, really.

And…I was clearly trying to distract myself from the awkward conversation at hand.

"So," I said as I got out a little metal pot and set it up over the fire Tin'amen had just coaxed to life. "I kissed Lio. We're all good with that?"

Lio looked down at his hands, his dark skin flushing a beautiful deep burgundy. Singing Crow and Tin'amen shared a look, but it was the metal guy who spoke, as dispassionate and to the point as ever. "None of us have made any promises. When this is all over and you've retrieved the crystal ball for the wizard, you'll leave. Return to your own planet. It seems pointless to set limits on our romantic relations, when they are only temporary."

Ouch. Maybe he really *was* heartless, if he could so coldly dismiss the bonds we were all forming.

But…it wasn't like he was wrong. The whole point of this trip was to restore them all to normal and get myself home. I would fly off into space, and they would return to their people, to their families or whatever lives they'd had before magic and circumstance fucked them over.

I sighed. "It isn't…I…."

Singing Crow crossed by the fire to come sit on a log by my side. "You don't have to apologize, Daniel," he said softly, his new way with words making my heart ache. Making me wish for a vicious second there that he couldn't say anything, if it was just going to be dismissive. "We've all known from the start that you aren't really ours. Take what pleasure and comfort you wish, and we will all do the same."

He glanced at Lio with a wry smile. "It was only a matter of time before two people with such tender hearts felt drawn to each other."

Tin'amen huffed at the talk of tender hearts, but the scarecrow ignored him. "Sharing these things is beautiful," Singing Crow added. "It is a gift. Not something to be ashamed of."

Lio finally looked up and met everyone's eyes, fidgeting with his hands in his lap. "Crow people are so poetic. Their brains are all filled with words and grand ideas."

Singing Crow huffed a dismissive laugh. “My head is empty. Filled with hot air and useless things.” Then he grinned. “But enough about that. Are we eating now, or making love?”

I rolled my eyes. “Oh, stop it,” I muttered. “You degenerate. You know, when I first met you, I never would have guessed what a horny bastard you were.”

He shrugged a skinny shoulder, completely unrepentant. “Life is meant for living.”

Tin’amen gently nudged another log onto the fire, under the hanging pot. “Water’s boiling.”

Lio’s stomach growled loudly. I chuckled. “Priorities, scarecrow,” I said, getting out our cups and the fortified dried rations that would rehydrate to make a passable meal.

I was thankful for the excuse to focus on something else. No matter what Singing Crow and Tin’amen said, I wasn’t going to rush into anything with Lio. He was fragile. He probably only felt drawn to me because I offered comfort when he was falling apart. I didn’t want to take advantage of that.

I had already let myself seek comfort in the arms of a cursed guy and an emotionally stunted psychopath. I felt like I should at least try to show *some* restraint.

And besides, Singing Crow and Tin’amen’s words hurt. Honestly, I was used to being the throw away lay. But this time, I found myself wishing they’d at least *pretend* they wanted me to stay.

Chapter 18

I spent the next few days trying to focus on our journey and put my pining away. There was no use moping around over things I couldn't change. Might as well focus on the task at hand and figure out what I was going to do when I got off this planet.

I was damned sure not going to let Commander *Assburn* and his brother swindle a ten-year-old girl out of her inheritance and use it to stage the takeover of an entire planet! But all of that seemed distant at the moment, so removed from the strange reality that was Ozma-4 and its drama.

I was grateful when we came upon an unexpected bit of luck. The dimness of the afternoon light that managed to reach the forest floor grew brighter and I was pulled from my thoughts to realize the others had stopped. I joined them at the roadside to study a thick growth of blue-leafed bushes that were bursting with purple berries.

"Edible?" I asked, glancing at my companions. We had food in our packs, but it was stuff meant for travel, for soldiers and explorers and other people who'd lost their tastebuds in the line of duty. Fresh food was always a welcome treat.

Singing Crow nodded. "Yes, they're edible. And they are really nutritious—like fruit, vegetables, and meat combined.

They're good for restoring magical energy. My people dry them and use them for rations on long journeys."

I smiled at him. It was amazing what a wealth of knowledge he had about these things. It reminded me poignantly of the natives back on my home world, and how they'd been nearly wiped out hundreds of years ago, their wisdom and nature lore lost to time. I could *not* let that happen on Oz.

So many people needed help—my companions, the various native populations here, little Ciza back on Sumborto. It suddenly felt heavy, overwhelming.

Lio nudged me in the shoulder. "Daniel?"

I took a deep breath and plastered on my best diplomat's smile. It wasn't like this was the first time I'd had countless people depending on me. It had just been a while, was all.

"That's great," I said in response to Singing Crow's berry education. "We've been making good time. Should we stop and do some gathering to supplement our rations?"

Tin'amen's silver eyes pinned me to the spot, and I thought maybe he saw right through my fake smile. "Rest would do us all some good."

Right. Like he even needed rest. I was pretty sure he could walk for *days* and not get tired. But I didn't say anything. He was right. I needed to chill. Somehow.

Lio dropped his backpack and pulled out his collapsible food bowl. We all followed suit, grabbing any vessel we had at hand to gather fruit.

"Those trees there have nuts that are good roasted," Tin'amen said, pointing overhead toward some distant hanging globes that were a weird purply-brown color and covered in fuzz.

I arched my eyebrows at him. "And how are we supposed to reach them?"

He shrugged and started unfastening the belt that held his axe.

I hugged my bowl to my chest like I was clutching my pearls, as if the thought of him getting undressed was going to scandalize my poor, innocent soul. "What are you *doing*?"

He shook his head, a bit of a smile lifting one side of his pretty mouth. "Getting you some…nuts."

I gaped at him. "A joke? Again? And this one was *dirty!* Tin'amen, are you sure you're feeling okay?"

Singing Crow and Lio laughed. But Tin'amen just brushed past me, going to the indicated tree and wrapping the belt around the trunk. Then he began to climb.

"Look at him handle that wood," Singing Crow breathed in an overly loud whisper, just loud enough for Tin'amen to hear him. "He's so *good* at it."

I snorted. Lio shook his head at our stupidity and took his blushing self off to pick berries.

"No going off alone!" Tin'amen called from…way up near the top of the tree. How the fuck did he get up there so fast? He really did know his way around a big 'ol piece of wood.

I laughed and followed Lio before I could make any more jokes that might distract the silver monkey man. I didn't want to see if he could survive a fall the way he survived bee attacks and metal birds.

Lio and I picked berries in a silence that was anything *but* empty. I felt drawn to the big guy, and that hadn't improved since that kiss the other day. I thought he felt the same, if the lingering glances my way when he thought I wasn't looking were any indication.

But was it really okay to start something with someone who seemed so vulnerable? I stuffed the stupid thoughts down deep and tried to think about our current mission instead. But that was just downright depressing. Steal a magical object from the one woman everyone on this planet feared? Yeah. Piece of cake.

Just getting there was going to be a challenge. But once we arrived, that was when the real fun started. We had to somehow convince the wicked witch that we had pissed off the other colonial rulers and come to *her* for sanctuary—that we wanted to side with her, join her cause or whatever the hell you called being mean for fun these days.... My acting skills were going to be put to the test in new and horrifying ways. I just hoped the dead stepsister wasn't too much of an obstacle.

Singing Crow and a perfectly unharmed Tin'amen joined us a while later, and I felt some of my tension unwinding as we all joked and stuffed ourselves--and our bowls--full of sweet, juicy berries. Tin'amen was right. We needed this little reprieve from our death march toward doom. And Singing Crow was right, too. You should enjoy life while you could, however you could. Because who really knew how many opportunities you were going to get?

I was pondering that truth when a fat berry hit me in the cheek with a wet, juicy splat.

I turned my head to look at my companions, who were all innocently picking berries. No one met my eyes.

"Oh, I see how it is," I said in a low growl. "Ganging up on the human."

Tin'amen's silver gaze was as placid as ever when he met my eyes. "I'm sorry, what?"

A berry hit me in the other cheek while I was distracted. I smiled sweetly, scooped up a few berries, and turned to Singing Crow, who was studiously digging around in the bushes, supposedly hunting for hidden treasures. "Crow, sweetheart?" I cooed.

He glanced up at me and I smashed the handful of berries into his face.

As we laughed and scuffled, a barrage of berries bounced off the back of my head. "That's it!" I shouted, spinning and dashing away toward the road where we'd left our packs. "I'm outnumbered, time to retreat!"

But of course, they caught me. Every single one of them was faster and stronger than I was. I found myself tossed down on an open bed roll, breathless and holding a stitch in my side from laughing so hard. Tin'amen knelt over me like the big, scary killing machine he was. Then he ducked his head and kissed my chin, pausing to lick berry juice off my cheek.

And yeah, there was no way we weren't all getting naked *right now.*

I reached up and impatiently tugged at Tin'amen's shirt. "Off. I want to see all of you."

He pulled back and obliged, shucking his shirt, then staying where he was, kneeling over me so I could look at him. It was strange, how a trained killer could look so much like an angel. His silvery-blonde hair had come loose in our tussle, and it streamed over his broad shoulders and chiseled, flawless marble-white skin. The bit of dappled light that reached us through the forest canopy was yellow with the sinking sun, and it made his silver parts look almost gold.

I slid my hands up from his perfect alien abs to his chest, a smile stretching my face. "Damn, you're beautiful," I whispered.

One corner of his mouth twitched upward, and he reached out his oddly warm metal hand to caress the side of my face and jaw, fingers drawing inward to brush over my lips. "I'm a cobbled together abomination," he said evenly. "It's you who is the beauty, Daniel." His silver eyes shimmered with the gold light of the setting sun.

No heart my ass! The man certainly *sounded* like he had feelings. Big ones. Scary ones. Ones that could last beyond this stupid quest.

But that was just wishful thinking.

"Kiss me again," I begged, making grabby hands to urge him back down to me, desperate to shut off my damned depressing brain. *Living in the moment here, Danny boy, remember?*

Tin'amen bent and did as he was told, like a good little tin soldier. The press of his lips grew demanding, his tongue sliding over mine in a way that promised wickedness. I tangled my hands in that long, silky silver hair and it was like all of my problems suddenly ceased to exist.

When he came up for air, I was a needy puddle of goo, and he knew it. His knowing smirk did things to my fun bits, made my stomach drop with a little zing of anticipation. Then, he pushed away, sitting back and climbing off me.

I immediately sat up in an attempt to follow him, my lust-hazed brain intent on reeling him right back in for more of those drugging kisses. But then I realized what he was up to, and decided I wholeheartedly supported his decision.

Singing Crow had come to kneel beside us, and Tin'amen was rapidly stripping the slender man, pausing to press teasing kisses to every bit of golden-brown skin as it was revealed. I set to work on my own clothes, sending a glance toward Lio.

The big, sweet guy was watching, his eyes bouncing between me and the others, hesitance written in every line of his body. I finished unbuttoning my shirt but left it on. "Hey there," I said softly, pushing myself to my feet and stepping into his space. I looked up into those big green eyes and gave him a reassuring smile. "If you don't want this, that's okay."

He blinked down at me, his eyes riveted on my mouth. "I do." He reached for me, then dropped his hands at the last second. "I do want this. You. Them. But…." He looked around again, then ran a hand through his big, fluffy mane of golden curls.

"You're afraid," I said softly.

He met my eyes and nodded, his dark cheeks flushing with red again. "We used to share partners, back in the pride…we shared *everything*. So, this kind of thing wasn't unusual. But I've been alone ever since…well, since they've been gone."

I nodded. "I get it." Stepping closer to him, I put my hand on his broad chest, raking my fingers through his mat of curly golden chest hair, then going on tiptoes to press a kiss to his softly stubbled jaw. "I won't judge you. And neither will they," I nodded my head back toward the others, but didn't look to see what they were up to. Wouldn't want to get distracted. And I had a feeling that crow with full use of his mouth and his hands would be a *serious* distraction.

Lio's hands came to tentatively rest on my hips, pulling me closer as he bent down to meet my lips. I leaned into him with a sigh and his arms slipped around my waist, nearly lifting me off my feet. Kissing Lio was like honey, and sunshine on hayfields, and coming home for Sunday supper after months away from home on interplanetary missions.

I pulled back, dreamy and breathless, surprised at my own deep, visceral reaction to the man. "If opening up to others again after everything that's happened to you isn't courage," I breathed, "then I don't know what is, darling."

He smiled down at me. "Still feel like a coward. And an idiot."

I took his hand and tugged him along with me as I went to join Tin'amen and Singing Crow, who were currently making out with a tenderness and intensity that made my dick so hard it *ached.*

"Oh, lawd," I breathed, a little bit of Dotty sneaking into my voice. "I think I've died and gone to heaven."

They broke apart to come join us. I went along enthusiastically when Crow drew me into his arms. His yellow eyes were glowing, and his beautiful, completely *normal* mouth curled upward into a mischievous grin. "Hello, my beautiful Daniel," he murmured, leaning in to nuzzle at my neck in the way he had before he lost the beak. This time, soft lips brushed across my skin, trailing a path up to my ear, where he whispered, "I do not miss the beak."

I chuckled and curled my fingers into his soft raven hair, stroking over the small iridescent feathers that lingered there, apparently just a normal part of his humanoid form, rather than the curse.

"Not gonna lie," I said on an exhale, as his tongue darted out to trace my earlobe. "I'm with you on that." I put my hands over his, removing them from my waist and pulling them up between us so I could press a kiss to each palm. "But *these*…." I licked a long stripe up the side of one elegant finger before sucking the tip into my mouth and biting down playfully. "These are a work of art, and I cannot *wait* for you to touch me."

He laughed and stole a too-brief, playful kiss with his sensuous new lips before pulling back to free me from my pants. "Then I suggest we get rid of these, immediately."

Lio stepped closer, a big, warm presence at my back, pulling my shirt down off my shoulders and dropping sweet kisses there as he eased it off my arms. Singing Crow glanced between us with an appreciative leer before sliding his graceful hands inside my waistband and shoving my pants down.

He went to his knees in a motion so quick and fluid it startled me. My hands went instinctively to his shoulders to steady myself, but I needn't have bothered. Lio caught me, my back to his broad chest, one strong arm wrapped around my waist while the other hand slid up to caress my chest and play with my nipples.

I dropped my head back against his shoulder with a groan as Crow set to work demonstrating how well he could use his newly transformed lips and hands. He cupped my balls and sucked my dick into his mouth in a long, slow motion that didn't end until his nose bumped me. Then he looked up at me with those degenerate yellow eyes, winked, and *swallowed.*

I gasped, back arching, and he tugged at my sack, the pressure just sharp enough to keep me from shooting right then and there.

Strong fingers gripped my jaw and turned my head to the side, firm, commanding lips pressing to mine even as another set of teeth latched onto my earlobe on the other side. Tin'amen's kiss was relentless, dizzying. Like he had a point to prove.

I was way too lost in pleasure to puzzle out what he was trying to prove, but I definitely wasn't going to complain about whatever it was. When Singing Crow finally released my dick from his evil clutches, my knees were jelly, and my brain was even worse.

I mean, sure, I had *wanted* to stop thinking, right? But I hadn't really intended to forget my own *name.*

The bed rolls the wizard had supplied us with were ridiculously luxurious, thicker and softer than any sleeping bag I'd ever used. Of course…I *had* developed quite the habit of rolling around on the bare ground naked since I came to Oz. So maybe my standards were just a little skewed.

Regardless, I found myself on my back on one of the bed rolls, and it was definitely an improvement over trysting on a bed of moss or dried leaves, let me tell you. Sex is much improved without stones digging into your back or worrying about bugs crawling on your ass or…*oh my god Lio is hung like a fucking horse.*

My weird thoughts scattered, and I licked my lips, my mouth gone dry. “Um,” I managed, my voice breaking a little. “What is that?”

Lio knelt between my legs, looking down at the massive cock he was holding in his hand. “Um. My penis?”

I laughed and sat up, reaching out a hand to gently run my finger over the bumps along the length of his shaft. They were smooth if I went toward him, but when I dragged my finger back toward me, they lifted up like little fleshy barbs.

Singing Crow leaned over my shoulder from behind to see what I was doing, his long arm wrapping around my waist. “Feline shifter,” he informed me, as if I should just *know* this. “And before you ask, Mr. Responsible,” he said, suppressed laughter in his smooth voice, “yes it’s safe for humans. No, it won’t spew poisonous sperm, and trust me, you’ll enjoy the barbs.”

I swatted at him. “Oh, be quiet,” I said primly, lifting my chin for effect. “Practicing safe interspecies sex is no laughing matter.”

Singing Crow started to say something, then gasped as he was yanked away from me. I looked over my shoulder to find him on his knees with Tin’amen’s hand buried in his hair. Tin’amen pulled Crow's head back, making the slender man arch his back as Tin'amen delivered a sharp smack to his ass.

"Enough talking," the bossy metal man demanded. "More making Daniel scream."

I rolled my eyes as if *that* display wasn't the hottest thing I'd ever seen. "I'm not a screamer." I was so a screamer…if you did your job.

"Dan," Singing Crow begged, his voice gone all breathy as he sat back on his knees and patted the bed roll in front of him. "Please."

Funny how he'd reverted to one-word phrases again. I turned away, smirking. Lio caught my face in his hands and kissed me, then pressed me back again, my head ending up between Crow's knees.

Lio's big hands gripped my thighs, and I tilted my head back. I might be on some backward planet on a mission that would probably end badly, but I was nothing if not practical. I had made sure to pack lube along with our rations, and someone had dug it out somewhere along the way.

Thank the universe, because I was pretty sure Lio was about to break me.

Thick, well-lubed fingers teased at my hole as Lio planted a kiss on my knee. Singing Crow trailed a hand up my chest and I opened my eyes to see his upside-down smile. "You're so hot like that, Daniel. That big shifter cock sliding inside you is going to feel amazing."

I moaned as Lio stretched me with his fingers. Holy hell, the scarecrow really was a degenerate. I loved it.

Singing Crow gasped when Tin'amen did something I couldn't see. Then the scarecrow was crawling over me, his long cock bobbing above my lips as he sucked my own dick into his mouth. Oh. Oh, yes *please.*

I reached up and pulled him into my mouth at the same time as Lio started to slowly press that massive dick into my ass. The twin sensations of being filled and sucked off at the same time had me writing, my body not sure if we should be thrusting or trying to escape.

Then Lio was fully seated. Singing Crow moaned around my cock as Tin'amen fucked him from behind, driving the scarecrow's long dick further into my mouth. I relaxed my throat and reached up my hand to guide his thrusts.

Lio's slow, deep thrusts grew quicker and deeper, and he shifted my hips, drawing my legs up over his arms so he could peg my prostate, the fleshy nubs on his dick dragging inside me in the best way on every backstroke.

Singing Crow jolted as Tin'amen picked up the pace, slamming into him so hard I felt the force of it where we were connected. Crow moaned against my dick, pulling back to use his hand as he descended into pleading and sobbing. His dick was painfully hard and leaking precome. I sucked him harder, hallowing my cheeks, determined he was coming with me when we went over that brink into screaming orgasm.

But Tin'amen had other ideas. He folded forward over scarecrow, got the other man by the throat, and lifted him up off me, pulling him back so he sat splayed on Tin'amen's dick, his leaking cock on proud display.

Lio pulled out and lifted me like I weighed nothing, moving us closer to the other two, and arranging me so I faced Crow, my own position mirroring his as I was impaled once more on Lio's cock.

I made a noise some *might* confuse with a small yell. Still not screaming.

Singing Crow held onto my hips, and I wrapped my arms around his neck, leaning to the side as Tin'amen gripped my chin and pulled me into a kiss.

They were going to kill me with lust, I swear.

Singing Crow gripped my cock and I glanced down between us, watching those beautiful fingers stroke me, Lio still buried deep inside me. And that was all it took to have me shouting and painting Crow with my release.

Lio *growled* as he gripped my hips and lifted me, slamming me up and down a few more times on his amazing cock. Then his teeth sank into my shoulder, and I felt him pulsing inside me as he came.

I stroked Singing Crow off as he clung to me, Tin'amen's thrusts vibrating through the scarecrow's thin frame. Crow pressed his lips to mine in sloppy kiss as he spilled, shuddering through his orgasm.

Tin'amen's frantic movements slowed, his strokes slow and deep, his head bent forward over Singing Crow's shoulder, silver hair falling all around them in a curtain that hid his face. He stilled, his arms coming around the scarecrow's waist, holding him close as the stoic metal man gasped a soft sobbing sound and shook with the force of his climax.

Yep. Totally heartless, that one. I reached out and stroked his hair back from his face, getting a good look at the tender, raw expression in those silver eyes. Then I kissed his forehead and let his hair hide his face again, letting him have his flimsy shield.

Singing Crow kissed me, slow and languid. Lio pressed a soft kiss to my shoulder, his big hands stroking lovingly over my hips. I let my forehead rest against Crow's, my eyes slipping closed as I chuckled. "We're a mess."

Crow laughed with me, my kinky partner in crime. "I feel it was well worth the sacrifice, don't you?"

I huffed. "That depends…we'll see if I can walk tomorrow."

Chapter 19

It turned out walking was just fine. Sitting was a bit of a challenge, if we're being honest, but it wasn't like I had to do much of that.

Everyone in our strange little party was in high spirits the next day, despite the fact that the forest was growing darker and denser with every passing mile. It was also alive in a way that the woods I'd seen previously in Oz were not. Aside from the strange dark blue vines hanging from the trees—which moved their twisted lengths with sentient purpose, reaching for us as we passed by—there were also the animals. Most of them kept out of sight, shy and hidden but for the occasional crackle of footsteps or shush of wings as they scurried through the underbrush or flitted from branch to branch. But every so often, I'd catch a glimpse of critters that resembled squirrels or ferrets. And once I even spotted a fluffy critter that looked like a cross between a raccoon and a panda. It regarded us with large brown eyes as it slowly scaled a tree just off the road.

Lio took one look at it, then at me, and shook his head. "Venomous. Don't even think about it."

I sighed. Why must all the cutest, most pettable alien lifeforms also be the deadliest? It was heartbreaking.

Tin'amen snorted. As if he'd never considered petting something that would kill him before. What a liar. Everyone has. What? No? Just me?

Lio kept hold of my hand, as if I really would just march off into the woods like an idiot. But I didn't mind the excuse to stick to him. He was just so…solid and lovely. And a part of me wanted to cling even harder because I knew that Lio and the others…all of them considered me to be temporary. A fun time that couldn't last.

The novelty human who was just desperate for a good time.

I knew it wasn't fair to them, wasn't fair of me to be so sullen. So, I ignored the thoughts swirling in my worry-prone brain and focused on the sensation in my chest instead. The one that let me believe I could keep them when this was over. And that we were all going to walk out of it alive.

It was late afternoon, evening just creeping in, and we had just descended a hill into a small valley, a little dip in the road between two hills—when everyone froze.

There on the rise of the next hill, under the shelter of the ever-encroaching trees, stood a…beast. The closest thing I can say is wolf—the coloring was similar, the fur a mixture of grays, creams, and black. The shape was a close approximation—at least the head and snout. But the thing was easily hip-high, and it was at least twice as wide as an Earth wolf—its legs longer, and its lashing tail more like a giant rat's fleshy appendage.

Tin'amen held out an arm, shoving the rest of us back behind him as he drew his axe, his silver eyes darting about, taking in the situation in an instant. "Surrounded," he whispered.

My heart stopped then started again, kicking like an agitated rabbit, when a horde of forest creatures—including a lot more of those wolf-beast things—emerged from the shadowed places on either side of the road, encircling us, boxing us in.

"Fuck," I muttered, getting a hand on my taser. Wouldn't be much use if we were swarmed. But at least it was something. The sound of fabric tearing was loud in the sudden silence, as Lio shifted into his beast form.

We all waited.

The wolf thing in front of us lifted a paw, hesitated, then started loping toward us, its frost-blue eyes glowing and full of intent. Dog chow. We were dog chow.

Tin'amen burst into motion, spinning and dropping low, his arm outstretched, mowing down half the creatures on one side of the road in one fell swoop. *Holy fuck.*

Chaos descended. The lead wolf-beast thing howled in rage and rushed us. All the other forest creatures swarmed us, nipping and snapping, tearing at clothes and snarling, keen on avenging their fallen comrades. Or egged on by all the blood, maybe.

I was so not cut out to be a soldier. The figurative bloodbath of the diplomatic negotiations floor was more my thing.

I tased something that looked like a panther. It had gotten its teeth snagged in my pantleg and nearly yanked me off my feet—but thankfully it had missed the meat of my leg. I kicked out at a couple little ferrety things, and batted birds away from my face. I couldn't really tell how the others were faring, since I was too busy not dying myself.

That purple-black energy I associated with Crow flared nearby and several beasts were flung back into the forest. Apparently, his magic was getting stronger, now that his curse was removed. *Yay!*

A hawk-sized bird sank its talons into my arm and tried to fly off with a hunk of my flesh. I smacked it in the head with the butt of the taser. But the distraction was my downfall. A sleek, heavy feline the size of a panther slammed into me, making me stumble forward and trip. I fell hard, landing on my hands and knees, the taser skittering out of my hand, lost under the shifting feet of the horde.

The panther thing butted into me again, rolling me, then grabbed my wrist in its mouth and dragged me. It was almost as if he was trying to just…carry me away.

Which is when the cat dropped me at the feet of a massive wolf-beast. The thing planted a foot the size of a dinner plate in the center of my chest and held me down as I struggled to get away.

"Daniel!" Singing Crow's shout alerted Tin'amen, who chopped the head off another wolf-beast and came stalking toward me, wading through the mayhem like he was crossing a shallow river, his silver blade flashing non-stop, severing heads and parting flesh as he went.

There was death in those silver eyes. And I thanked every deity that ever lived that I wasn't the one in his sights.

Lio roared and tried to get to me as well, but then he screamed, torn off his feet and rolling into a tumbling ball of fur and flashing claws as he fought off two more of those panther things.

I struck at the wolf's leg, twisting from side to side, trying to wriggle free. Long claws extended, the prick of them through my clothes like a warning—hold still or get skewered. Message received.

Then the wolf threw back its head and howled again, the sound loud and eerie, carrying on the approaching evening breeze.

"Daniel," Tin'amen called, falling to one knee as he was overwhelmed by a swarm of furry rodent things, the beasts flowing over him like water, appearing faster than he could bat them away.

That was when the sound reached me. It was the scariest, weirdest shit I had heard yet—like the sound of high-pitched, off-key laughter. I reminded me of something…but my poor brain was *not* in the mood for reminiscing at present.

"Get the fuck off me," I snarled, finally managing to lever myself out from under the wolf's paw.

I surged to my feet, expecting to be knocked down again and slashed open. But the wolf just watched me with its glowing blue eyes.

"Daniel!" Crow's smooth voice was full of dawning horror. "Run! Get under cover! Down, down!"

But I was too slow. I stumbled a few steps forward out of instinct, following his advice, before something gripped my shoulders, and I was suddenly yanked off my feet.

The cackling sound was so loud it nearly drown out Tin'amen's roar of rage and despair, but I heard his voice crack as he called my name one last time.

I twisted and fought, trying to return to the ground before it was too late. But the grip on me was merciless, and soon we flew so high that the fall would kill me if I managed to get myself free. So, I went slack.

Oh, I thought in that utterly emotionless state that comes right before and right after a time of intense panic, *monkeys. That's what they sound like.* The flock of creatures around and below me…they were massive, flying monkeys.

I looked down at the forest and its miniature trees, hoping Tin'amen, Singing Crow, and Lio were still alive. But I doubted it now. There were so many wolves. I'd seen it all from above. How outnumbered they were. How helpless they were against that sheer number of beasts.

So much for granting wishes. For helping them. For returning home, or helping little Ciza thwart her planet's takeover.

My companions were likely dead or dying. And I was probably going to join them very soon. Why the beasts didn't just kill me on site was a mystery. But maybe the monkeys were taking me back to the nest to feed their young or something.

What a fitting end to my absolutely anti-climactic life.

Chapter 20

It soon became obvious that I wasn't being carried to the monkeys' nest. A structure with tall, golden spires like something out of a children's fairytale rose up from the dark thicket of the wild forest. And we were headed right toward the tallest tower.

Thrilling, really. I felt like the damsel carried off by the dragon in one of my favorite erotic romance novels. Too bad I wasn't in costume. But these things couldn't be helped, I suppose.

The monkey that was carrying me set me down with surprising gentleness, all things considered. We'd been flying long enough that it felt weird to stand still again, the thick soles of my borrowed hiking boots planted firmly on the flat roof of the tower. This one didn't have the epic spires that the others had. I wondered if it was designed specifically for aerial landings. What other winged monstrosities did the wicked witch command?

I didn't get long to ponder it. A pair of blue-skinned guards with short spears approached, their weapons crackling with electricity—or magic, I suppose—as they drew close.

They were built differently than the one glimpse I'd had of the wicked witch of the west, but they shared her blue skin. Was she part native? Or was it a coincidence?

"Come on," one of the guards said evenly. "Witch is waiting for you."

I huffed. "Well, we wouldn't want to keep her waiting, now would we?" I said sarcastically. They acted as if I was late for an appointment, rather than the victim of a vicious attack and kidnapping.

Too bad I'd dropped my taser. I really should have kept up on my defense training once I left the service.

The guard waved his spear impatiently and I sighed, moving toward the indicated door. We marched down a spiraling set of wooden stairs—one guard in front and one behind. I was surprised to find warm wood and soothing colors…not the cold, dank castle vibe I had expected from the infamous wicked witch of the west.

Interesting.

We reached a landing, and I was led down a warmly lit hallway to a set of tall wooden doors, intricately carved with all manner of flora and fauna. One of the guards knocked, then opened the door and ushered me inside.

The witch sat at a simple, polished wood desk, her blue-black hair falling forward to partially obscure her face as she stared into a glass orb on a metal stand. Well, there was the crystal ball I was supposed to steal. But it wasn't like I could just grab it and waltz back out the way I'd come.

The witch flicked a dismissive hand at the guards, but didn't look up from the orb when they left. I supposed I could make a run for it, but there was probably security all over the place. And I had no idea how to even get out of here. The palace-like structure looked huge from the outside.

And besides…something was niggling at my brain. I was curious. And the urge to go poking around in things that piqued the part of my mind that *insisted* on answers was something I'd never been able to ignore.

I waited not-so-patiently for the evil woman before me to finish whatever she was doing, using the time to study my environment. The room appeared to be an office or a study. It was open, but not incredibly large, with wall-to-wall bookshelves stuffed to bursting, a small fireplace, and a window seat that looked like the perfect reading nook. There were items I did and didn't recognize strewn about on every horizontal surface—stones, vials, a mortar and pestle, half-burned bundles of herbs, a flint, a small knife, various bits of things that might be crustation shells, or animal horns or claws.

It was like a mad scientist, a bookworm, and a hoodoo magic practitioner got together and had a baby. I found myself smiling slightly for no apparent reason.

I'd been kidnapped, for fuck's sake. I should be pitching a fit worth of a make-up covered, sequin-wearing diva right now. Not smiling like an idiot. But it was just…I *knew* everything I was being told didn't add up. And here, I thought, might be proof that I was right. The missing piece of the puzzle.

Except, the others were still out there. Wounded or dead. And this was no time for a smug I-told-you-so moment. My smile faded as my eyes returned to the witch.

She sat back, tapping one slim finger on the base of the crystal ball. "Your bloodthirsty companions have been subdued," she said, brushing her shoulder-length black hair out of her face and slipping on a gold circlet to keep it back. The accessory was a bit strange—bright and jewel-encrusted against her gothy, witchy esthetic. Everything else was black. Black hair, black lipstick, and a high-collared black jacket thing with long skirts. The light, dusty blue of her skin was even brighter against all that lack of color.

I studied her strong, androgynous features as she stared at me with piercing gray eyes.

"Considering we were attacked," I said dryly, "I think they have reason to be a bit bloodthirsty."

She scoffed, rising from her desk and pacing toward me in a billow of long jacket and flowing harem pants that was just epic. Real stage presence. I held my ground, crossing my arms over my chest and raising my chin defiantly. I was well used to people in power trying to cow me into submission. Wasn't happening.

"Attacked!" she snarled, circling me, those long-fingered hands waving in agitation. And…yep. Too many fingers. Six, I think. "I sent my creatures to escort you to the castle, and you respond by mowing them down in cold blood! Humans. No respect for life. No awareness of their place in the ebb and flow of creation."

I arched my brows at her. "*Okaaay.* Look, lady. A bunch of wolf…things…came bearing down on us, surrounded us and were about to eat us for dinner. I wouldn't really consider that a friendly escort. Besides, who are you? The beast master?"

She didn't seem to get the ancient Earth fiction reference, but, eh, hadn't really expected her to. And here she thought *humans* were uncultured. She stopped her pacing and *billowing* long enough to face me, lifting a blue hand to the circlet on her head. "It is my magic. To communicate with all the living creatures."

I cocked my head as I studied the circlet. "An amplifier?" I'd heard of them, but never really paid that much attention. In order to believe that there were devices that amplified magic using a combination of science and sorcery, you would first have to, oh, I don't know…*believe in magic.* But I'd seen enough on Oz to erode my conservative levels of skepticism.

She nodded once, sharply, her gray eyes delving into my own, before she resumed her pacing, flicking the long skirts of her jacket out behind her in a nervous tick. "I asked the beasts to bring you and your party here because I didn't trust you idiots to make it safely on your own. There is a colony of drainers not far from where you were."

I frowned. "Drainers?" Didn't sound good, whatever it was.

She stopped and looked at me, then shook her head in disbelief. "Yes. Night drainers. You are the most ill-prepared spy I've ever encountered. Who sent you to Oz, human?"

I couldn't help it. It had been a long day. Hell, a long *exile.* I burst out laughing, bent over with the force of it, gasping for air. Tears leaked from my eyes, and I held my aching ribs as I was wracked with cathartic laughter.

When I managed to get myself under control, I straightened, wiping my eyes on my dirty sleeve and letting out an occasional wheeze. "Spy? *Spy*? I was sent here by EARTH. They *exiled* me here as *punishment,* you ridiculous woman. What could I possibly be here to spy on?"

She narrowed her eyes at me. "I'm not a woman. And you know damned well what you're meddling in."

I blinked at her…uh, him? Them. "Pardon," I said absently. "Witch is a feminine word where I'm from."

They rolled their eyes. "Humans." Spinning, they paced back toward the desk. "*Wicha,*" she spelled out patiently for the translator, "is a term for magic users. Why should gender matter?" She muttered, "Idiot humans," as she picked up a long, smooth stone that turned out to house a hidden blade. She flicked the blade out like a jackknife, then headed toward me again.

I stepped back and toward the door. Fucking knives. I *hated* knives. A bunch of thugs from Galfor Prime had decided to try to torture information out of me once. They hadn't gotten far before I was rescued, but I still hated bare blades.

The witch stopped and frowned at me, then followed my gaze to the knife. "I'm not going to *harm* you, moron." She gestured with the blade, indicating the window seat. "The wizard sent you, didn't he? Take off the boots."

I blinked at the witch. "The boots?"

They rolled their eyes as if I was the most dim-witted being they had ever encountered. "Yes, the boots you murdered my sister for. Are you really that dense?"

I huffed and went to sit where I was directed, unlacing my boots and yanking them off. If they wanted the damned boots so bad, they could have them. I wasn't getting fucking sliced up over some dead chick's footwear.

I chucked the boots on the ground at the witch's feet and pulled my legs up, curling into a ball and hugging my knee while I watched the weird witch with the knife.

They studied me for a long time, frowning, before they bent and picked up one of the boots. I watched the witch inspect the sole of the boot before tossing it aside. Then they picked up the other one, looked at the bottom, and let out a little hiss of happiness.

I frowned as the witch worked a blade into the recess between the boot and it's overly thick sole. My eyebrows rose when they grinned and a portion of the sole slid out, revealing a hidden compartment. Then the witch withdrew a cloth-wrapped bundle. Shaking off the cloth onto a nearby end table, they grinned, revealing teeth that were a bit sharper than human, their expression gleeful. “Finally!”

They held up a finger-sized vial filled with cloudy purple liquid.

For fuck’s sake. I was a mule all along. I *knew* there was a reason everyone kept asking me what I took from the dead witch! “What is it?” I asked softly. “Pollen? Another drug to control the natives?”

Grey eyes met mine and the witch laughed, the melodic sound just a bit unhinged. “A drug? Hardly.” They held up the vial, shaking it slightly to make it glow. “This, my dear, sweet, moronic human. This is a permanent cure to pollen addiction. *This* is the downfall of the bitch of the south and her corruption.”

I watched, wide-eyed, feeling both elated and like a complete fucking moron at the same time. “The what now?”

The witch carefully tucked the vial away into a locked drawer in her desk, then sent sparkling green energy over it with a wave of her hand—magic. Probably to prevent theft or to protect the vial. Though, that thing must be absolutely shatter-proof, if it had held up to my traipsing around with it *inside my boot.*

“A permanent antidote,” the witch said as they straightened. “Created by a scientist magic user in the east who absolutely *refuses* to get involved with politics or to be named, but who agreed to share his invention so it could be enhanced and spread to all of Oz. An end to all the imbalances and power plays. At least until the south and north find some other way to control the people here. East was carrying it to a drop off location when she was murdered.”

The witch turned and paced back over to me, still holding that damned knife. “Now, let’s find out who you’re really working for, shall we?”

They lifted their arm and I cringed backward, cold sweat popping out on my brow. I tried to get control of myself, to square my shoulders, uncurl my legs, and make an unaffected face. But I couldn't move. All I could do was sit there and relive the feel of a sharp blade parting my flesh.

The witch scowled. "What in the world is wrong with you now? Surely whoever sent you didn't send such a timid mouse into this mess."

Their eyes narrowed, following my own gaze to the knife they held. Moving very slowly, they set the knife aside on a nearby bookshelf and held up two blue, six-fingered hands. "Is that better?"

I swallowed hard, uncurling my legs and sitting up, refusing to let out a sigh of relief. "You can torture me for information all you want," I said evenly. "But it's a waste of time. I'm no spy."

The witch arched one slim black eyebrow at me. "Torture? Oh, stupid human. I have much easier ways of getting answers. Come."

They turned in a swirl of black skirts and strode over to the door, opening it and stepping back. "After you, exile. I'm eager to hear your story." They smiled evilly. "I promise, nothing sharp will enter the conversation."

I stood, fists clenched. But the two guards were waiting outside, crackling spears in hand, and what choice did I have? I suppose that depended on how badly I wanted to survive this.

"The others," I said calmly. "My traveling companions. Are they dead? Did your beasts finish what they started?"

The witch's brows drew together. "Dead? No, of course not. Maybe a bit worse for wear—which is only fair after the murder they committed. But they are being led here. Now, come!"

They whirled and strode out the door in that purposeful way of theirs, as if they just expected me to come to heel, like a good dog. Not that there were many other options.

And if the others were alive, maybe I should focus on staying that way as well. I followed the wicked witch of the west deeper into their evil (if a bit too comfortable and welcoming) lair.

Chapter 21

I was led through numerous winding halls, down a staircase…or fifty…and eventually out another set of doors. The doors closed behind us, leaving me and the witch inside…an atrium? I could see the guards stationed outside through a filmy stained-glass window.

I watched in complete confusion as the witch strolled into the warm, humid room, unbuttoning their jacket. They chucked the garment over the back of a garden bench, leaving them in just the loose pants and a short, cropped bandeau top. Black, of course.

The witch twisted their long hair up into a knot, then turned impatiently to me. "Well? Come. All the carnivorous plants are in the back. You're safe for now."

The "for now," wasn't really reassuring. And…*carnivorous plants?*

I followed slowly after the witch as they led me to the center of the garden. Plants of all sorts burst from every available plane, crawling along the ground at our feet, growing over rocks or raised planters, and trailing from hanging pots, their vines crawling along the metal girders that held up the glass ceiling. I plucked at my shirt, pushing up my sleeves as sweat began to form. It was so hot and humid in here it was like being in the tropics back home. I could see why the witch had immediately stripped.

I tried not to notice how lithe and defined that long torso was, or to wonder what was under the bandeau. *Not the time, Daniel,* I chided myself. *You're probably about to be tortured, no matter what they say.*

The witch twisted and reached above them, the column of muscle along their spine flexing beneath that smooth blue skin. I watched warily as they gently retrieved a bit of red blobby stuff that could only be some sort of fungus from a little hanging pool.

Turning to me, they held out a hand. "Ingest this, please." At my skeptical look, they arched a black brow in challenge. "Don't think I can't force you."

I sighed. This was probably how I died. Ingesting alien hallucinogens. Stepping closer to the weird blue sorcerer, I slurped down slimy red stuff from their six-fingered hand.

I wrinkled my nose, looking up to meet amused gray eyes. "That tastes like ass."

They arched their brows. "Are you well acquainted with the flavor of ass, human?"

"Ha, ha," I said dryly. "But yes. Kind of. I've definitely done some rimming in my life."

Oh my god! What was *wrong* with me?!

The witch laughed, the sound rich and lacking in mockery. "Oh, do tell." They gestured at another conveniently placed garden bench and I hurried to take a seat, my face flaming.

"What do you want to know?"

Oh god. No. What are you saying, Daniel? Shut up!

"Hmm," the witch said, those gray eyes just *full* of amusement. "Interesting as the topic of your sexual exploits may be, I have more important things to talk about." They settled on the seat next to me, sitting sideways to face me, one long, lean arm over the back of the bench, eyes on my face.

"Who sent you to Oz, Daniel?"

I huffed. "EARTH exiled me. Snatched me off the stage and dumped me here. I'm not a spy!"

They looked down for a moment, thinking. "Why did they exile you?"

I rubbed my face with my hands, the truth pouring out of me, filled with bitterness and fatigue. "I used to be a pretty well-known diplomat. I helped resolve disagreements and keep the peace between planetary interests. I stopped more advanced races from taking over and exploiting natives. Everyone hated me. Because I was damned good at what I did. And because I had an actual fucking moral compass."

I sighed, but the words kept coming. I was *compelled* to answer the witch's question. "I left EARTH service five years ago. It was that or be dishonorably discharged. They wanted me gone. Too inconvenient when I wouldn't sacrifice my morals to better their political interests in my negotiations. I went off and started doing all the things I couldn't when I was a professional representative—I was living my most flamboyant, fabulous life. I was finally able to be myself."

I tried to clamp my lips shut. That was too much information. The witch didn't need to know all about my poor repressed self. But I just couldn't stop talking.

"A friend sent me information while I was in the Emerald City. I think EARTH sent me here because a commander in EARTH is about to undo some work I did a while back and swindle a little heiress out of planetary mining rights. He'll end up starting an interplanetary war. They needed to prevent me from interfering. But they couldn't just outright kill me, because

I might have information they'll eventually need. So, they put me where no one can find me but them. And they've been blocking communications so I can't get word out."

I glanced up to find the witch watching me with a strange expression, head tilted, bottom lip caught between their sharp teeth.

"You're *really* pretty," I blurted.

Fuck my life.

The witch let out a surprised chuckle. "Thank you. Communications are always blocked on Oz. That might not be EARTH's doing. South and North deny they have anything to do with the constant comm issues, but that's bullshit. Is it possible you were sent here to spy without knowing it?"

I blinked at them. "Uh." My mind spun, tracing possibilities in the web of lies that was politics. "Maybe?" I said truthfully. Now that they had planted the idea…what if EARTH wanted inside information on Oz and its colonial rulers and they were betting on my nosey, interfering self to recon for them unwittingly?

Stars. This fungus was ridiculously effective.

"How did you end up with the wizard?" the witch said, leaning back a bit, feigning indifference.

I shrugged. "Everyone said he had all the answers, the cure to every ill. Worth a shot, right? He said he could get me off Oz, send me to the IMAD station, and help my companions. But the wanted me to steal something from you." I glared. "I had no idea I was running substances in my damned shoes! Is that why you kept attacking us? Why you sent the hornets, and the spooks, and the metal birds?"

They sat forward, removing their arm from the back of the bench and regarding me curiously. "Hornets? Metal birds? I sent the spooks to convince you to leave the shoes where one of my people could pick them up. But the others…that wasn't me, I'm afraid. Probably North and South. They must have realized there was a reason East was out of her territory."

"Huh." I just stared, feeling a little floaty. "Do you have to be so…." I flailed my hand helplessly. "All of that?"

They sat up, regarding me with confusion, then anger. They spread their arms, inviting my inspection of that lithe, androgenous body. "Oh, I beg your pardon. Do tell me, what part of my being upsets you? It's not as if I haven't heard it all before!"

I put a hand over my face, but my mouth just did its own thing. "You're really hot. It makes it hard to hate you for being evil when I kind of want to touch you."

I groaned. "I want to die now, please."

More rich laughter spilled between us. "Are you always so… sexually adventurous, Daniel? Or are the fungi affecting you oddly?"

I tried to glue my damned mouth shut with my hands, but the amused witch pried them off my face and the words burst out in nearly a shout. "I've always enjoyed sex and it's stupid that a lot of humans still think it's taboo, even in this day and age! I love fucking! What's wrong with that?"

I closed my eyes and dropped my head back, praying for this to all just be over soon. The whole room felt like it was pulsing. "Also, the mushrooms might be making me high. Is that normal?"

The hands on my wrists gave me a light squeeze before releasing me. "You don't need to be embarrassed. And you've nothing to fear from me as long as you don't endanger my people or the natives of this planet."

They stood and I opened my eyes. "When will this shit wear off?" My body had started to tingle, and I wasn't sure if I wanted to masturbate, or crawl out of my own skin.

They frowned down at me. "You do look flushed. There shouldn't be any adverse reaction in humans. But some people react differently than others. How do you feel? Are you in pain? Any trouble breathing?"

I glared at them as the truth spilled out of my mouth. "Horny as *fuck.*"

They worked to suppress their laughter, but I could still tell it was there. "I apologize. That's…unusual. Come. I'll give you a place to sleep it off and a tonic to banish the effects of the fungus."

I followed the strange witch out of the atrium. They grabbed their jacket along the way, shrugging it on, but not fastening it, and shaking the knot out of their long blue-black hair as they went.

My dick was so hard it hurt. I kind of wanted to just cut the fucker off at the moment. Lusting over my captor was low, even for me.

The witch waved away the guards and led me to a room a few halls away from the atrium. When they opened the door, I was greeted by the sight of a small, tidy space filled with light wood and warm, earthy fabrics. "Try to rest," they said. Then they paused and gave me an apologetic wince. "I'm sorry. But I've learned that the north and south have spies everywhere. No one can be trusted, no matter how friendly they appear. The fungus was necessary. It's the only way to be sure a person speaks the truth."

I waved them away, too dizzy and too horny to be properly angry. "Whatever."

They turned to leave, but hesitated, one long-fingered blue hand resting on the doorjamb. “And Daniel?”

I looked over my shoulder at them to find a soft smirk on their handsome face. “What?”

“I’m not offended that you want to fuck me. It’s refreshing, actually.” They winked and shut the door behind them.

“Fucker,” I muttered. I would have preferred knives to this humiliation.

Then I shook my head at myself. “No, you wouldn’t,” I muttered. Stripping, I rubbed one out and fell face first into bed, feverish and wishing that I wasn’t alone.

Chapter 22

Have you ever gotten so drunk or so high that your soul left your body, and you did something irrevocably embarrassing? The sun on my face woke me the next morning and it took me a while to recall why I had this lingering sense of shame fliting around the edges of my awareness.

Then it all came back to me, and I wondered why I even bothered waking up. A blue-skinned servant or employee of some sort had come around sometime last night with a steaming drink that tasted like spearmint and citrus, and insisted I drink the whole thing in one go—witch's orders. It had fizzed and crackled on my tongue like electricity, and it made my whole body feel a bit…jittery. But apparently, the witch's magical brew *did* help me metabolize the mushrooms and get them out of my system, because once I got up, I felt remarkably energetic and well for someone who had been stoned the previous evening.

Too bad my new mental clarity let me recall in vivid detail how I'd hit on my enigmatic captor and told them how much I loved rim jobs and fucking. *Classy, Danny boy. Real classy. And you wonder why they threw you out of the diplomat gig.*

Not that I had ever let myself lose control like that when I was working in a professional capacity. Being human wasn't allowed when you were in the political spotlight. That's why I much preferred the spotlight that came with makeup and heels—the drag community was big on self-acceptance and embracing all your quirks and flaws as part of what made you fabulous.

I missed it. That sense of belonging and acceptance. Even if I had to wear a costume to find it.

A brief exploration of my room revealed a small bathroom with a sweet little bathing nook. I took full advantage of a hot bath and soft towels. If this unsuspecting drug mule was gonna be a prisoner for the foreseeable future, I might as well enjoy it.

Afterward, I dried off and stood there, not wanting to put my nasty, stained old clothes on. I stared at myself in the pretty, vine-framed gold mirror as I braided my hair back out of my face and secured it with the hair tie that had somehow miraculously survived my capture. My hair was getting longer than it had ever been, but I was definitely vain enough to admit I liked it that way. Anything to avoid thinking about actual, important matters.

A soft knock sounded on the door before it opened to reveal the witch, looking all lean and imposing in a full-skirted, torso hugging black dress today. I squared my shoulders and pretended I didn't care that I was wearing a towel. I also pretended I didn't have the slightest recollection of what I'd said to them the night before.

"Come to free me from captivity?" I asked coolly.

They arched their black brows and came into the room, holding out a pile of cloth. "You might want to wear something more than a towel, if you're planning your escape from the horrible, wicked witch."

I took the bundle of clothes and stared into those interesting gray eyes. "Where are the others? Have your beasts decided to eat them after all?"

They strolled away, pacing around my room, touching things here or there with those long blue fingers, their motions conveying bored indifference. "They are still traveling. I'm afraid it takes much longer to get here on foot than…what is it your people say? As the crow flies?"

That smirk probably meant no good for anyone. I huffed. "They had better not be harmed."

The witch made the circuit back around the room to me, stopping in front of me to give me a curious look. "You seem rather anxious about the wellbeing of your companions, Daniel. One might almost think you were fond of them."

Nebulas, what game were we playing now? I arched a brow. "One might be correct. One might *also* recall that I am a trained diplomat and civil rights activist. Perhaps I am fond of the idea that *all* sentient beings should treated with care."

That got me another smirk and one lifted brow. "Oh? Even witches, Daniel? Should witches be *treated with care?*"

I narrowed my eyes. They had started that sometime during our conversation last night…calling me *Daniel* in that strange tone of voice. I wasn't sure what it meant, but it got under my skin. "Depends on the witch," I said evenly. "The ones who send murder hornets, metal birds, and killer wolves after me and my friends can fuck right off. Can I get dressed now? Or were you going to stay and watch?"

They tossed their long black hair out of their eyes and spun, the full skirts of their dress doing that *billowing* thing again as they moved back across the room toward the door. "After last night, I thought you might *want* me to watch," they murmured, chuckling.

I gritted my teeth together. "I have no idea what you're talking about."

They glanced back over their shoulder at me as they hovered near the threshold. "No? Pity. You said the most delightful things. Shall I remind you how fascinating it was to hear all about your obsession with—"

"No!" I snapped. "Get out so I can get dressed."

That wide mouth curved into a wicked expression that was oh, so fitting on the dark, androgenous witch. "You may come downstairs and have breakfast if you wish. The guards will direct you." Then they turned and headed out the door. "Despite what you believe, Daniel, you aren't a prisoner here. I will send you on your way back to the wizard as soon as your friends arrive."

Then the weirdo witch was gone.

I let out a sigh. I was a mess. "Losing the plot, old boy," I muttered to myself.

If what the witch said was true, all I had to do was hang out here in relative safety and comfort—I hoped—until the others arrived. Then we could all go back to the Emerald City and get our wishes granted by the asshole wizard. Of course, I had to steal the witch's crystal ball first. And I was pretty sure I'd told them that last night while I was on my little fungi trip.

So, steal from the witch. *Then* I could get off this planet and figure out how I was going to stop Commander *Assburn* from swindling little girls and ruining interplanetary peace treaties.

One thing at a time, I reminded myself. It was a good mantra in times of overwhelm. Focus on the most immediate problem first, then move on to the next most important thing and so on. The panic lessened when you directed all your energy to the thing you could do right now.

And right now, all I could do was go eat some breakfast, hope it wasn't poisoned, and see if I could get the lay of the castle for later thievery.

I unfolded the pile of clothes, surprised do find a simple shirt and trousers in a soft, comfortable fabric. I had half-expected a dress to match the wicked witch's costumes. I was relieved. Of course, I looked amazing in a dress and heels, but I wasn't sure I quite had the legs or the slender physique to pull off that level of dark drama. I was more of a sequins and glitter kind of girl.

My borrowed boots had been returned, but the pile of clothes also included a pair of flexible house slipper type things. I eyed the thick soles of the boots I'd worn for *weeks* of hiking and went with the slippers. I probably wasn't going to attempt an escape any time soon, so comfort won out.

Dressed and loins girded for espionage, I left my guestroom-slash-prison cell. There was a guard out in the hallway, though not—surprisingly—right outside my door. She seemed to be just guarding things in general, rather than making sure I didn't leave my room.

Her blue skin was a shade or two darker than the wicked witch's skin, and she was quite a bit shorter, with proportions closer to a tall moonkin. Native, probably. "Good morning," I greeted politely. "I was told I might find breakfast somewhere?"

She eyed me up and down as if assessing my threat level, then jerked her head toward the end of the hall. "This way."

I was surprised when she kept her electric spear thing tucked away and led me off down the hall. "Are you here just to keep me from making mayhem? Or is there some other threat that warrants guards all over the place?" I asked curiously.

She huffed. "You? No offense intended, human, but you're hardly a threat."

I shrugged. "I'm definitely not offended, since I'm about the least threatening person you'll ever meet. What is it then? Why all the security?" Maybe the witch was building an evil army. I doubted it, from what I'd seen of the strange creature so far, but who knew?

The guard shook her head. "You really don't know? What kind of a spy are you?"

I huffed. "I'm *not* a spy. I'm an exile. A refugee. An unwilling guest."

She gave me the side-eye. So suspicious. "That's exactly what a spy would say."

I groaned. "Is everyone here so eternally frustrating to deal with?"

She grinned, then got her expression under control again, the professional blankness back on her face. "Probably. But we come by it honestly."

We stopped at the end of the hall, at an intersection of hallways that could lead anywhere. This place was like a maze. The guard gave me the once over again. "I'll give you some advice, human. If you really are as clueless as you say, it might help."

She leaned on her spear pole, her blue eyes narrowing. "Lots of people have come in here over the years, playing friendly, cozying up to our witch, pretending to be friends, or lovers, or who knows what. In the end, they're all only after one thing—to trick or kill the wicked witch of the west. Most of us guards and staff, we've been around for a while. We've seen it happen over and over again. So, we all learned to be suspicious of anyone who tries to worm their way in. The last asshole tried to kill them in their own bed after a good fuck." She twirled the spear, and her look was clear. Threaten her beloved employer and I was as good as skewered. "Do us all a favor and don't get friendly with the witch…*refugee*."

I blinked at her in surprise. But she lifted a hand and spoke before I could formulate words, gesturing toward another hall. "Down that way to the end, there's a staircase. Take that down to the first floor and the smell of food will get you to the dining hall." She arched a brow at me. "Don't wander. And don't get 'lost' along the way."

I sketched a sarcastic bow her way. "Thank you for your assistance and your amazingly useful threats and warnings, lady guard." I headed off to breakfast with her laughter echoing in the hall.

When I finally reached the lower level and found the dining hall, I was greeted by yet another un-wicked sight in the supposedly evil castle. A couple of long wooden tables were arranged in the large, open space, the settings informal, and every surface filled with trays of meat, bread, fruit, nuts, pastries—you name it. The air was filled with chatter and laughter, as a couple dozen people socialized and ate. They all seemed to be the same race as the guards, with skin tones that varied from a blue so deep it was almost black to a shade so light that it was nearly white. They were all quite a bit shorter than your average human, but their heights varied from moonkin-like stature all the way up to a few people who were just under my own five-eight.

The chatter quieted a bit when they noticed me, and I didn't miss how the open faces suddenly became guarded and wary. A server of some sort came to hover at my elbow, a pitcher of fruit juice in her hands.

"Daniel?" she asked, her light blue eyes frank and appraising as they studied me from her lined, good-natured face.

I nodded. "Yes, ma'am. I was told I could get some breakfast?"

She jerked her chin toward an open seat at the nearby table, between two gruff-looking men with scruffy blue beards and a belt of weapons each. “You can sit over there. Our witch told me to look out for you. Don’t cause any trouble, now, understand?”

I held back my sigh. Gods, did *everyone* here think I was some sort of deadly assassin or something? I mean…were they blind? I was one step removed from a twink. And any muscle mass I did have was gym sculpted and purely for show. “I promise,” I said, hand over my heart. “The only thing I’m a threat to is the food.”

She grinned and reached up a plump hand to pat my cheek. “Good boy. Off with you now, I’ve got things to do.”

I laughed and did as I was told, while the serving woman hustled off to deliver the juice to the other table. I took my seat between the two gruff-looking men, bracing for more scrutiny. Ignoring their curious looks, I dished up a plate of food and poured myself some juice. Then I looked up and caught the eyes of the woman seated across from me.

“Excuse me,” I said pleasantly. “But could you tell me if any of the items on my plate are dangerous for humans?” What I wouldn’t give to have Toto and his scanners right about now. I pushed my plate her way for inspection. “I understand some of the fruits on Oz can cause stomach upset.”

Her eyes widened, but she studied my plate. “Uh, I think it’s all safe. But I’ve never spent much time around humans.”

I pulled the plate back and nodded. Probably as good as I was going to get. “Thank you.” Time to see if I was about to be poisoned. I tried a bite of some sort of hash that consisted of tubers and assorted vegetable matter. It was spicy and delicious. Hopefully I survived it.

The rough-looking guy on my right nudged my arm and shoved a small platter of something purple and gelatinous my way. “Try this. Goes with the hash.”

I met his dark blue eyes for a moment, then shrugged and scooped some of the jelly onto my plate. It was sweet and spicy, and complimented the hash perfectly. “Thank you,” I said enthusiastically. “I love trying new foods whenever I visit a new place. This is delicious.”

The guy on my other side spoke around a mouthful of toast. “Been to a lot of new places, then?”

I sighed. Here we went with the wariness and veiled threats again. “Before you even ask, no I’m not a spy. No, I don’t mean anyone here any harm, including ‘your witch,’ and for god’s sake do I *look* like a threat? I used to be a diplomat, before I was exiled to Oz and blackmailed into coming here by the wizard—which, apparently ‘your witch,’ knew all about anyway. So please, chill the hell out.”

Everyone within earshot stared at me. Then the nearest ones burst out laughing.

The guy on my left shook his head. “Calm your britches, kid. We were all told you’re a guest here. We’re supposed to keep an eye out so you don’t wander off and get yourself into trouble. That’s all.”

I huffed. “I’m not some helpless child.”

“Might as well be, when it comes to shit around here that’s no good for a human,” the guy on my other side said. “Just stay inside the castle so we don’t have to hear about how we let you get too close to something deadly, yeah?”

I rolled my eyes and ate my breakfast. What a strange evil race this was. As far as vile and spooky went, the lair of the witch was a complete disappointment. When I was done eating, I set out to explore the place—after being forced to promise I wouldn't leave the castle grounds for my own wellbeing. I wandered hallways and stairs, peered out tall windows and gazed at paintings done on high, vaulted ceilings. Nature was everywhere, painted on the walls, carved into the extensive woodwork, and making itself known in potted plants and trailing hanging vines.

The usual rich person displays of vases and priceless knickknacks were replaced with singular pieces of natural beauty—a large, pearly pink shell here, a twisting black and gold horn there, a bit of fur, an animal skull, a snakeskin. It all said a witch lived here—one a bit more in line with the nature-worshipping beings of Earth lore—but none of it felt ominous. Somehow it just worked.

I crept around at first, afraid someone was going to take offense to my snooping and *spying*. But every time I passed a guard or a worker of some kind, they just nodded at me and watched me until I passed by. Eventually I got more comfortable and forgot I was in the lair of a supposed monster.

I came to a door on the top floor of the wing where I thought I had landed with the monkeys. The door was partially ajar, and I was so lost in exploring that I had long-since given up caution.

I didn't realize where I was, until I had already pushed the door open and strode inside. The witch's study. The room where they had me brought the first night I was here. It was, thankfully, empty. And just as warm and inviting as I remembered, the sun currently warming the window seat, which contained an open book, as if its owner had set it aside meaning to come back, then forgotten it.

A spark of light caught my eye and I looked over at the witch's desk. At the crystal ball that had reflected the sunlight, casting little rainbows across the gleaming wood floor and the soft fur rug. My feet carried me toward it without conscious thought. I licked my lips as I stared down into the smoky depths of the thing. Here it was. My ticket back home.

But for some reason…it felt wrong to just take it. My damned moral compass chose that moment to remind me that the witch hadn't turned out to be all that evil after all. Maybe a touch wicked. But they hadn't *actually* harmed me. And…they may be working on *helping* the natives of Oz. Pretending for one moment that I could actually get away with it and they didn't notice it missing…could I actually take a valuable magical object from someone who might, just maybe, possibly be trying to help me, in their own weird way?

A soft noise startled me, and I spun, elbow knocking into the crystal ball and sending it tumbling off its stand. Long blue finger caught it and the wicked witch twirled the smoky orb in a fluid motion, passing it from hand to hand with the grace and mystery of a magician. "Careful, Daniel," they purred, that lean body far too close to me. "You almost made a mess."

I closed my eyes and let out a shuddery breath. "I wasn't going to take it. I was just looking."

They reached around me to return the ball safely to its stand, brushing against me, their compelling voice right near my ear. "No harm done."

They straightened and put a smidge more space between us, and I could draw a full breath again. "I was only looking. I'm sorry."

The witch tilted their head, their shiny blue-black hair falling forward over one shoulder. "You're just full of curiosity, aren't you, Daniel? I know you were sent here to fetch it," they said softly. “Why not just take it when the opportunity presented itself?”

I swallowed and tried to calm my racing heart. No matter what I used to believe about magic and science, I *knew* this person was powerful. Dangerous. But I couldn’t seem to make myself lie.

“I thought about it,” I said finally, my eyes meeting theirs. “I thought it was too easy, but it was probably the only chance I’d get. I thought that it was the only way I’d be able to get home, to heal the metal man’s heart and the lion’s fear…but I couldn’t take it. It felt wrong.”

Genuine surprise showed on the handsome, angular face before me. “Wrong? To steal from evil incarnate?”

I huffed a laugh. “I’m not sure what you are, but I’m fairly certain evil isn’t it. Scary sometimes. Eccentric, maybe? But I’ve seen evil. You’re not evil.”

Long fingers tucked a stray strand of hair behind my ear, then trailed lightly along my cheek and jaw. “You’re a strange one, Daniel. Are you always so altruistic?”

I chuckled again, bitterly this time. “Unfortunately, yes. Which is how I ended up exiled, remember?”

“Oh, I recall,” they said, stepping closer again, lean hips brushing mine. They smelled like incense and the stimulating scent of ozone right before a lightning storm. “That willful *goodness* in you is intoxicating.”

Their long fingers slid from my jaw, through my hair, destroying my ponytail to grip the back of my head and tilt it upward. “What were you really doing in here?”

I shuddered, unable to stop my stupid body’s reaction to danger and beauty. “Exploring. I didn’t realize where I was at first. Didn’t mean to trespass.”

They tilted my head back further, forcing me to gaze up into stormy gray eyes. “You were here to gather intel. To find my weakness. To report back to North and South. Maybe the wizard has changed sides.”

I couldn’t look away from those mesmerizing eyes, so filled with bitterness and…hope. Geesh, mistrustful, much? Hadn’t they *just* done the whole truth fungus thing? “No,” I breathed. “I wasn’t. I was just curious. And I have no idea what the wizard is up to. I only want to go home.”

“Curiosity killed the cat, Daniel,” they purred one long arm sliding along my side, hand planted on the desk to cage me in while the other hand continued to grip the back of my head, holding me still. I arched my back as they pressed into me, bowing me backward over the desk. “Do you know the rest of that old Earth saying?”

My voice was low and husky as I replied. “But satisfaction brought it back.”

The witch’s lips twitched upward in a wicked smirk—right before they met mine.

Holy fucking shitballs they could kiss. I clung to lean, silk-clad hips as they *owned* my mouth, that lean, tight body pressed the length of mine, literal *electricity* sparking between us. I drank it in, all logical thoughts fucking right off out of there. Sharp teeth bit down on my bottom lip, and I groaned, leaning into the witch, begging with my body. Please, please, *please!*

Then they released me, drawing away in a flutter of long black silk skirts and magic. “Careful, Daniel,” they drawled, their voice low and husky. “I’m certain *this* isn’t what you came for, whatever other goals you might have.”

I collapsed back against the desk, shaky and flushed. A harsh laugh escaped me. “You *still* think I’m here to spy on you? For what? Believe me, if I ever see either of those other witches again, I will gladly punch them in the face for all the shit they've sent my way."

I pressed a hand to my lips, which were still tingling from that *kiss*.

The witch looked…torn. That unaffected, powerful mask slipping enough to let me see how vulnerable they really were. "Everyone always has ulterior motives, Daniel. I'm not a complete fool."

They waved at the desk. "Take the ball, if that's what you want. I can make another."

I left the damned crystal ball right where it was and stormed over to get in the powerful magic user's face. You know, like a smart person would. Planting my hands on my hips, I glared up at them. "People suck," I said succinctly. "I get it. Been there. Done that. I'm sorry if some other guys have waltzed in here and made you feel used. But I'm not them. That's not how I roll." I reached out and booped the tip of their, long, sharp, ridiculously adorable nose. "Apparently, I'm stupidly attracted to my captor. Take it or leave it. But don't fucking insinuate I'm that much of an asshole, to seduce someone for intel." I crossed my arms over my chest. "What? Do we need to revisit the whole slimy mushroom thing again? Because at this point, I'll do it willingly just to get everyone around here to stop calling me a spy!"

I may have stomped my foot. You can take the boy off the runway, but you can't take the queen out of the boy. Or something. So I was a bit of a diva. There were worse things in life.

The witch stared down at me with a blank look on that pretty face. "Did you just…are you *diplomatting* me, Daniel? Is that what this is? Did you just use *psychology* on me to get me to want to reel you right back in and kiss you senseless?!"

I smirked. "Did it work?"

They shook their head. But a hand came to rest on my hip, gently tugging me closer. "I can't afford to dally with you, tempting as you are. You'll only leave when you have what you need." They held up the other hand to stall my protests. "Not an insult, a truth. You came here for a reason. To deliver the antidote for the wizard and return with the crystal ball. Has that changed?"

I sighed, feeling petulant. "No." Then I lifted my eyes to meet theirs. "But someone recently told me you have to live life while you can—take what joy you can when it's offered."

They closed their eyes. "I'll take that under advisement, human."

Human. Not Daniel, spoken in that alluring, teasing tone. Just human. Other.

I tried not to be hurt. I mean, honestly what was with me lately, forming crazy attachments to people I'd just met? Insane people? People with *issues*? *Girl, you're a hot mess.*

I swallowed and stepped back, not knowing what to say when the person who had kidnapped you turned you down for sex. What was the protocol here?

The witch slipped right back into their striding and billowing act, walking across the room to retrieve their book, then plopping down on the window seat to resume reading, as if they hadn't just had that talented tongue down my throat. "Feel free to explore," they said dismissively. "You may borrow any of the books in here, if you wish, to pass the time until you return to the wizard."

I managed not to roll my eyes. Yeah. Reading. *That's* how I wanted to pass the time.

But, you know, the witch's comment *did* remind me that I had few guys out there worrying about me. Not sure how they'd react to me screwing the enemy, even if they *had* implied they didn't care who I got busy with.

Cause I was just going to leave, right? It was only sex, after all. Funny, how the evil creature I'd just met seemed to be the only one who had a problem with the idea of fucking me then saying goodbye.

I picked a book at random and went to find my way back to my borrowed room. Alone.

Chapter 23

It turned out, my motley crew of friends and lovers didn't reach the castle that day, or the next…or the *next.* I stopped myself from going crazy by attempting to relearn everything I could about Oz and its people from the perspective of the other side—from the supposed villain.

It really was a re-education. I was beginning to see how vilifying the wicked witch of the west had served the interests of the other colonial rulers…and the interests of whoever was benefitting off-world from North's drug trade. They needed somewhere for everyone to focus, some evil villain to shift the scrutiny off their own shady shit. And I was beginning to see why West made the perfect target.

The witch—whose name was Vix—spent most of their day pouring over books, learning and tweaking their magic, and tending to both the plethora of creatures who called the black forest home *and* the local native people, who called themselves the winvies. The locals had quickly flocked to West when the witch arrived on Oz, drawn in by the foreigner's shared skin-tone and their shared connection to and appreciation of nature.

The witch of the west had been protecting the winvies and their land, and buffering them from the witch of the north and the witch of the south, ever since.

Vix was a giant *nerd,* happier in their library or the quiet reaches of the forest than in any city or political venue. And they had absolutely no patience for false pretense or playing nice just to save face. It was probably so easy for the others to paint them as wicked, to build up fear around the powerful magic and deep stillness that was the witch of the west.

And…Vix was very physically different from the other rulers. Their skin color, their cool, honest personality, and their lack of a clear gender—it all made good fodder to set them apart and make them into the "other."

I mean, really, bad people the galaxy over needed to come up with new tactics, because the old "divide and conquer" technique was just getting stale. I'd seen it so many times in my life. Oldest trick in the book.

But still effective.

I wondered at the wizard and how he played into all of this. He seemed to be the opposite case—one who played the healer and savior, while privately acting the villain. But…was it all just an act? Vix said they were working together. That the wizard was helping to undo the work of the others. But they wouldn't say more than that. It was infuriating not having all the answers. And the longer I stayed in Oz—the more people I met and lives I peeked into—the more I *cared.*

Tin'amen was right. Sometimes caring was a liability. It distracted from your goals. Like my goal of getting the hell out of here!

But still, I was drawn in by the enigmatic witch. With nothing better to do, I found myself spending hours following Vix about, drinking tea and watching them work, asking as many questions as I could about life on Oz, while the not-so-wicked (at least in that sense) witch wove spells and science together to heal animals and protect winvies, and sometimes just because something got their attention and curiosity demanded that they create it.

I laughed over the wooden horse that currently danced on my tea saucer as the witch watched with that little half-smirk that said they were pleased with themselves.

"Are all Valkon people as skilled at magic as you are?" I asked, in awe. I knew the Valkon people were magic practitioners, energy manipulators. But I had never heard of anything as fascinating as what I saw the witch perform every day.

Their smirk faded, and Vix's expression darkened a bit. "No. It's why I was sent here. Out of the way. My hybrid genes resulted in magic that doesn't fit into our society's standards and expectations. I cannot call lightning or create water from thin air. I can't manifest more than the tiniest flame or call a wind. The Valkon are elemental masters—particularly my family. But my magic is twisted, combined with other things. No one else I know can speak with beasts." A bitter smile accompanied that statement. "It makes me beastly myself. Base. Beneath them. And it's quite an embarrassment for the ruling family to have produced such a bastard child." Their gray eyes lifted to meet mine from where they sat across from me on the window seat. "It's what comes from mating with a human, you see. My carrier muddied their blood."

I gaped at them. "What a load of ridiculous bullshit!"

Vix chuckled and rose, stretching that lean body, clothed today in dark gray shades—a clingy, stretchy top with a high, lacy collar and long sleeves, the front cut up shorter and the sides and back trailing to long points over a panel skirt and clingy black leather pants.

Seriously, the clothes. I was a bit jealous. Not going to lie.

The witch paused, cocking their head to the side, then went to the window to gaze out at the trees, which were starting to whip about in a strong breeze. I stood and went to join Vix as the wooden horse went still, its animation magic lost when Vix's attention was directed elsewhere. "What's wrong?"

Vix licked their lips, gray eyes flicking up to the clouds of the same color, which were gathering rapidly, flowing past the castle and to the east. "Cyclone," they said distractedly.

Then they flowed into motion, scooping up their discarded gold amplifying circlet and plopping it atop their head. They stood at the desk and activated the crystal ball, peering into the smoky depths as it swirled and cleared.

"What does it do?" I asked, coming to stand across from them and get a look at the globe.

I was shocked to see Tin'amen. And he was apparently arguing with a wolf-beast, mouth moving and metal arm gesturing wildly to the side.

"It projects what I'm seeing," the witch said, attention still on the ball. "I can hear and see what my beasts see, and it is clearer with the amplifier. But this helps me sort it all out and replay it, so all my own thoughts aren't jumbled up on top of theirs." They waved me around to their side. "Come. Look. They're almost here, maybe half a day's walk or less. But there's a cyclone headed right for them."

The witch cursed softly under their breath, alluring voice nothing but a bitter growl. "North. She hacked into the weather controls a few years back. Suddenly the cyclones pop up whenever it best suits her to cause an accident."

I blinked at Vix in surprise. Had North caused the cyclone that made me crash land my pod right on top of one of her rival rulers? Somehow, I didn't doubt that at all. But I had more important questions. "What now? Do they have somewhere to shelter?"

The witch was silent for a time, then they waved a graceful hand, peering intently into the ball. "No," they said firmly. "That's too far for the men to run. Take them to the old cave. The rest of you scatter. Take shelter wherever you can find it. Go to ground. I'll lend you speed. Go. Now!"

The witch sat suddenly, elbows on the table, gaze fixed on the ball. "Daniel, bring me that blue stone on the shelf behind you, please. And the orange one just there." A jerk of their head directed me to an array of stones scattered across a table.

I grabbed the indicated items and brought them to the desk. The witch gripped one stone in each six-fingered hand. "The knife, love. Push it over to me."

Again, I did as I was told.

I could feel energy rising, flowing out from where Vix sat, making the hair on my arms stand on end and my breath come short. "I'll need to bleed, Daniel," they said, voice urgent, but soft. "If the knife bothers you, you should leave."

I huffed. Like I was going to just step out while they sat there trying to *save* people. "What can I do to help?"

Those gray eyes flicked up to meet mine briefly before returning to the scene playing out on the crystal ball. "Catch me if I faint. I usually manage to crack my head pretty good when I do this spell."

I rolled my eyes and stepped closer, wanting to put a hand on their shoulder for support, but unsure if that would include me in whatever energy circuit they had pulsing around them at the moment.

I watched as the witch set the stones down, calmly, efficiently slashed a long cut across each palm, then gripped the stones again coating them in ruby red blood.

Shit got real weird after that. Vix channeled power to the forest creatures somehow, lending them speed and strength as they strained to outrun the cyclone and make it to cover.

A massive wolf-beast carried Tin'amen on its back. Lio shifted to beast form to keep up. And Singing Crow…my beautiful, raven-haired man became a massive black bird, wings flapping erratically to fight against the strong winds. I watched silently, hands curled into tight fists as I willed them to make it to shelter. To outrun a *tornado.*

The vision in the crystal ball grew chaotic, as debris and a few small trees went flying in front of whatever beast the witch was seeing through. Their vision shifted, the witch jumping from creature to creature to keep a clear view.

I registered the labored breathing of the person at my side, and reached out without thought, my hand gripping their thin shoulder. I hissed at the sensation of raw energy crawling over my skin. But I held on. Stars, was this what they were feeling as the magic ran through their entire body? I fucking hoped not!

Vix let out a ragged sob when a rocky outcropping came into view through the driving rain and flying debris. I watched with my heart in my throat as Tin'amen, Lio, and Singing Crow, along with some of the bigger animals, all crawled into a cave that burrowed into a hillside.

Safe. They were safe.

The smaller creatures had scattered, off to find shelter in burrows and the smaller hidden places that were readily accessible to animals of their size.

The witch closed their eyes and the vision in the ball cut off, the surface once more going smoky. They let out a shuddery sigh, dropped the rocks they held, and pushed to their feet.

"You okay?" I asked, reaching out in concern.

"Yes," Vix muttered, voice shaky. "Fine. I just need to lie—"

They listed to the side, and I dove in, getting an arm around their narrow waist and propping them up. "Lie down. Yeah, I get the picture."

Did I mention I'm not a big guy? The witch was lean, but lanky, all long limbs and flowy clothes. It was a bit of a struggle getting them over to the window seat.

I got them arranged there, long limbs up on the cushion, and a small, light blanket draped over them, then I darted to the door and yanked it open.

A guard stood outside the door, on the other side of the hall, far enough away to provide privacy, but close enough to come when called. I forced myself to get my breathing under control and ignore my racing heart as I explained the situation. The guard frowned, but didn't seem terribly upset. He clasped my shoulder and reached around me to some sort of comm system that was built into the wall by the door.

I had noticed the little button before, but I assumed it was either a panic button or a local comm to announce visitors or something, since I'd never see it used.

A familiar voice answered, and it took me a moment to figure out that it was the friendly woman from the dining hall. The one who greeted me every morning like an eagerly awaited guest, rather than some sort of unwanted semi-prisoner.

"Witch has done it again," the guard said shortly.

I arched my brows at the snort and the string of muttered curses that came from the other side of the comm. "I'll bring something up. Is someone with the fool at least?"

The guard flicked a wry glance at me, then looked back to the comm. "They've got their human here."

The voice on the other end of the comm immediately lost its edge and went all sugar and sweetness as she cooed at me. "Oh, hello, Daniel, dear. You go keep our witch company and I'll be right up."

I met the guard's eyes and he shrugged at her change in demeanor. "Of course, ma'am," I said politely. "Thank you."

The guard returned to their post with a muttered, "Idiot's gonna die one of these times."

I was getting the idea that this wasn't the first time the witch had overstretched their magical abilities. Given what they'd said about their family, I wasn't surprised. We often do stupid things just to get the people closest to us to finally see us as "good enough."

I left the study door partially ajar, pulled up a chair by the window seat, and watched the strange, beautiful witch sleep. Their breathing was worryingly shallow, and their angular face was drawn into a sharp frown of pain or frustration. Long black lashes rested against high cheekbones, and I couldn't quite keep myself from reaching out and touching that smooth blue skin.

No hint of stubble met my fingertips as I leaned over the unconscious witch. If I remembered correctly, Valklons were quite a bit different physically than humans. I hoped that meant they were hardier. Because blue though they might be, my witch looked paler than usual.

A soft throat-clearing had me jerking away, blushing faintly at having been caught looming over the unconscious witch. "Are they going to be okay?" I asked immediately, party to cover my creeper moment, and partly because I really was concerned.

The serving lady—Ama—bustled over with a tray that was piled so high I could barely see her eyes over the top of the contents. She placed the tray on a nearby end table and came over to inspect the damage, lifting one of Vix's blue hands and flipping it over, her small fingers searching out a pulse. Finally, she shook her head, placed the hand back down on the cushion and turned to pour out some fragrant, herbal tea.

"They'll be fine," she said easily, a bit of her earlier irritation coloring her words. "Overdid it, is all. The idiot doesn't respect their own limits." She handed me a cup of tea and gestured for me to drink it. "That's for you. They won't wake for a bit yet. What fool magic were they doing this time, to end up so flat out?"

I grimaced and took a sip of the delicious tea. "Saving my friends, actually. There was a cyclone. I'm not sure what they did, but they somehow helped the creatures in the forest move faster so they could get to safety."

The woman tutted. "Shared a bit of their own soul energy with the beasts, I suppose." She brushed a strand of blue-black hair from the witch's face and a motherly smile crossed her own features. "Our witch would do anything to protect those who depend on her. Even the little furry ones. Not many understand that *all* life should be precious—not just the ones you consider important."

I sighed and sipped my tea, feeling responsible for the witch's condition, since they had gotten this way saving *my* friends.

Silly, since we weren't even traveling here voluntarily. But still…I quite liked this witch. And I really didn't think there was an evil bone in their body.

Ama tucked a few shiny blue stones into the cushion around the witch to boost their recovery. Then I was left with strict instructions to watch over the witch and call for help if their breathing changed.

The door clicked closed and I sat alone, staring out the tall stained-glass window, hoping the others were safe. Hoping the person beside me pulled through this okay. Wishing I could *do* something, rather than just sit here being useless.

Vix moaned softly in their sleep and one hand twitched, clawing at the blanket. I scooted closer and wrapped my hand around those long blue fingers, trying to let some of my warmth seep into their cold skin.

Eventually, I got up to build a fire in the fireplace. Then I settled in again, gripping one of the witch's hands and fighting back a yawn.

Chapter 24

I woke to the pleasant sensation of someone petting my head. I smiled dreamily, my eyes still closed. I had always loved to have my hair brushed or my scalp massaged.

A soft, barely audible chuckle rumbled against my ear and the petting continued, long fingers combing deeper, threading through the waves and untangling the mess.

I sighed in contentment. Then I lifted my head in surprise, staring into a pair of sleepy gray eyes. “You’re awake!”

Vix smiled softly and pushed on the back of my head, urging me down, their voice still heavy with sleep. “Come back. It was nice, waking to find you here.”

I took stock of my current position, sitting in the chair still, but with my upper body draped over the window seat. “I’m going to be permanently stooped over.”

I sat up to rub my stiff back, immediately regretting how that took away the fingers combing through my hair.

The witch shifted over on the big window seat and held out an arm. “Come here.”

I don’t think either of us was really awake yet, or we probably both would have known that was a terrible idea.

I shucked my shoes and climbed up to lay beside Vix, my head pillowed on their lean shoulder, one arm around their trim waist. They pulled me close with a sigh.

"You're really okay?" I asked softly. "You scared the shit out of me."

A soft chuckle. "I apologize. I'm not used to working magic with an audience."

I huffed. "And what? You usually just pass out on the floor alone and sleep it off?"

When they didn't answer, I pushed myself up onto my elbow so I could look them in the face. "*Seriously?!*"

"Oh, stop worrying over me, Daniel. I'm perfectly fine."

I shook my head. "*Someone* needs to worry about you, you moron. What if you hurt yourself? What if you didn't wake up?" I slapped at their shoulder, feeling more than a little pissed off. "Maybe you already gave yourself brain damage. That would explain the recklessness!"

Long fingers wrapped around my wrist to keep me from smacking them again. "Daniel."

I stopped my tirade at the odd tone in the witch's voice. "What?" I snapped.

"Do you *actually* care what happens to the wicked witch? The one who kidnapped you and held you prisoner in their evil tower?"

I stared into those stormy gray eyes. "You're an idiot."

Then I was kissing the witch like my life depended on it. Not sure who started that. But I sure as shit wasn't going to complain.

Vix's lips slid over my own, softly this time, both asking and yielding. Their arm around me tightened, urging me to roll so I lay on top of them, our bodies pressed together, legs tangled in the blanket. I pulled back at last, bracing myself on my arms to look down at the witch. "Are you sure you should be doing this right now?"

They closed their eyes. "No. Not at all. You'll just leave the moment your friends return. But I've never exactly been one for making safe choices. Hence the using magic until I pass out."

I sighed. "I didn't mean are you sure about *me*, idiot. I meant are you sure you're up for, you know, *exertion*…after all the passing out."

I found myself yanked down and pinned under a long, lean, wicked body, sharp teeth at my neck, and a rock-hard lump pressed against my own very interested dick. "I'll manage," Vix breathed against my throat, making me shudder as goosebumps broke out on my skin.

"By all means, then," I said airily, my head spinning with lust and adrenaline at the feel of those sharp teeth pricking my skin, "manage away!"

No matter what my wicked witch said, I could feel the bit of tremble in those long arms as they hovered over me, and I knew they were still depleted. Not that they would *ever* admit it, as stubborn as the witch was. We didn't bother wasting time on undressing fully or lingering over foreplay.

I slid my hands up under that long shirt, palms sliding over the smooth, lean muscles of their back until I met with more stretchy fabric. Another bandeau top. It reminded me that I really knew nothing about the androgenous witch's sexuality or gender. I slid my hands back down to grip their tight, round ass as they thrust against me, teasing us both.

"I don't know anything about how this works," I managed to mutter between heated kisses.

One of those graceful, clever hands had found its way under my own shirt to tweak a nipple and I hissed. "I find that very hard to believe, after all that talk of rimming," the evil witch said with a smirk.

I rolled my eyes and tugged at their shirt in illustration. "I *meant* with a Valklon. With *you*, ass. I don't even really know your gender!"

Vix chuckled and obligingly leaned back on their knees long enough to pull off the shirt, revealing that leanly muscled torso and the little wrap they wore over their chest. "Does it matter to you?" They asked curiously, as they started unwinding the bandeau. "Gender? I've never really understood. Humans generally have strange ideas about these things, from what I've been told."

I smoothed my hands up their sides, loving the feel of the coiled strength in their lean form. "But you're half human, aren't you?"

They shook their head, their long black hair spilling around their chest and shoulders as they cast the bandeau top aside, revealing two pair of small breasts where a human woman would have just the one set. "I never knew my human giver. Only my carrier, who was Valklon."

I licked my lips. Huh. I was pretty firmly gay. I thought. Usually, boobs weren't my cup of tea. But this was the *witch* we were talking about. Vix was hot no matter what. So maybe I was a bit more open than I realized?

"Giver? Carrier?" I said, making myself focus. "Explain please."

I hated that all this talking was needed, honestly. I just wanted to *finally* fuck my witch. But these things had to be addressed. Because, you know, alien anatomy and all. Though, if the witch was half human, that meant the parts were probably compatible.

Vix leaned forward and kissed me again, and I instinctively drew my hands up their torso to cup their breasts, my thumbs brushing over one set of nipples, then the other. They moaned softly and arched into my touch, then slid a hand down my pants to grip me firmly and give me a stroke, twisting their wrist in a way that had my toes curling.

"Asexual xenomorphic species," they muttered impatiently. "We have carrier and giver cycles. I'm not on my carrier cycle, so you can't impregnate me. You can fuck me, or I can fuck you. I have the appropriate parts to approximate the experience of being with a male of your species, if that is what you prefer." They smiled dryly. "And trust me, I have gone without long enough you won't catch anything from me. Can we please stop talking now, Daniel?"

The purr in that voice when they said my name nearly undid me. But no. They were admittedly reckless, so one of us had to be responsible about this. "I *have* been sexually active. With like three people. I'm fully vaccinated, so the risk is low. But you should know."

Vix leaned in and bit my shoulder, hard. "Magic, Daniel. My body would burn off any threat. Please. I need you."

Okay. Hearing the scary, powerful, sometimes stand-offish witch *beg*? I almost came on the spot.

We laughed and rolled about awkwardly as clothes went flying. The witch was right—they were made differently than I was. With similarities to both a human male *and* a human female. But somehow, together it all just worked. I didn't go examining things too thoroughly, since we were both done waiting. All I knew was there were no external testicles, something resembling a vagina, and a long, hard, slightly ridged dick that I was more than happy to sink down on and ride until we both saw stars.

Luckily, Vix's study was filled with all sorts of essential oils and base oils for spell ingredients. Those long fingers were just as graceful as ever as they worked me open, the witch delivering sharp, biting kisses to my lips, neck, and chest all the while.

When I felt like I couldn't take it anymore, I pushed them down on their back, pausing to take in the sight they made, their shiny blue-black hair spread out on the velvet cushions, gray eyes intense as a rising storm. I sank down on their cock slowly, head thrown back and breath shuddering out as they filled me.

Those six-fingered hands squeezed my hips as Vix kept themselves from hurrying me, from thrusting up into me, giving me time to adjust. I grinned down at the beautiful witch. They were pale still. "Let me do the work, sweetheart," I said with a wink. Then I started moving, swiveling my hips and driving Vix deep.

It didn't take long, honestly. We were both a bit pent-up and strung out. I came first, a sharp shout breaking past my lips as I shot my load across the witch's abs and those beautiful little tits. The witch gripped my hips with bruising force and drove upward even deeper as my ass clenched around them.

They said my name reverently, like a prayer…like a spell. Magic shimmered along their skin, blue-white and dazzling, slipping out to caress me before it broke, sliding back inside the witch again, leaving me feeling like I was standing on the brink of a cliff, all exhilaration and crisp, sharp air.

I pitched forward, collapsing on the witch's sticky chest with a whoosh of breath. "Oh." I was all I could manage. But it was enough to express the absolute feeling of *wonder.* I felt like I'd just seen god.

Those long-fingered hands smoothed over my back. “Oh,” the witch echoed quietly, the tone one of absolute agreement. And a little sadness.

I didn’t want to move, but I did manage to eventually scoot off the poor, exhausted witch, clean us up with my discarded shirt, and pull the small blanket up over both of us before we passed out again.

Chapter 25

I didn't wake up to the nice feeling of fingers in my hair this time. Instead, I jerked awake to the sound of angry voices and a loud, echoing bang.

It took me a minute to figure out where I was. I blinked at the ceiling. Right. I was lying on my back in the deep window seat in the witch's study. The wicked witch of the west had their head pillowed on my shoulder, long legs tangled with mine beneath the small throw, and one long arm draped over my chest and neck, fingers lying along my jaw, tangled in my hair.

A *roar* shook the place. Then an angry, commanding voice shouted, "Where *is* he?!"

Oh. Um. Well. This was about to get awkward.

I gently nudged the witch, who was still sleeping, so exhausted they were snoring lightly through the commotion in the hallway. "Babe," I said idiotically. Who called the most powerful witch in Oz *babe*? Apparently, I did. "Hon, I'm sorry but you need to get up." Was that any better? Probably not.

The witch groaned, still clearly not done sleeping off the energy depletion and mind-blowing sex. Poor thing.

I managed to shimmy myself up to sit with my back against the wall, but Vix just went all ragdoll, flopping their head on my lap and wrapping that long arm around my hips, muttering something about emerald beetles and purple moss. Despite the situation, I grinned down at the witch like an idiot. How cute. They talked about spell components in their sleep.

Another loud bang, and this time I realized what that sound was. A door being flung open so hard it was nearly ripped from its hinges, rebounding off the wall. Tin'amen stood in the doorway, an enraged lion-beast on one side, and a darkly murderous-looking scarecrow on the other.

I lifted a hand and waved weakly. "Hey."

The guards behind my motley crew of angry friends-turned-lovers seemed grumpy, but not inclined to commit murder—yet. Apparently, they had been told not to harm the yahoos, even if they were acting like complete lunatics.

"Daniel?" Singing Crow arched his brows and tilted his head as he took in the scene before him.

I cleared my throat and swallowed, my mouth suddenly gone dry. Okay, so…they *had* said they were good with me sleeping with whoever, right? That what we had was just good fun. That they had no claim on me. But I still felt like an ass, over here, sleeping with the enemy.

I held up a hand. "I can explain."

Tin'amen strode across the room, smashing a small table covered with gemstones out of his way with his axe as he went. The noise finally seemed to get through the fog that held the witch under. Vix sat up slowly, unfocused gray eyes going sharp and narrowed as they took in the chaos around them.

"Daniel," Tin'amen said, his voice cold as he halted near the end of the window seat. "Are you okay? Did the witch…force you? Have you been cursed or enchanted?"

I opened my mouth to tell him to stop being dumb. But the witch in question beat me to it, drawing themselves up regally, the blanket pulled up to cover their breasts, sparks of anger filling those gray storm cloud eyes. I felt magic spark along their skin as their voice cracked out, filled with bitterness and rage. "Yes. He's spelled. Clearly, I am so vile that I have nothing better to do than kidnap travelers and bring them away to my evil tower so that I may have my way with them!"

The room fell silent.

"Why else would any sane man fall into my bed?" They clambered over me, and I reached out, trying to stop them. But they were on a *roll*. They cast the blanket away, yanked on their pants and long shirt. Then they grabbed up a jacket they had left draped over the back of a chair at some point and threw that on too. Sure, they were probably just doing it for the sense of security and armor. But they could now *billow* as they paced to their desk and sat, hands steepled and sharp features as imposing as I'd ever seen.

"Well?" Vix snapped, those gray eyes avoiding me entirely. "You've come to rage at me for the all the wrongs I've done, metal man. Don't let me stop you."

I rolled my eyes and got to my feet, finding my own pants and tucking my dick away before stomping over barefoot to stand beside the desk. "Oh, knock it the fuck off," I snapped at the martyr witch.

I thought I saw their lip twitch with restrained humor, but I ignored them.

"And you!" I snapped, pointing at Tin'amen. "Pick up the mess you just made and sit the hell down."

He arched a silver brow at me, but grudgingly scooped up the gemstones off the floor and tossed them on the witch's desk before slamming his ass down in a nearby chair.

"I'm not under any damned spell," I snapped. "For fuck's sake, the witch just about killed themselves using the magic that let you all escape that twister North sent after you. Everyone take a deep breath and be happy the guards haven't stabbed you with their electric jabbies by now!"

Lio shifted back into man-form and lunged across the room, grabbing me up and squeezing me so hard my ribs creaked. "You're really okay, Daniel?" he sobbed into my hair. "I was so scared for you. I thought…I thought…."

I worked an arm free of his crushing hold and patted his wild blond curls. "I know. I'm sorry. You're okay?"

At his nod, I sighed. "Good. Put me down please."

After I was set back on my feet, Lio looked around, realized he was naked, turned bright red, and went all lion-beast form again.

I shook my head.

Singing Crow walked across the room to join me, wisely giving Tin'amen wide berth. "Daniel."

I nodded to him uncomfortably, afraid I really had fucked things up by, you know…*literally* fucking things.

Then Crow held out his arms and I let out the breath I'd been holding. I let him pull me into his embrace, sighing when the caress of his dark magic touched my senses. He had grown even more *himself* since I last saw him, the curse well and truly broken. I could feel the wildness in him in a way I hadn't noticed before. "You're different," I breathed.

He stepped back and gave me a wry smile. "I felt a presence in my mind when I was in bird form—as we were fleeing the cyclone." He glanced away from me, at Vix. "It was as if pure magic flowed through me, making me stronger, faster. I think it burned away any lingering effects from the curse that had yet to fade."

The witch pressed their lips together and kept that cold glare on their face.

I shook my head. "You sent your magic to all the animals. Even them. Didn't you?"

I glanced at Lio, and he nodded his massive head. Vix had shared their soul magic not only with their people, but with mine as well. I let go of the grip I was trying to get on my diplomatic presence and took the three steps necessary to reach the witch, wrapping my arm around their tense shoulders and pulling them into an awkward side hug.

"Thank you," I breathed. Then a bit louder. "I think it's time you stopped pretending and let people know who you really are. We're all on the same side."

Vix huffed, their voice dry and cold. But I felt the tension leaving their lean body, noticed the way they leaned into me slightly. "I have no side but my own. People can't be trusted, Daniel."

I risked life and limb to slide my fingers through that silky blue-black hair, pushing it back from their face so I could see their eyes. "Not true, and we both know it. At least try. For me?"

Tin'amen snorted and I shot a glare his way. He held up his hands in defeat. "Far be it from me to interfere with the way your excess *heart* infects anyone who comes near."

Singing Crow shoved him in the shoulder. "Good thing it does, or you'd be insufferable. You're bad enough as it is."

The witch looked to the guards who still milled about on the other side of the room looking lost and confused. "Go," Vix snapped. "I've got this well in hand."

"You got *something* in hand, I'm sure," the scarecrow muttered with a leer.

I glared at him as the guards left and the wonky door was pulled closed—as much as possible. "Shut it, Crow."

He just smirked.

The wicked witch of the west put their head in their hands and let out a tired sigh, and I was reminded how exhausted they were. "Your companions are strange," they muttered to me. "But somehow they suit you."

Vix lifted their head with apparent effort, sitting up straight again. "Call for Ama, Daniel. She can show your companions to a room large enough for you all to share. You can leave again as soon as they are rested."

I opened my mouth to protest, my heart squeezing at the desolation I thought I sensed behind that cool mask. But those gray eyes met mine, and the look there stopped me before I could speak. They were tired, pleading. "We will speak again before you leave."

I swallowed, gave a sharp nod, and spun on a bare heel to find a place for the rest of the crew. But I felt like I'd just been stabbed in the chest.

Dismissed. Again. Just as I knew I would be, in the end. Because everyone on this planet had made it very clear that they didn't want me to stick around.

Chapter 26

The room that the staff found for us was, indeed, big enough for us all. We were provided with bathing things, clothes, and several heaping trays of food and drink.

I watched it all arrive with a sort of dull awareness, still worried about how I'd left things with Vix.

I had grown used to the wicked witch's hospitality, but the others were showing all the shock and confusion I'd first felt when I arrived here. I pasted on a polite smile, thanked the staff, and shooed them out the door, pausing to take one of them aside and ask them to tell Ama to send something fortifying up to the witch. I had a hunch Vix was currently sulking alone somewhere, loathing themselves or trying to lose themselves in work—maybe trying to perfect the pollen treatment. They had been exploring ways to enhance the effectiveness with magic, so the addiction problem could be eradicated that much faster….

I turned to find several sets of eyes on me. "Go," I said, waving them away, toward the attached bathing suit. "Get cleaned up and comfortable. Have something to eat. I'll explain everything once you're settled in."

"You're a bit rumpled yourself, human," Tin'amen observed, his expression blank. "You need to bathe as well. Will you join us?"

I sighed. I had planned to return to my own borrowed room to scrub away the evidence of my promiscuity, actually. “That depends,” I said, lifting my chin and crossing my arms over my bare chest. I would *not* let myself feel guilty for something as natural as sex. “Do you want me in there because you missed me? Or just because someone else touched your shiny human toy?”

Lio shifted to man-form and wrung his big hands, unconcerned that he was now completely naked. “Daniel? Why are you angry? We came as fast as we could….”

Singing Crow sighed and paced closer to me. “He’s not angry at us, Lio. He’s embarrassed.”

I scoffed. Even though he was totally right. I might *try* to be all enlightened and cavalier about wanting what I wanted and all that jazz…but deep down inside, the prejudices of the society I was raised in persisted.

Tin’amen shook his head. “This is another of those strange human *feelings* things, isn’t it? Maybe I’d rather not have a heart after all.”

Lio shuffled up to me and hesitantly took my hands, prying them away from my chest. “Daniel?”

I slumped. “I’m such a slut.” I glared up at the big softie, then each of the others in turn. “But I’m not sorry. I don’t regret it. There’s more to the witch than you know.”

Singing Crow laughed. “Like breasts? I thought you preferred males, my dear Daniel. But that’s nothing to be ashamed of. I enjoy females as well.”

I rolled my eyes skyward and prayed to every deity and celestial body I could think of to save me from this weird conversation. “You know what? I thought you actually understood for a second there, Crow.”

He shrugged. "I've told you, my people don't view sexual intercourse the way yours do. It was a bit of a shock to burst in expecting to save you, only to find you naked. But that's it. All that matters is that it was consensual, and you are unharmed."

I rubbed a hand over my face, then looked at the others. "And you two? You don't care that I slept with the enemy? Well, the person we *thought* was the enemy. They're not, really, you know."

Lio looked confused. "You share the three of us. And we have no formal claim or agreement."

I swallowed hard. "Yep." Even though I *wanted* there to be something more between us, damn it.

Was I really the only one who was upset over this? Of course I was. Because I was the only one who considered what we had some sort of actual relationship. Stupid, Daniel. Rookie mistake in any negotiation, assuming the other side thought and felt as you did.

Tin'amen set his axe aside and started stripping. "No one is angry, Daniel. I have every confidence that you will explain your interactions with the witch. Your body is your own to do with as you will."

Singing Crow winked at me. "*We* were hardly celibate while we were away from you."

No, I didn't suppose they were. And I wouldn't expect them to be. Even if I *had* meant more to them, it would only be natural to seek comfort together.

They just…truly didn't care. But they still considered me a friend. They still wanted me here with them. That was something, I supposed. After the wound of the witch's dismissal, I'd take what sense of belonging I could get.

We took turns showering and soaking in the big stone tub helping each other wash up. I let the others hog the warm water, and managed to only blush a *little* bit while I washed away the traces of my other lover.

I was starting to feel like a regular old Casanova over here, what with all the conquests. I'd never been a prude, but having four lovers at the same time was a bit much, even for me.

I forced myself to relax, to accept the fact that no one was upset and that—for at least a little while longer—they could still be mine. I was *just* selfish enough to take advantage of that fact for as long as I could. We traded gentle kisses and sweet touches, getting reacquainted, my lips and skin relearning the lost touch of the people I'd missed so badly over what felt like months, but had barely been a week.

We didn't have sex. I think everyone was a bit strung out. And I didn't even know half of what they might have been through on their travels.

"Did you know the wolfbeasts can speak, Daniel?" Crow asked as we all settled around a small table, clean and dressed.

I shook my head. "No. But…can they always do that? Or was it magic?"

They looked at me and I chuckled. "I forgot. I need to fill you in on some things." I gestured at the food, and they all dug in ravenously while I brought them up to speed on everything I'd learned during my time at the castle.

"So…" Singing Crow said slowly, once I'd finished my tale. "You were carrying the cure for pollen addiction in your boot this whole time?"

"Yeah. I think Vix is finalizing the formula." I shrugged. "I felt kind of stupid, not gonna lie. But the witch has been working on it constantly. They called it a 'base' for the antidote. I don't know what the whole scheme is once they craft the final version of it. But it involves the wizard somehow. Vix plans to send us back to him."

"The witch's magic is…wow," Lio said around a mouthful of food. "There are legends of natives among the winvie people who used to be able to communicate with all the animals on Oz. But that knowledge has been lost."

Crow nodded thoughtfully. "Legend says that's where the various shifter tribes came from—that we are all descended from the nature-talkers. The magicians who could speak for the planet."

Tin'amen shifted in his seat, ever the skeptic. "The witch of the west isn't from Oz, they aren't native."

I shrugged. "No. But they have a really strong bond with the people here. Maybe they were taught?"

Crow's eyes lit up and I could see that clever, rebel brain of his working. "Maybe they could teach others. Maybe we could learn to live in harmony with the land again—to commune with mother Ozma."

I held up my hands. "Whoa. Down boy. One problem at a time. Everyone *hates* the witch of the west. The people of Oz have been systematically indoctrinated against Vix by the other rulers, and Vix has had zero support from their family back on Valklon, from what I understand. I doubt anyone's going to want them teaching anything at this point."

Besides, we'd have to convince Vix first. And my witch was *not* a fan of the idiot masses. For obvious reasons. I probably wouldn't feel too charitable toward them myself after years of lies and violent persecution.

"We should return to the Emerald City as soon as possible," Tin'amen said, no expression on his face as he broke my heart.

"I'm sure you want to get home, not get further embroiled in Oz's political problems."

I licked my lips. "Sure. But you know I want to help any way I can, right?" They might not care if I just scurried off to my own life, but Oz was *their* planet, and I wasn't going to leave the people I loved to live under oppression and manipulation.

Wait. What? I kicked myself mentally. I could *not* fall in love with these men. It was already too late to prevent getting attached. But *love*? *No, Daniel. No way. Don't do it.*

"Well," I said, standing and glancing toward the dark window. "You're probably all tired. A good night's sleep in a real bed will feel wonderful. Trust me on that one. I've been living like a spoiled princess while you guys were out there in the wilderness." I gestured at the massive bed. "Get some rest."

If I didn't know any better, I'd think I sensed disappointment when I went to the door.

"You're not staying with us, Daniel?" Lio said, eyes on the floor and cheeks red. "We missed you."

I closed my eyes and tried not to go all mushy. "I'll be back," I promised. "But I need to…take care of something first."

Then I slipped from the room and padded back toward the witch's study.

Chapter 27

For a brief, crazy moment, I was afraid Vix had retreated to their rooms somewhere in the far reaches of the massive castle and I would have to track down a staff member and convince them to reveal the recluse's hideout.

But no. Of *course* they hadn't gone off to rest.

I found the handsome, frustrating creature right where I'd left them over an hour ago—sitting at their desk, bent over some musty old book, muttering to themselves.

"You know," I said, leaning against the doorjamb and gesturing at the untouched dinner plate that sat by their elbow, "I'm pretty sure that was meant to be eaten, not used as decoration."

They didn't even look up. "I didn't ask for it. The staff is just fussing needlessly."

I sighed and walked into the room, going to stand before the desk. "*I* asked for them to bring it to you."

"Then *you* are needlessly fussing."

"We're leaving tomorrow," I said evenly, watching the way the witch's shoulders tensed and their breath caught.

"Good. I'll make appropriate arrangements."

"You're coming with us."

That finally got them to look at me. "I beg your pardon?" they said, gray eyes searching my face. "I think my ears were damaged at some point this evening."

I huffed a dry laugh. "Hardly. I want you to come with us." I dropped into a chair near the desk. "You and the wizard have some plan for the antidote, right? Wouldn't it make things easier if you were in the Emerald City?"

Vix sighed, finally letting some of their lingering tiredness show through the tough mask. "Yes, we…I'm to perfect the contents of this potion, and he is to supply the manpower and large number of raw components that go into the final distilled ingredients—enough so we can broadcast it quickly and widely in a single strike."

Those gray eyes were vulnerable as they admitted softly, "I planned to go to Emerald City anyway. But I had meant to let you and your companions travel without my infamous presence to attract trouble."

I huffed. "Ridiculous. Just…we'll all go together. I've explained things to the others—how wrong everyone is about you. It'll be fine."

The witch drummed long fingers on the desk…and I couldn't help but recall that soft, strong touch on my body. "I will consider it," Vix said, finally. "But you must understand that no one can know I'm in the city. North and South go to great lengths to ensure the wizard and I don't spend time together scheming."

I nodded, grinning. "I can see that. I imagine the two of you together would be downright *wicked*, a hazard to the health of anyone who stood in your way."

They laughed, leaning back in their chair. I stood, rounding the desk, and shoved the plate of food their way. "Now, eat something before you waste away."

That earned me an eye roll. "I'm not hungry."

I looked over the plate and chose a chunk of juicy golden fruit that resembled pineapple. "Ah." I held the fruit in front of those delicious lips and made baby noises.

The murderous glare was kind of adorable.

But then the witch leaned forward and took the fruit, making sure to suck one of my fingers into their mouth. And there… *there* was the wickedness everyone always accused them of, but I doubt few ever saw. "Happy?" they snarked, sitting back.

I smiled and leaned down to kiss the sweet juice off those wicked lips. "Mmm…getting there."

I reached for the plate again, but Vix snatched it away. "Shouldn't you be off reuniting with your companions, rather than courting another embarrassing incident? What if they come looking for you?"

I sighed and bent to kiss the tip of that ridiculously long nose. "Listen carefully," I said, pulling back to look them in the eyes. "I am not ashamed of what happened between us. I am not embarrassed to be seen kissing you." I paused, tilting my head as I considered the veracity of that statement. "Okay, well, I *was* embarrassed at first, but not because of you. It was because I was afraid the others would be mad if I fell for someone outside our group. But I've been told that is a purely human hang-up."

I kissed them again, loving how they leaned into it, how they clearly longed for what I was saying to be the truth. "So," I said against their lips, "I don't give a rat's ass *who* sees. You're amazingly sexy, evil witch."

I stepped back, putting some distance between me and the silent witch. "Maybe *you* don't feel that way, though, and that's okay. If I was just a one-off for you, fine. You're still coming with us though, either way. I'm not using sex to coerce you or trick you, or whatever else your twisted brain might say."

I sucked in a breath. Honestly, I *thought* maybe they still wanted me after all. But I could be totally wrong. "I'll see you tomorrow morning, and you can tell us all what we need to do to help get ready, okay?"

A perplexed, wistful expression crossed Vix's angular features. Then they nodded. "As you wish, Daniel."

I crossed to the door and left, returning to the room to cuddle up with the others, a smile playing about my lips.

The witch was coming with us. I had heard it in the way the lilt returned to Vix's voice when they spoke my name.

Maybe I wasn't just a throw-away after all....

Chapter 28

The return trip to the Emerald City was a bit quicker than the hike there, since we were able to ride the witch's wolfbeasts. The witch used their magic to enhance the creatures' speed and endurance, sending us rushing through the dark woods in record time. But once we left the forest, we had to leave the wolves behind.

"It's not safe for them outside the forest," Vix said grimly. "They are hunted—seen as symbols of my evil. And traveling that way would only draw attention."

I sighed wistfully as we started the last stretch of the journey on foot. Cars would be helpful, but the witch had explained that they long ago worked magic into the lands between the black woods and the Emerald City to prevent motorized vehicles approaching.

"They used to try to send spies or outright attacks on a near daily basis," Vix said tiredly. "It was the only way to keep them from easily mounting attacks. And any beast they might ride will abandon their mount before they get close enough to do any harm."

I was amazed once again at the scope of their magic…and at the terrifyingly strange and dangerous circumstances that they just took as a given.

One good thing about all the walking, though. It gave my witch time to get to know the others. And my suspicions were right. Once they got past the hard shell, they clearly saw the sweetness inside, just like I did.

As we sat by our small campfire that night, I watched Crow and Vix from across the fire, where they sat side by side on an overturned, half-rotted log. I couldn't hear what they were saying as they spoke softly about magic and spell weaving, but I liked the sight of them together, oddly similar with their thin frames and dark hair, but yet vastly different. Crow held out a hand, letting a flame of black and purple flare to life there. Vix tilted their head, examining it, running their nimble fingers along the edges as if feeling along Crow's magic.

The witch tilted their head and said something, gesturing up at the sky, then down at the earth. Then Vix put their hands on either side of Crow's conjured flame and coaxed it to burn brighter. Crow's face lit up with wonder, but he apparently got over-excited and lost focus. The fire went out with a soft *pop* and a sprinkling rain of purple sparks.

They both started laughing, and the witch patted Crow on the shoulder. I just shook my head at them and hoped they didn't blow us up.

"It's rare to encounter magic users who can manipulate the energy as tangibly as Crow can," Tin'amen said, dropping an armload of dead branches he'd scrounged from the edge of the thinning wood behind us. One corner of his mouth twitched upward, and I thought maybe he was having as much fun watching the two dark-haired hotties as I was. "The crow people are in tune with the natural world. They use magic in their daily lives, but they also use tech when it's needed. I think many of them have begun to abandon their traditional ways and lean on tech more often. To find someone of the witch's power who is willing to teach him nature magic is a great gift."

Crow glanced our way and waved, still looking like a kid presented with the biggest candy you could imagine. I waved back like an idiot. But the witch was talking again, those long-fingered hands dancing in the air, and Crow was of course riveted once more.

"We're lucky to have met you," Tin'amen said softly, drawing one leg up and resting his arm on his knee. "You have a way of bringing people together. A side effect of that overly large heart of yours, I suspect."

I nudged him with my shoulder. "Oh, hush. Your heart is every bit as big and mushy as mine. You just refuse to admit it."

Strong fingers curled around my jaw and turned my head, forcing me to meet those intense silver eyes. "I'm broken," he said softly, his voice lacking any emotion. "Damaged. You know this."

He sighed and leaned in to press a soft, surprisingly sweet kiss to my lips. "And yet you allow me to stay by your side and continue to benefit from your beautiful heart."

I huffed against his lips, going back in for another kiss, since I could never seem to get enough. "I'm actually not sure why *you* stick around and help *me*, darling. But if you want to put me on a pedestal and worship me like a treasure, by all means, don't let me stop you."

He smiled then, a full smile, rare and blinding as the sun. "I'm afraid too much attention might go to your head. It's a terrifying thought. But I also shudder to think what you might be like if you felt neglected."

I poked him in the chest. "Did you just call me needy?"

Lio stood from where he had been lying by the fire in beast form, soaking up heat. Shaking out his impressive curly coat, he padded over and sat before me. I stared into his reflective green eyes in question, having to look *up* to look him in the eye, since I was sitting and he was *massive*. I yelped when the monster cat leaned in and licked me, his rough tongue dragging over my cheek.

I swatted him away and he shifted, the burly, naked man kneeling at my feet and laughing at me. "What's wrong, Daniel?" he said, sweetly innocent. "Tin'amen got a kiss. Don't you like my kisses? You'll hurt my feelings."

I rolled my eyes. "Well, we definitely wouldn't want that."

This time, his kiss was all man, warm and sweet, and somehow reminding me of sunshine and golden honey and the tall dry grasses of home.

I pulled back, flushed and dreamy, only to be pulled into Tin'amen's arms again as Lio ran his big, warm hands up and down my thighs. Fingers tangled in my hair, pulling my head back, so I was looking at Crow nearly upside down. I hadn't even noticed him joining us. His lips on mine were demanding and hungry, and I nearly fell over backward off the backpack I was currently sitting on. But Lio and Tin'amen caught me. Then they just went ahead and pushed me down anyway. So much for the assist.

"Oh, fuck!" I muttered, when someone rubbed my dick through my pants, while another someone undid the button there and someone *else* stretched out his long, pale body beside me and started kissing me again.

I flapped a hand weakly, pushing away from the sudden attack to sit up and catch my breath. They were going to be the death of me. And I was all for death by orgy, believe me. No better way to go. But there was a problem here.

I looked across the dancing flames of our little fire to meet a pair of gray eyes, the shadows around them making them look nearly black. The witch was calmly sitting there, watching, clearly unsure of their place amongst the rest of my little harem. And probably *still* thinking I hadn't meant it when I said I wanted them for more than a curiosity fuck, or a means to an end.

I untangled myself and stood, yanking my unbuttoned pants back up like an idiot. I lifted my chin, squared my shoulders, and made my way around the fire to stand before the infamous wicked witch. "Enjoying the show?" I asked dryly.

They looked up at me and leaned back, planting their hands on the ground behind them, the picture of unconcerned boredom. "Not the worst performance I've attended. Anything has to be better than the school-aged winvie's annual stage show celebrating their gourd harvest."

I gaped at them. "Did you…did you just compare my impending *orgy* to a kids' school play?"

One corner of that wicked mouth curled upward. "Did I?"

I shook my head. "How do you *do* that?"

They arched their thin black brows at me. "Do what, Daniel?"

There they went again, saying my name like they were talking about some kind of dessert. "Distract me! How do you deflect every damned conversation away from yourself?!"

That got me a full smile. "You make it quite easy."

I bent so our faces were just inches apart. "Are you going to join in on the festivities, or just sit here being all…distant and evil?"

A flicker of seriousness finally showed on their face. "I wasn't sure I was invited." At my growl—because how many times did I have to say I wanted them?—they held up a hand and added, "the others…."

I straightened, moving in to sit straddling Vix's lap. "I know you find them attractive. I've seen you looking."

The look that got me said it all. "So," I said easily, leaning in so only they could hear me. "Do you want them too? Or is it only okay if it's me touching you?"

They swallowed, licked their lips. Those lovely hands came up to grip my ass and press me closer. Long lashes fluttered downward, hiding those storm eyes from view. "Your other lovers *are* quite attractive."

I smirked. "Then watch how easy this is." I leaned in and kissed the witch, our tongues tangling as we wrestled for control. They slid one hand up to grip my hair and tug, and I groaned, rubbing against them through our clothes.

I smiled when I felt a second set of hands on my back, a warm body pressing up against me, pinning me between them and Vix.

I knew damned well that the others shared my infatuation with the sexy witch. All they needed was a signal, someone to give the okay. I pulled back and watched in smug satisfaction when Crow settled in next to Vix, reaching out to cup their face and pull them into a kiss.

I was right, the two of them were a perfect set, all lean, dark beauty and grace. Lio was next, sitting on the witch's other side and patiently waiting to be noticed. When Crow released our witch, the wicked smile on the witch's face was so hot I nearly combusted. But when the witch turned to the quiet, shy Lio, gave him a small, encouraging smile, and tugged him in by that glorious mane of curls…yeah…fireworks.

I mourned the lack of real beds. I had gotten so spoiled back at the witch's castle. What I wouldn't give to have all of them completely naked and spread out on soft pillows and sheets like a buffet. My heart gave a little pang at the thought. I might never get to see that. It was all wishful thinking, since the moment we reached the Emerald City we would all go our separate ways.

I sucked in a breath and willed my wounded heart to keep beating. If this was all we had, then I was damned well going to enjoy every moment of it, soak it all in and save it up for when the memory was all I had left.

We tumbled down into the tall grasses and wildflowers at the side of the road, and all I could see when I looked up was the beautiful sight of my unexpected lovers, framed by dark petals in the flickering firelight—wild poppies, of all things. It seemed only fitting for a tryst in the wilds of Oz.

I found myself on my back as Tin'amen's strong fingers prepped me, the warm, living metal of his other hand bringing my cock to aching hardness in slow, sure strokes. The witch knelt by my head, leaning down to kiss me, their touch giving away their barely restrained hunger.

How long had the wicked witch of the west been deprived of touch, of affection?

No longer. Vix straightened and leaned back, pulled into Crow's arms, the witch's back to Crow's chest. Murmured conversation ensued between lingering kisses and caresses, and I caught enough between my sobs of pleasure to realize the witch was explaining their sexuality and needs to Crow. I was beyond curious just what it would mean when they eventually moved out of their "giver" cycle to their "carrier" cycle. But for now…I was just happy we were all safe from accidentally impregnating the infamous evil witch.

Stars and comets, that would surely complicate things.

I lost my train of thought when Tin'amen leaned down to kiss me, breaching me with his steel-hard dick. I gasped and writhed, wanting to both escape *and* impale myself at the same time. One hand cupped my face as he pushed in, slow and unrelenting, kissing me so hard I could barely breathe.

Then he was pushing away slightly, making room for Lio to stroke my chest and swipe the flat of his tongue over my nipples. The witch let out a shuddery sigh, and I glanced up and back in time to see them reach backward and loop their arms over Crow's neck as the other man pressed inside them. The witch was alien and strange, with their blue skin and four breasts jutting out in a wanton pose, that long cock twitching with pleasure—but holy hell were they hot.

I groaned as Tin'amen pressed deeper, then slid out, slow and teasing, his strong hands gripping my thighs. Lio sat back on his heels to stroke his massive dick, heat simmering in his green eyes, sparks dancing there in the firelight, his wild mass of springy blond curls standing out against his dark skin, like some wild alien god of the prairies.

He stretched out beside me, head toward my feet, and I reached for him, stroking his cock as Tin'amen drove into me. Vix fell forward onto one hand, and I twisted my head, urging him and Crow to shuffle closer until I had Vix's cock in my mouth, Tin'amen in my ass, and Crow fucking our lovely witch from behind. My hand that was still awkwardly stroking Lio was brushed aside as Tin'amen leaned over me, kissing a path along my jaw before he turned and started sucking Lio's cock, all the while fucking me in sure, slow strokes.

I have no idea how, but we made it work, all connected, twisted and contorted and pressed together until I didn't know where I ended and they began. Breathless gasps and moans, the slap of skin on skin, and the wet suction of lips and tongues around rigid flesh. My cock jumped and throbbed against my stomach, trapped against the hard ridges of Tin'amen's abs as he ground into me, dragging one of my legs up so he could thrust harder, pegging my prostate and sending little *zings* of pleasure through me.

I couldn't see Lio through the silver fall of Tin'amen's hair. But I could see Crow and the witch above me, Crow's graceful hands coming around to cup the witch's breasts, making the witch shudder in his arms and come down my throat, a spill of wild magic dancing in the air around us.

I swallowed down the salty sweet release and Vix pulled out of my mouth, leaning back onto Crow as the beautiful shifter rode out his own orgasm, clutching the witch's narrow waist and thrusting upward in short, jerky motions as their magic visibly entwined around them.

I felt my balls draw up tight, my own release building at the sight of my beautiful lovers coming apart in each other's arms. Tin'amen pulled off Lio and gripped both of my legs, hooking my knees over his arms and folding me in half as he pounded home, wild and lost in the tide of lust and magic around us. He came with a shout that had me coming so hard I saw stars, hot jizz splashing my own chest and stomach.

Before I could even come back down from the euphoria, Tin'amen was gone and Lio was there, his hot tongue lapping up my cum, nipping at my jaw and neck. The sweet, usually timid shifter was gone, replaced by someone who was nearly animal. He growled low in his throat and manhandled me with ease, flipping me over onto my knees and slamming his huge cock into my well-used hole.

I spasmed and cursed at the startling, yet absolutely arousing, invasion. He buried a hand in my hair and tugged, the other big hand just above my ass, near my hip and low back, anchoring me as he pulled out, inch by inch, only to slam back into me. I groaned and met him thrust for thrust, my dick already twitching back to life, more than willing to try for another go.

I was nothing if not motivated.

Lio's hands gripped my hips and he helped slam me up and back as he thrust, his speed increasing until all I could do was hold on for dear life and take the punishing, mind-bending pleasure.

I screamed as I came, a string of nonsensical curses pouring from my lips at having two orgasms ripped from me in such a short period of time. I felt Lio swell impossibly bigger inside me, just before he spilled, pulsing so hard I could feel it.

Stars, just the sensation of that alone had my dick wishing it could stand up again and demand more. But we were thoroughly and utterly spent.

I went limp, Lio only just managing to catch me before I could faceplant on the ground. A couple of amused chuckles followed, but I was way too wrung out to muster the appropriate snarky response.

Instead, I let Lio pick me up like a fainting female in one of those museum quality black and white Earth films and carry me to a bedroll closer to the fire.

I remained in a floaty state of bliss as the witch was deposited next to me, crankily muttering how they weren't helpless the entire time. Then Crow settled in on my other side, kissing my cheek before reaching out to take Vix's hand and bring it to his lips for a soft kiss. "Let him fuss," the bird shifter said, wry humor lacing his voice. “Lio’s lost to his beast at the moment. Being all territorial and rounding up his herd.”

I snorted. Crow just called us a herd. And Lio the cowardly lion-beast *protective*. Tin’amen dragged another bedroll over and plopped down behind Crow. I let out a surprised *oof* when Lio’s massive body covered my own, sprawling in the middle of us all like some kind of puppy pile.

I grinned like a dope, even though I couldn’t breathe under the approximately three hundred pounds of man slab sprawled atop me.

I wished I could fall asleep like this every night. But as I drifted off, I knew it couldn’t be. They were forever burned into my senses, my heart. But these men could never really be mine.

Chapter 29

Aside from some sweet, adorable apologies and worry on Lio's part after giving me the pounding of a lifetime…the remainder of the trip to the Emerald City was surprisingly uneventful. I really expected something to go horribly wrong—maybe more attacks from North and South. But I had contacted the wizard the first day outside the black woods on our borrowed comm, only to be reassured that the wizard of Oz was "keeping them busy." I had no idea what that meant, and I was kind of afraid to ask, given how evil and full of joy his smile had been when he said that.

I had learned something valuable from all my time in the diplomat gig foiling evil plans—when you partner up with villains, sometimes it's best not to know all the details. Plausible deniability and all. Although…given what I now knew of the wicked witch of the west, and that Vix worked with the wizard, I had to wonder if at least part of the wizard's evil persona was created to shield the reclusive witch.

I had a suspicion that the witch was also doing something to shield us. Vix seemed to be tired, but they brushed it off when I asked. Like I really believed they'd admit it if they were overtaxing themselves again to protect us all. Ha.

As we approached the city, the witch pulled on a long gray jacket with a hood.

"Do you really think people will know who you are on sight?" I asked curiously. I mean, sure, the wicked witch of the west was like some kind of scary legend. But there were lots of people on Oz who looked all kinds of strange, not to mention a whole colony of blue-skinned winvies not that far away. And communication and information didn't seem to travel too far or too fast on this backward planet with all of its isolated, divided colonies.

The witch just gave me a grim look. "Better safe than sorry."

But Tin'amen wasn't about to let them get away with hiding things from me. For once, I was sort of glad for his bluntness and inability to sugar coat things.

"There have been multiple failed assassination attempts against them," the tall, silver god said simply. "And a few were almost successful. North and South have eyes everywhere."

I gave the witch an unimpressed look. "You were just going to not tell me you've almost been *assassinated*? *Multiple* times? Is that why you never leave the castle?"

They started to agree with that assessment, but Singing Crow chimed in. "Actually, I believe at least a couple of the more successful attempts were inside the castle, if the gossip was right."

The witch glared at him. "Overblown stories. Only an idiot poisons a witch with a strong connection to nature. I slept it off." And I definitely heard a muttered, "After I kicked them out of my fucking bed."

I shook my head at Vix. "I swear to fuck, you have *no* sense of self-preservation."

Sure as hell made their hesitance where friendships and relationships were concerned seem a lot more logical. Geesh.

We scanned in at the gate, and my eyebrows climbed into my hairline when the witch did some little energy trick that made the scanner think they were a moonkin seamstress here to barter for imported silk. They *really* didn't want anyone knowing they were here. Tin'amen took up his usual position in front of us all, one hand on his axe and a sharp glare on his face as we entered the city.

I got a weird sense of déjà vu when Lio crowded in on my side in lion-beast form. I glanced down at him with a sigh. "You know you can't stay that way. They'll just make you change back."

He made a chuffing sound at me that sounded like a *scoff*. "Are you…did you just give me *attitude*? I swear, you've been spending too much time around this lot," I said, waving to indicate our companions. He just purred.

"Fine," I muttered. "I'm not the one getting tased when they come to force you back into man-shape."

"Don't worry, Lio," Tin'amen said in a serious, even voice, not even looking back at us. "Daniel will hold you while you cry your cowardly little eyes out."

I gaped at him.

"I'm pretty sure that's the whole point," Singing Crow added with a smirk and a wink.

I narrowed my eyes suspiciously at Lio, then put a hand to my heart as if mortally wounded, going full-on diva voice. "You've been *playing* me this whole time! Using my big heart to get to all my other *big* things. I feel so used."

The witch snorted, not looking at me, their gray eyes scanning the place much like the metal soldier was. "I worry for you,

Daniel. Surely you can't be *that* simple."

"Not you too!" I gasped. "I thought you were different. I thought you wanted me for more than my looks. I might faint."

"Are you feeling well, Mr. Westerfield?" A dry voice interrupted. Good thing, too, because my last statement had hit a little too close to truth for comfort. I *did* want them to want me for more than a good tumble in the weeds. Or on the window seat. Whatever.

We all stopped when one of the wizard's flunkies stepped into our path. It took me a minute, but I identified him as the same uptight ass I'd had fun annoying the first time I came to see the wizard. I grinned and stepped forward to slap him on the back loud and hard, like we were best friends, and I was an intergalactic football player or something. "Mr. Uptight! Look at you! So good to see you again. How's the wife and kids?"

He shook me off and jerked his boring uniform jacket straight, his greenish-colored complexion going a bit red in the face. "I don't have a wife and kids." Stepping further away from me, just to be safe, he gestured ahead of us, toward the gates of the wizard's lair, where a couple of guards had been stationed to herd us through.

I walked through the gates and into the entry to the wizard's dome-shaped place of business with the others just as the afternoon sun was beginning its descent toward the horizon. We had been walking for four days, and I was dirty and tired. Lio, Crow, and Tin'amen must be even more road weary than me, given they had only had one night to rest at the witch's castle before we returned here. But despite my fatigue, my whole body buzzed with nervous energy.

Steal the crystal ball from the witch and deliver it to the wizard and our wishes were granted. That was the deal. Was it a deal breaker that I hadn't stolen the orb, even if I *had* delivered my unknown cargo and brought the witch to the wizard in person? What if he refused to help us?

As much as I wouldn't mind staying on Oz, Lio and Tin'amen still needed help. And there was still the little matter of the corruption in EARTH and the looming threat of a war over mining rights on Sumborto that I could probably prevent—but it would take leaving Oz to do that. It would take returning to the stuffy existence of a hired cajoler working for largely corrupt and self-interested galactic powers.

It didn't seem fair, really. That I had to give up so much, when all I wanted was to help people. If I was sucked back into EARTH employ, I'd even have to give up Dotty…and the drag persona had become a big part of who I was. She was the freedom to be loudly and unapologetically me.

We were led down to the bowels of the building again, past the parts that were for public consumption, for show, and to the parts that seemed truer to who the manipulating wizard really was. I expected more of a fuss about the addition to our little band of travelers. But then, the witch *was* supposedly in-league with the wizard. Though I had no idea how easy an alliance it was.

We entered the wizard's office study to find him seated at his desk, just like before, still looking just as imposing and powerful. His suit was different today, cut more like those I was used to here on Oz, with exaggerated shoulders, and a navy and silver pinstripe this time. His black eyes studied us from an expressionless face as we approached his desk. Our escort left, pulling the tall wooden doors closed behind him with a bang.

"Dotty," the wizard greeted, one corner of his mouth lifting in a smirk. "Or should I say Daniel, now? You seem to have made an addition to your rogue crew of misfits."

I smiled sweetly at him. So, I hadn't exactly told him the witch was coming back with us. I wasn't sure what his reaction would be. And the stars *forbid* the witch actually divulge information about themselves and their relationships with others *voluntarily.* "Oh, I thought you might want to see an old friend," I cooed, batting my eyelashes like I was wearing my biggest false set. "Aren't you thrilled?"

The wizard stared at me for so long I thought he had gone catatonic. Thinking, maybe? If so, he was scrambling furiously for what to say. It was kind of funny.

His eyes slid to the side, to look at the witch in all their tall, slender, androgynous, dark-clad glory. Too bad they couldn't billow right now. No breeze. But the hooded jacket today was just as epic as all the others. Very dramatic.

The wizard stood and came around his desk, pacing closer, halting in front of Vix. "The wicked witch of the west," he said gravely. Then, a slow, sensuous smile graced those frightening lips. "I've missed you, my dear."

I blinked at them. Vix crossed their arms over their chest and lifted their chin defiantly. "I wish I could say the same." Unfolding, they swung their pack around so they could rummage through it, coming up with a cloth ball. "I think you were looking for this."

The wizard took the bundle and tossed the cloth aside, revealing the crystal ball that I had *not* stolen. His eyes flared with something, the inky black becoming red for a heartbeat before they went back to black again. "Ah…busted," he breathed.

I shook my head. "Why did you bring it?" I demanded of the witch. "I told you I wasn't going to take it!" It was a magic artifact, clearly important to the witch.

Vix's gray eyes narrowed dangerously. "Because this asshole wanted it. I can make another one. There's nothing special about the crystal ball, Daniel."

I frowned. Then why....

The wizard cleared his throat uncomfortably and spun, taking the crystal and lovingly tucking it away into a padded wooden box he took from his desk drawer. His eyes were on the box as he spoke, his voice nonchalant. "The orb allows the user to see through the eyes of those connected to it."

The witch huffed, for some reason. I glanced between them, an awful suspicion forming in my head. "I thought the orb let you see through the eyes of the animals you were communicating with," I asked the witch slowly.

Vix didn't look away from the wizard, their hostile glare never fading. "It does, but not how you assume. I said it helps me sort out what I'm seeing. I can divide my conscience using the orbs—sort what I'm seeing in my head and the eyes of the creature I'm viewing through. But there are other uses. It's a focus. Any strong magic user can link up to another magic user through it, if they have a deep enough connection."

I blinked at them. "So...."

"The interference that blocks the comms in the black woods makes it difficult for us to communicate," the wizard said, matter of fact as he packed away the orb like a treasure. "With this I can contact the witch at any time."

"And see through my eyes," Vix said in a waspish voice. "Because Dewin is a nosy, interfering—"

"Infatuated," the wizard added. "Addled, obsessed, madly in love—"

"Asshole," the witch finished, their sharp teeth coming together with a not so comforting click. Like they'd like to take a bite out of the wizard's flesh.

I just stood there, shaking my head. Because *of course* the two of them had some sort of…thing. History? Whatever. I mean, stars and planets, *look* at them. Both oozing power and sex appeal like breathing. I shook myself. Didn't matter.

"Well," I said, squaring my shoulders and acting as if I couldn't care less—spoiler, I could care less. A lot less. I really could. I was dying to know what the hell was going on. But it was none of my business. "Dewin…." Because of course the wizard's name was something so quaint and…*nice* sounding. "You have your magic ball, I did my drug mule thing, the witch is here to work on manufacturing the antidote or whatever. I think you owe several of us for services rendered."

He smiled at me. *Smiled.* Like a real smile. And it was the weirdest thing I'd ever seen in my life. Evil and beneficent all at once, with his black eyes and his mobster vibe alongside his good looks and manners. "Of course, my dear. Would you like to rest first? Or should we get on with it?"

My head started to pound with the threat of a massive tension headache. Put it off a while longer, maybe shower together and lounge about in an actual bed with my lovers…or hurry the fuck up and get out of here, end it all?

I was going to have to play professional diplomat again soon. Might as well rip the bandage off now and start being practical. "Now, please."

Lio whined.

I gripped his hand and gave it a squeeze. "It's okay, big guy. I'm sure whatever he has planned will help. He did remove

Crow's curse." Somehow, slippery as he seemed, I had a feeling the wizard kept his promises.

And after seeing how he had lifted Crow's curse, I definitely believed in his magic.

"Alright, then," the wizard said, clapping his well-manicured hands together and turning to the shelf behind him. "I've prepared everything for your return." He pulled down a slim case and turned back, opening it. "For the lion-beast and the metal man," he said with a soft smile. He ran a finger fondly over the twin necklaces that sat on top of the emerald-green velvet. "Who wants to go first?"

Tin'amen stepped forward without hesitation, while Lio wrung his hands, clearly afraid of the magic and what it might do.

The wizard smiled that wistful smile again at the stoic look in the Tin'amen's eyes. They were about the same height, and he clapped the man on his metallic shoulder. "You feel as though you've lost your heart. Your ability to feel."

Tin'amen nodded, a muscle in his lean cheek flexing as he clenched his teeth. Clearly, he was as worried about this transaction as Lio was. He just refused to show it.

The wizard turned to me, flicking a glance at the others as well. "And what about you? Do you believe the man before you has no heart? No capacity to feel great joy, or tenderness, or love?"

I shook my head immediately. "Absolutely not. He's brimming with emotion. He's just afraid to show it. Or maybe he doesn't even *know* when he's showing it. When he's protecting us, caring for us. Giving his all."

Singing Crow patted the metal man on the shoulder. "I feel cared for when I'm with you."

Lio nodded, his bushy curls bouncing with the violence of the motion. “I feel protected.”

I smiled at Tin’amen’s confused expression. “I’ve felt so much tenderness from you. You’re not a heartless man.”

Vix spoke up, waving an expressive six-fingered blue hand. “Even *I* can see that you are completely selfless. A hallmark of a big heart.”

The wizard turned back to Tin’amen, one corner of his mouth lifted in a wry smile. “You see?”

Tin’amen shook his head. “I…don’t. I don’t see it. I still feel empty inside…here.” He patted his chest, over his heart. “As if South took my heart and turned it to steel.”

The wizard nodded, his expression laced with sadness, bittersweet. He unfastened the necklace and stepped in to hook it around Tin’amen’s throat. The tiny pink gemstone charm that hung from the chain, seated in the hollow of his throat, was cut into a heart shape. “This will help,” the wizard murmured, pressing a finger to the charm and making it glow.

Tin’amen showed no hint of surprise on his stoic face when the wizard reached out and cupped his metallic cheek. “All I feel is warmth,” the magician murmured. “Not the coldness you fear.”

Then he drew away and turned to Lio, the second necklace in his hand. “And you, my fine shifter. You believe yourself to be a coward because of the lingering fear that colors your soul after your mistreatment at the hands of those despicable carnival folk.”

Lio nodded his head, green eyes downcast. “I’ve lost my courage,” he murmured, his deep voice full of shame. “I startle at everything. I’m a disgrace to my pride.”

The wizard turned to the rest of us again. "Is it true? Is the man a quivering coward, a failure as a protector, devoid of worth?"

I rolled my eyes. "Of *course* not. I've never once seen him run from trouble when we needed him."

Tin'amen reached out and surprised us all by ruffling Lio's wild golden mane. "You have fought beside me many times, despite your fear, when lesser warriors would have frozen up and been overrun."

Singing Crow gave Lio a lopsided grin. "You always speak up, even when it's hard for you."

I crossed my arms, feeling ridiculously vulnerable, but knowing he needed to hear this no matter how embarrassing it was. "You've always made me feel safe, Lio. Sheltered. Treasured. You show me—hell, all of us—your vulnerabilities, and that's about the most courageous thing a man can do."

The witch nodded agreement to my words. "Have you ever heard that old saying about courage?" they mused, gray eyes studying Lio. "I believe every culture has some version of it. It says that courage is not a lack of fear, but rather, being scared to do something and doing it anyway."

The wizard nodded. "It isn't fear that makes a coward, my dear beast. It is inaction. And you never fail to act, even when your heart is nearly bursting with remembered terror. Even if you *did* fail to act in a moment like that, no one would blame you. You're far too hard on yourself." He unclipped the necklace and held it out. "This will help."

Lio pulled his hair back out of the way and let the wizard secure the necklace around his neck. The charm that pressed against his dark skin was golden this time, round and glittering like a miniature sun. The wizard touched it to activate it.

Lio froze in surprise, his green eyes jerking up when the wizard playfully tugged on one of his golden, spiral curls, stretching it out, then releasing it again to watch it spring back into place. "The color suits you, I think," the wizard of Oz said with a wink. "You're like the sun yourself, aren't you?"

Then he stepped away, becoming all business once more. "The truth is, gentlemen, there is nothing wrong with either of you. You've been hurt. You've each erected your own kind of barrier to protect you from the world and the ones who harmed you. You simply can't see that you aren't broken, you can't see how beautiful you are, inside and out." He shrugged, as if he hadn't just spouted *actual* healer speak. "The amulets will let you see what others see in you. When you doubt your heart, or your courage. When coldness or fear gets the best of you—the magic in the amulets will remind you that it is all a distortion. Until such time as you can see that for yourself. One day, when you no longer need the amulet, you will be healed."

I watched with no little awe. This was…amazing. A combination of psychology and sorcery that, if it worked, was truly like a magic wand for trauma.

"They're real?" I couldn't help but ask. I was probably ruining the placebo effect, but I had to know. "Not a placebo? Not snake oil and magic tricks?"

It was Vix who answered, voice soft and wry. "It's real, Daniel. Dewin actually *is* a talented healer with an affinity for getting to the heart of what a person truly needs."

And I trusted *Vix* enough to believe it.

The wizard of Oz gave me a wry smile. "We all wear the masks we must wear to get through life, my dear Daniel. We all play our parts. And for now, my part is to be the great salesman.

It is…sleight of hand, distraction from my more…savory endeavors."

I shook my head in disbelief. *Nothing* was what it seemed on this damned planet.

"And now for you," the wizard said, effectively derailing my thoughts and making me break out in a cold sweat and fight to keep my breathing even.

"I have a way to get through the communications blockade on Oz and get a message out to the space station—a carefully maintained and hidden weak spot in the security net. I can only send messages on a very strictly monitored, random schedule so as not to give away this little fact to the others. When you left on your little trip, I advised the nearest IMAD station of your predicament." His black eyes delved into mine, as if he could read my thoughts. "Do you still wish to leave Oz and seek justice, Mr. Westerfield?"

I swallowed with a dry click, everything in me screaming out a vehement *"no."* But I had a duty to do. And everyone in this room had made it plain, on more than one occasion, that my time with them was temporary.

"Yes, please," I said, somehow managing to keep my voice from breaking and my hands from clenching into fists. All my training came rushing back, letting me mute out my feelings and get the job done.

The wizard tilted his head, as if my answer surprised him, but his face showed nothing but polite agreement. "Very well. They are standing by. I will message them tomorrow afternoon to arrange your removal. Congratulations," he said, taking my hand and bowing over it. "You are a free man. Our bargain is complete."

Too bad that made me feel like I was going to be sick.

"Thank you," I said evenly. Only years of practice playing my part kept me from bursting into tears.

The wizard straightened, giving my hand a light, invisible squeeze, as if he could sense my imminent breakdown. "There. That's all settled then." He nodded to West. "And we will get started on setting up a space for you to work so we can ruin North and South's hold on this dear little planet tomorrow." He turned to smile at us all like a congenial host. "Until then, please be my guests. Get clean and dressed, and we'll have a feast to celebrate all we have accomplished."

Somehow, as I followed the butler dude to my guest room, I didn't feel quite as festive as the wizard's tone implied.

Chapter 30

The wizard of Oz was true to his word. We didn't just have dinner, we had a *feast*. I had always enjoyed trying new foods on every planet I visited in my time as a diplomat, and I dug into the spread with a gusto. Sure, I'd been on Oz for a while now. But most of my gustatory experiences had been travel rations and whatever we could pick from alongside road. The wizard clearly had a chef and access to a full range of spices and flavors that I'd never tasted elsewhere.

I focused on the food, reveling in each new burst of flavor on my tongue, from sweet, to savory, to the tangy bite of the wine, in an effort to forget that this was probably going to be my last night on Oz. IMAD was going to arrange a quick transport for me tomorrow, in and out before EARTH even knew I was gone. They'd get my story and sort all the details once on was on the station. The wizard had stressed to them the importance of making sure the other rulers weren't aware that the wizard had made contact with IMAD. Who knew what would happen if they thought Intergalactic was in league with the wizard?

I spent all of dinner avoiding the elephant in the room. But eventually, I couldn't put it off anymore. The feast was held in a room clearly built for socializing. Rather than one large table, there were several smaller tables with benches and groupings of comfortable chairs. I could imagine the place being used for political schmoozing, poker nights, drinking parties, you name it. Right now, the tables were covered with tablecloths of emerald and burgundy, each table piled with food and drink. The wizard had invited his staff to eat with us—a strange and wonderful gesture from someone so high up the food chain. Groups of people came and went, sitting and eating for a time before going back to work. There was even music, and a small space cleared on one side of the room for dancing.

I sat on a padded bench at a corner table, with Singing Crow, Tin'amen, and Lio. The witch had been reluctantly drawn into a dance with the wizard, scowling the entire time. Which, with them, probably meant they were ecstatic. Who knew? The two of them were certainly a striking couple as they moved around the small dance floor with a fluid grace that I could certainly never achieve. Must be their non-human heritage.

I had stuffed myself to bursting, so using food as a distraction was no longer an option. And I thought it best to get this conversation over with before I had any more wine, since I was already buzzed.

My chest ached and my eyes stung. But I knew this was for the best. I couldn't take comfort tonight in the arms of the men I was going to abandon tomorrow. We had shared light touches and glancing kisses all evening, but there had been a feeling of boundaries, of distance, nothing progressing any further. As if everyone instinctually knew this was it. This was goodbye.

As it grew late, most of the staff left, replaced by a table of quiet workers who were probably preparing for various night shift or early morning duties. Someone turned the music down low, and it had changed from the upbeat, lively clamor of earlier to a more sedate, sleepy pace filled with low wood flutes and slow, deep-thrumming drums.

My companions were yawning, all of them nearly falling asleep in their cups. I would be too, I suspected, were it not for the nervous, buzzing anxiety that was present, reminding me that I was going to be leaving Oz tomorrow, resuming my role as a retired EARTH diplomat, speaking with the higher IMAD authorities to levy serious accusations against high-ranking EARTH officials.

I took another sip of my wine, wondering how my glass got so empty.

"We should go to bed," Crow finally said around another yawn.

His yellow eyes met mine, and I saw the question there. I felt the others looking at me as well. Tin'amen stood, his chair scraping against the hardwood floor, loud to my fuzzy, anxious brain. He pushed in his chair and paused, waiting for the rest of us. The others joined him, but I stayed where I was.

"Daniel?" Lio said, his deep voice hesitant.

I shook my head. "I'm not coming," I said evenly. "I have to…prepare for tomorrow. I…it's better this way."

The silence seemed absolute, the soft sounds of music and muted conversation washed out by the pulse pounding in my ears.

"If that's what you want," Tin'amen said, finally. I glanced up to find his silver eyes on me, his perfect face as devoid of emotion as I'd ever seen it. Proof that the only one I was hurting here was me. "We will see you tomorrow."

He turned and walked away, sedate and easy, broad shoulders straight and his long silver ponytail swaying. My chest tightened.

"Are you sure you want to be alone?" Singing Crow asked, his pretty hands curling around the back of his chair, yellow eyes searching my face.

I pressed my lips together, but gave him a short nod as I ran my finger around the base of my wineglass. "It's been…I've enjoyed our time together. But I need…."

I couldn't seem to put into words *what* I needed. He waited for a moment, then when no answer was forthcoming, he executed a courtly bow, turned, and followed after Tin'amen. I felt dizzy.

Lio stared at me for a moment, twisting his hands as he fought to find his courage. I was surprised when he blurted, "Come back with us? Just one more night? I don't want to sleep alone."

I hardened my heart against those pleading green eyes. "Lio. You're not alone. You'll have Singing Crow and Tin'amen with you. And probably the witch…."

I glanced toward the dancefloor to find the wizard and the wicked witch had stopped dancing to argue about something in harsh whispers. "Yeah…the witch too, I'd wager."

Lio took a deep breath and let it out. "Okay. You're right. Goodnight."

Then he was gone too, shoulders slumped, and head bowed. Vix nearly plowed into him as the witch exited the dancefloor with long, angry strides. Lio said something to Vix. The witch pinned me with sharp, stormy gray eyes, then they gave me a curt nod and left with Lio. And that was that.

I stared into my wineglass, having trouble breathing.

The bench I was sitting on rocked a bit as the wizard of Oz lowered himself to sit beside me, a full glass of the tangy-sweet wine in each square-fingered hand. He met my eyes, offered me a glass—which I eagerly took—and let out a long sigh. "Not going to bed with your harem?" he asked dryly, taking a sip of his drink.

I shook my head. "No."

"Did you fight?" he asked, his deep voice still tight from whatever argument he'd had with the witch.

"No," I said, taking a fortifying gulp of fruity alcohol.

He huffed. "Then why not? You clearly love them. Seems like you'd want to spend the night together before you're off to IMAD tomorrow."

I set the wineglass aside and turned on the bench pulling one leg up to rest across it so I could face the wizard. "That's the problem. If even *you* can see that I'm falling in love with the idiots, why can't *they* see that? They've made it abundantly clear it was just sex. A temporary fling until we got our lives back. I can't spend another night getting even more attached to them, wishing I could stay."

Black eyes met mine, and a wry smile lifted one corner of his chiseled lips. "You're a beautiful mess, Daniel Westerfield the Fourth."

I just blinked at him. "What would *you* know?" My voice was petulant, my emotions swinging even further into maudlin now that I'd sent my lovers away for good.

He sighed. "You never asked for your TOTO back, you know."

I started. "Oh!"

He chuckled and patted my knee. "Don't worry. I'll return him to you before you leave tomorrow. The modifications you've made to the unit are really quite endearing. He's almost like a real pet. Or a friend. I'm not sure." He waved a hand and I wondered if he was as far along the journey to piss drunk as I was. "The point is, I hacked the fuck out of your drives."

I barked a laugh. "Oh? I'm pretty sure EARTH was trying to break into him before they ditched me here on Oz, but my buddy Freddie wouldn't help them. I never could figure out exactly what they thought they'd find." I paused for more wine. "And? What sinister information did you find stored there, Mr. Wizard."

He arched a dark brow. "Never call me that again. I wasn't looking for military secrets." He grinned. "I wanted to know more about you. What made you tick. See if there was something in there you were hiding, sure, but also see if there was some strength or weakness I could use."

I huffed. "You're a terrible person."

He just shrugged one broad, suit-clad shoulder. "Maybe. I've certainly been called worse. But you…you are most definitely *not* a terrible person, Daniel."

I scoffed at that. "I just sent my lovers away so I wouldn't be sad when I wake up tomorrow. Sounds pretty awful to me."

He patted my knee again, then gave it a squeeze. "No, no. You see…that's what I found. That's what makes you so valuable and so perfect at everything you do." He looked like he was so proud of himself, like he had discovered some amazing secret of the universe. I couldn't help but smile at him. "You," he said, leaning closer as if imparting this huge secret on me. "Are just *good*."

I blinked up into those fathomless black eyes, confused. What were we talking about again? Wow. Maybe I needed more wine. Because having him all up in my space was making me all hot-and-cold. "What?"

"That's it," he said, smiling to reveal even white teeth with sharp, defined canines. "You're deeply, irrevocably, unmoveably, *good*." He winked. "That's why the corrupt entities of EARTH want you out of sight and out of mind. That's why you were forced out of your position in the first place. And it's why those idiots who just left won't ask you to stay. They know you're too good for them. That you have greater potential in you. That you could happily go on to save the whole universe from itself. And what are they in the face of such wonder?"

I laughed, draining the rest of my wine and stealing his cup from his unresisting hand to drain that too.

"You don't know," he said evenly, a soft smile playing about one corner of his mouth. "And that's what makes it even more amazing. You don't even know how you draw people in and make them feel like lesser beings with every decision you make, every word you speak."

"How *much* did you stalk me while you were poking around in my files?" I breathed, suddenly concerned for his mental stability.

He just laughed again, sliding his hand from my knee, up my thigh. "Too much, honestly. It just made me want to know you. It made me see what everyone loves about you." His smile turned bitter, his black gaze distant for a second there. "Even the witch."

I sighed and tried *not* to notice that hand on my thigh. "You fought."

His gaze lost that distant look and his attention returned to me. "We did. We always do. Just like you can't see the good in you, they cannot see the beauty in themselves, the perfection of who they are. They don't believe me when I tell them. They push me away because they are afraid of being hurt, and Vix knows I have the power to absolutely devastate them, if I wanted to."

I nodded. I could totally see that. If loving someone was terrifying to the witch, loving someone *powerful* who may be a threat to their position would be just unfathomable.

Poor wizard. He was screwed if he really cared for Vix as much as I suspected.

"It's painful, isn't it?" I blurted. "When your affection just… bounces off them and falls on the floor."

He shook his head. "A weird way of saying it, human. But apt, nonetheless. They don't even realize what they're about to tread on. It's horribly painful. But still, I keep trying."

I nodded. "What else can you do?"

Talk drifted then, down strange and twisted roads, to my childhood and his. To the films and pictures he'd viewed of me as a child and young adult, trying so hard to impress the family I loved, to raise us all up out of the existence of poor Kansas robo farmers to something more. I had triumphed. I became a high-ranking government official whose name was known on planets far and wide as a skilled and caring negotiator and champion of equal rights.

But they didn't get to see that, or to reap the benefits. My parents were killed in a farming accident just as I was accepted into the diplomatic corps. The first big paycheck I would have spent on finding them a new place to live, was instead spent on funeral expenses. Still, I tried every day to honor their memory. To remember why I had worked so hard to get where I was.

Until EARTH pushed me out of my position. Until I was left adrift to find myself again on the drag stage. I had built a new, different life, one that focused on the part of me that had felt repressed and bottled up all those years. It still wasn't *all* of me, because my drag personas weren't really the whole Daniel…but it was something. And then it was gone too, and here I was trying to find my feet again.

It was really uncanny how well the wizard understood. "I wasn't raised on Oz," he told me, a wistful smile on his face. "I came here as a kid with my dad. He was a healer, and he had been asked to consult on a tricky case of energy sickness in one of the natives' upper classes."

He had, apparently, been orphaned here when his father died trying to cure the person's sickness.

"I was taken in by an old healer woman who lived away from all the fighting and influence of the colonial rulers at the time. She taught me things I never would have learned back home on Ulrita Prime." He shook his head, and I could sense both fondness and sadness in his voice. "When she died, she told me Ozma had adopted me. That I was a native now. And that it was my duty to protect the planet and its people. I guess I took that a little too well to heart."

He had been adrift then too, a teenager with a cart of medicines, alone on an alien world that had somehow become his home. Over the years, this crazy man had managed to not only find a place for himself, but to build it into a thriving city where pollen addicts came for cures, and the outcasts of Oz came for refuge and order, to escape the colonial rulers and their games.

I gaped at him. "How *old* are you?" The Emerald City was nothing but a little village when he came here…how long did it take to build a thriving city?"

He winked at me. "Old enough, kiddo. My kind live a lot longer than humans. And with the healing energy flowing through me all the time…I've got a nice, long life span."

I was dumbfounded. I mean, sure, there were lots of alien races whose life expectancy far exceeded the couple centuries humans might hope to achieve if they were lucky. But I was always in awe of them. They saw time differently.

"The witch," I said slowly.

He shrugged. "I have the time to be patient. They will eventually admit their feelings for me. We'll be together. When the time is right."

"Wow."

I started when he took my hand, drawing it away from my empty wineglass. "It is well and truly past time for us to shut this little party down," he said, finishing his last glass of wine—and the pitcher we'd emptied while we talked. "I have a proposition for you, Daniel the great negotiator."

I arched a brow at him, feeling all floaty and warm. "Oh? This should be good."

He smiled a devious smile. "Since you refuse to go to the others, come to bed with me instead. We don't quite know each other well enough for there to be strings attached. And I promise to thoroughly distract you from your worries until sunrise."

I swallowed convulsively. He *was* ridiculously, darkly attractive. And I *was* really regretting the decision to sleep alone.

"That's…I…." I felt my entire body flush with embarrassment that I was even considering it. *And* with how matter of fact his proposal was. "Why?"

He smiled, the expression almost wolfish, with those sharp canines and dark, mysterious eyes. He still held my hand, his thumb stroking over the back of it in slow, hypnotic circles. "Truthfully? I've found you attractive ever since you waltzed in here in that dress and demanded my attention. And…I also don't wish to sleep alone tonight. I've suffered my own painful separation long enough."

I sighed, but I found myself leaning in, tilting my head up for his kiss. He tasted like the wine, sweet and tangy all at once, deceptively intoxicating, and like magic on my tongue. He released my hand to run his palms up my thighs, his mouth leisurely exploring every nook and cranny of my own with a thoroughness that left me breathless.

My hands came up to cup his face, to hold him close as I deepened the kiss, chasing the bite of the wine and the cloying sweet-darkness that was all him. When I pulled back, I knew I was wide-eyed and trembling. "The wicked witch will curse us."

He shook his head. "Hardly. That would imply they care." He leaned in to press a kiss just below my ear before whispering, "Besides, I'm quite sure it will only give them fodder for late-night fantasies, if they start imagining us together, Daniel."

I gulped. No promises. I hadn't made or received *one* promise or agreement with anyone I'd fucked in the last month or so. They had all made it clear that I could just disappear tomorrow, and they'd hardly miss me. They'd all be back to life as usual.

"Let me fuck you senseless tonight, my dear, sweet man," the wizard purred against my throat. "You won't regret it. I won't ask for anything more or less than what you want to give. Just come to bed with me."

Okay, so…he probably could have asked me to do *anything* in that dark, smoky, seductive voice, and I'd fucking hop to it. It was really no surprise to me when my traitor mouth and my traitor body conspired to blurt out. "Let's go," like an overeager idiot.

Chapter 31

The wizard of Oz chuckled and led me out of the party room and deeper into the building, past the guest rooms, to a place in the deep heart of the underground that was clearly his personal sanctuary. It wasn't the light, public healing face of the place, nor the dark, ominous trickster wizard vibe of the part of the underground I'd seen before, but a combination of the two that somehow felt more real, truer to who he was—a little bit of darkness and a little bit of light, a little bit of comfort and a little bit of charming seduction.

His bedroom was filled with deep colors and rich, decadent fabrics. The big, circular bed in the middle of the room was covered in black silk sheets and a puffy down comforter in a deep, emerald green. I shivered at the thought of rolling around naked in all that decadence with the tall, alluring man behind me.

He pressed up against my back, all heat and invitation, his arms wrapping around my waist to pull me up snug against him. "You smell like cinnamon and sugar," he murmured into my hair. "Like the sweet rolls you Earthlings are fond of."

I laughed. "Cinnamon rolls? You think I smell like a cinnamon roll?" I wasn't quite sure what to think of about that. Maybe not the manliest scent in the world…but I liked it.

He stroked a hand over my stomach, sliding up under my shirt to caress my abs. "Mmm…it's your aura. Everyone has a unique flavor to me. Yours is delicious."

I leaned back into him. "Well, I don't do magic and auras. But you taste like sweet wine and feel like every sensual pleasure I can imagine, all wrapped up in one."

I laughed at my own stupid words, but he just hummed against my skin again. "Come here and have another taste then." He turned me to face him, kissing me deeply, then started slowly undressing me, touching and teasing every bit of skin as it was revealed.

I slid my hands inside his suit jacket and pushed it off his shoulders. He shrugged, and I winced a little when the clearly expensive clothing hit the floor, but he just ignored it, my own shirt and pants joining it in rapid succession.

His hands ran over my skin, trailing magic, tingling and warm everywhere they touched. I shuddered in his arms, running my hands through his hair, toying with his nubby little horns, before pulling him down into another slow, deep kiss. Nothing about him felt desperate or rushed. It was like he had all the time in the world to take me apart.

He maneuvered me backward until the back of my legs hit the bed, then pushed me down, my feet still on the floor as he knelt between my legs. He worked his way toward my cock as slowly and thoroughly as he did everything else, planting kisses and trailing his magic fingers over my inner thighs, the sensitive groove of skin over my hip bones. Then he rolled my balls in one hand, his wicked dimples deepening before he guided my dick into his mouth with the other.

I gripped the soft bedding and groaned, trying not to immediately thrust up into the warm heat of his mouth. He pulled back, purposefully letting his sharp canines drag over my sensitive cock before he swallowed me down again, earning a hiss from me.

I writhed, but he pinned my hips down with his big hands, upping the pace, swirling his tongue around my tip every he pulled back. I curled upward, abs flexing, hands tangling in his artfully arranged chestnut hair and tugging. “Gonna cum,” I managed on a breathless pant.

He just chuckled and ignored my hair-pulling, sucking so hard I felt like he was trying to turn me inside out. I came with a shout, flopping back on the bed like my strings had been cut, my brain short circuiting.

He stood in a graceful motion and started stripping, ridding himself of the rest of his clothes before returning to me, standing between my knees, stroking his impressive dick with one hand, while the other gripped my leg and lifted it to rest on his shoulder.

At his wicked smile, and a jerk of his head, I grabbed the indicated pillows and wiggled them under my hips, elevating me even more and taking some of the strain off my back. He was fucking gorgeous, all chiseled lines and broad perfection, with a dark mat of chest hair and an Adonis vee to *die* for. In the low lamplight, he looked human, yet entirely *other* at the same time, the black pools of his eyes flaring with brief sparks of red, and what I was just now realizing was a small halo of deep emerald green magic pulsing around him.

“Oh, my fuck,” I panted when he stroked his cock again, releasing a fat, pearly drop of fluid.

He smirked at me and ran a thumb over his dick to collect the droplet, then reached down and slowly rubbed the slickness over my ass. “You’ve never been with a Ulritian before?”

I shook my head vehemently, my hair coming loose with the motion, probably a tangled mess by now from all the thrashing. He pressed his thumb inside me, making me arch against him and moan.

"We won't need lubricant," he purred, pulling back his foreskin even further to reveal how wet his dark, swollen cock really was. "I make my own."

"Sweet molasses," I muttered. Now I'd seen it all.

He rubbed his cock against my hole, his finger still working me open, spreading his slick to ease the way. Then he started pressing home, one hand gripping his huge dick, while the other took my growing erection in hand and stroked in slow, torturous movements. "You are so beautiful like this, Daniel," he said, his voice low and rich with lust as he slowly filled me. "You'll come so prettily on my cock." He winked. "I'd die to see you with the others, so stuffed full you can do nothing but whimper and beg for more."

Aaannnd the wizard was a dirty talker. Why was I not surprised? My dick was fully hard again already, buzzing from the pulse of magic that leapt from his skin to mine. He squeezed me as he stroked, riding that line between too much and not enough as my body stretched to take him.

Then he was in, and we both let out a sobbing breath. "Fuck me," I pleaded. "You don't have to be so slow and careful, wizard."

He just smiled a taunting smile, and started to move—his pace set to tantalize and tease, to torture us both. I arched up, pulling my feet up to rest on the mattress so I could thrust up to meet him, urging him on.

He finally relented, falling forward to cover me as he thrust deeper and faster, bracing himself on one elbow, the other hand buried in my hair, dragging me into a filthy kiss.

When he pulled back, his eyes were completely red and his energy, his *magic,* flared around him, dancing over my skin like a hundred hungry caresses. He stared into my eyes as he lost himself in my body, driving me toward the brink. Then he thrust hard one last time and stilled, pulsing inside me, whispering a string of endearments and curses, his head thrown back and muscles cast in stark relief as he went rigid with his orgasm.

I came again as he poured himself inside me, not even needing to touch my dick. My body spasmed, overcome with pleasure, and magic, and *release.*

I gripped his broad back and closed my eyes as emotion overwhelmed me. The chemical rush of orgasm, the dwindling buzz of the alcohol, combined with the stress of the day…it was just too much for my poor, overwrought system to bear. I hiccupped a choked sob and felt hot tears escape my eyelids, despite my best attempts to keep them in.

The wizard of Oz had just well and truly fucked me into the mattress and here I was, bawling like a baby. Good thing he wasn't expecting a real relationship here, because this would definitely scare him off. Nothing like someone crying after sex to make you feel like an asshole.

He pulled away, only to come back with a towel. I couldn't stop the waterworks, even as he helped me clean up and tucked me into his bed. I was surprised when he slipped into bed next to me and drew me into his arms, like it was perfectly normal. "It's okay," he murmured, his own voice sad. "It will all be alright, Daniel, just let it out. I'm here."

Well, I suppose if I'd never see him again after tomorrow, then there was really no point in being embarrassed or trying to save face. I cried myself out, my heart aching at everything I would be leaving behind tomorrow.

When I finally managed to get myself under control, I pulled away and rolled onto my back, staring up at the starry sky painted on the bedroom ceiling. I stared at the pretty arcs of painted magic and wonder, feeling as if I could just reach out and touch the stars overhead. “I’m sorry,” I said at last. “That was…wow, that was amazing. I didn’t mean to ruin it.”

He tucked one arm under his head and gazed up at the stars as well, the other hand rooting around in the blanket until he found mine and gave it a squeeze. “No need to apologize. You didn’t ruin anything. We fit well together. But I know your heart is heavy.” He turned his head to look at me. “Daniel. I’m going to ask you what the other idiots *want* but are too afraid to ask.”

I met his eyes in confusion. “What?”

He smiled softly. “Come back to Oz. When you’ve done what you feel you must to fix things out there in the universe. Come back here and stay.”

I blinked at him in surprise, tears threatening to well up again. “They don’t want me, Dewin. They have their own lives. I was just a fling. A good time with an alien species until they could get their lives un-fucked. They’ll forget all about me when I’m gone.”

He just gave me that enigmatic look he got sometimes, like he knew more than any normal person could ever hope to understand. “Don’t tell them,” he said, somehow managing a shrug while lying flat on his back. “Let them go about whatever you think they have to do. Get word to me when you’re on your way and I’ll make sure they know. What they do with the information will be up to them. But I’m telling you right now—they’ll be here, waiting.”

I sighed. "I wish you were right. But I have no idea how long this is all going to take. I'll be lucky to be a distant memory by then. They'll have new lives. New lovers. I'm just the throw away."

He arched his dark brows at me. "The throw away? Is that how you see yourself, Daniel?"

I put a hand over his mouth. "Don't. Don't magic-psychology me, dude. I can't take it right now."

He huffed a muffled laugh, and I removed my hand from his face. "Besides, if I come back here and they still want me, where does that leave you? Don't you want the witch for yourself? Aren't we technically rivals in that fictional situation?"

He lifted my hand and kissed the back of it. "If the witch wants you, I will never stand in the way of their happiness. Or yours. But don't forget who is doing the asking here."

I smiled at him, knowing it was a doofy, idiotic expression after two mind-blowing orgasms, a good cry, and all this *niceness.* "Why? Why are you asking?"

He grinned that wolfish grin, sharp canines on full display. "Because I'm selfish. I wouldn't mind a repeat of tonight myself, Daniel. Minus the tears and self-doubt."

I rolled my eyes.

"Think on it," he said, curling onto his side facing me, our heads close and his hand tucked under his pillow like a child. "Let me know you're coming back. You'll see. It will all work out."

He was wrong. All I'd do was get my hopes up and get them crushed. Again. But I felt myself utter the words anyway. "Okay. I'll try. When I'm done with what I have to do."

Then, I fell asleep in the wizard's arms, dreaming of what could be…if only.

The next day, IMAD sent a pod for me. I stood on the landing site outside Emerald City, determined, terrified, and heartbroken. I had no idea what would happen once I got off Ozma-4. Would IMAD believe me? Would they do anything with the information Freddie had illicitly gathered and take the word of two weirdos against the word of a renowned EARTH commander? Or was I about to end up murdered or in prison? Could I even make a difference?

And would it ever stop hurting? The missing them? Because I already missed them all, even though they were standing right here, waiting to see me off.

I missed the easy camaraderie. I missed the sweet gestures and little touches that my poor, desperate brain construed as loving. I missed the easy acceptance of all that I was. I hated the feeling of yawning distance that spiraled out in front of me.

As the IMAD pod landed, I turned and embraced each of my friends and soon to be *ex*-lovers. Singing Crow was first. And I recalled how I'd found him that first day, staked out for the birds, his beautiful body twisted by a curse. I pulled back and cupped his handsome face, meeting his bright yellow eyes. "Stay out of trouble, okay? Don't let them silence you, but be smarter about it from here on out."

He smiled. "I'll use my brain."

I nodded and moved on to Tin'amen. "You have a heart," I told him, gripping his shoulders. "Follow it. Don't let anyone use you, ever again."

He lifted his metal hand to touch my face. "I'll try to follow your example."

I forced myself to smile through the yearning and turned to Lio. He pulled me into a bone-crushing hug. "I'll try to be brave," he promised into my hair.

I pulled back and patted his wild mane of bright curls. "You already are."

Then I turned to the witch, who was watching us all with narrowed gray eyes, their posture tense and wary. The skirts of their long, dark navy jacket billowed in the wind and their blue-black hair fluttered epically. "You," I said with a fond smile. "Just stay exactly the way you are. Only…maybe let people take care of you once in a while?"

Vix gave me a curt nod. I started to turn away, but long blue fingers curled around my upper arm, pulling me back around and into a tight hug. My arms went around the witch's narrow waist and we said nothing as we squeezed the life out of each other.

I clenched my eyes closed, willing the tears to dry up before they could fall.

A polite throat clearing pulled me away from the witch, who released me and stepped back. The wizard of Oz approached, his usual congenial expression in place. "The pod crew is getting impatient, I'm afraid. Best to get out of here before we draw unwanted attention."

I nodded, but I couldn't speak. He pulled me toward the pod, halting me before I could climb aboard, gripping both my shoulders and giving them a squeeze. "I hope to hear from you soon, Mr. Westerfield."

Then he shocked the hell out of me by bending down and pressing a short, playful kiss to my lips. "Good luck!"

I clambered into the pod as fast as I could, not willing to risk looking at the men on the landing pad and see their reaction to that kiss.

My time on Oz was over. Everyone always went on and on about my big heart. Too bad I was ripping it out of my chest today and leaving it behind.

Chapter 32

Six Months Later

"Thank you for your service and dedication, emissary Westerfield," fleet admiral Orlianderg growled in his rough Arkranian accent. "You've chosen a complicated planet for a permanent posting. Are you *sure* this is what you want? After all you've done to restore order, you could have your pick of any of the available posts."

I nodded. We'd been over this before, so it was all just idle chit-chat at this point.

While exposing the corrupt parties within EARTH, and stopping the grab for young Miss Ciza Bule's planet's mining rights, I had been offered a position with IMAD.

I was still rather stunned. Most people spent entire lifetimes trying to get hired into Interstellar. All *I'd* done was save my own reputation and produce a copy of the iron-clad inheritance agreement I had helped draft years ago—an agreement that Commander Ashburn thought he had destroyed all legal copies of. It didn't matter anyway, since I had drafted the original myself and could still quote it from memory. Once IMAD was involved, it was all over for Commander *Assburn* and his relative.

My one request upon joining IMAD as a diplomatic emissary had been that I got to choose my permanent placement—where I would stay, for the most part, and work on that planet's issues, only traveling away from my home base when urgently needed, and consulting with other diplomats from IMAD via comm. And you better *believe* the coms situation on Ozma-4 was the first thing I had worked to get fixed.

Somewhere along the way, with Freddie's help, I had uncovered the fact that EARTH was responsible for the tech that North was using to block communications on Oz, making it look like it was due to natural causes or tech failure, when in reality it was the higher-ups in EARTH scrambling things in exchange for a hefty cut of pollen that they were using to get control of *other* natives on *other* planets.

It was a fucking mess. And I couldn't believe it had gone unchecked for so long. But the royal governing families involved in the colonization of Oz were all bitter political rivals, and the stars knew the lengths those idiots would go to in order to carry out their petty feuds.

I ended my call with Fleet Admiral Orlianderg and took a moment to fix myself using the view screen in the corner of my feed. I stood in my suite on the diplomatic transport, the viewscreen showing the cream walls with their innocuous paintings of nebulas and suns. I had just come from a meeting with the captain, followed by a video conference with several IMAD leaders about the order of priorities at my new post. I was still in full dress uniform, and I hardly recognized myself, the image both familiar and foreign to me. The man on the view screen looked compact and competent in his tailored dove gray suit with the bright gold vest, brown hair brushed to a shine, but curling over his shoulders in loose waves.

IMAD was a *lot* more open and less military about the physical appearance of their employees—probably because the entire organization was made up of hundreds of different races and cultures with hundreds of different standards of beauty and professionalism. I was even allowed to wear makeup, which was fun from time to time, channeling a little bit of Dotty into the more uptight interactions. The man in the view screen currently wore dark navy eyeliner that made his blue eyes look piercing, and a bare hint of lip gloss, for good measure.

I swallowed and jerked my jacket straight, feeling more nervous than I had any time in the last six months. Then I made myself stop fussing and asked the AI to connect my next call.

The wizard of Oz looked even more smug and imposing than ever, seated at his desk wearing a deep burgundy suit, his little horns barely showing through is carefully styled chestnut hair. I lifted my chin as his image filled the screen. "Good afternoon, Emissary Westerfield of IMAD," he purred, his ridiculously attractive dimples deepening. "I understand you wanted to speak with me?"

I used a practiced, calm, warm diplomat voice, falling back on my training to keep my emotions from getting the best of me. "Esteemed wizard, I am approaching Ozma now. I believe the captain has sent an ETA for landing along with security protocols for my transfer?"

He smiled, slow and hot. "Yes. Our people received the transmission, and an escort will be waiting for you." He winked. "I also sent word to your other…contacts…here on Oz as soon as I received word of your impending transfer."

I drew in a slow, measured breath. I didn't ask if he'd gotten a response from any of my "contacts." I couldn't. He was so sure of my reception back on Oz. But I still had my doubts. I had sent messages a few times, in care of the wizard. But I had never received a single response in return.

"Thank you," I managed evenly.

The wizard's black eyes regarded me with that patient, waiting expression of his. "Welcome back to Oz, Emissary. Happy landing."

I nodded and ended the call, a slurry of equal parts excitement and dread churning in my gut, making me jittery and slightly nauseous.

I had recently helped IMAD negotiate a treaty on a planet inhabited entirely by sentient, man-sized poisonous *slugs*, and I'd been less terrified.

When we finally landed, I picked up my carry-on and followed my escort off the ship. The rest of my things would be transported over the next week or so, but I didn't own much. Most of the furniture and supplies for my IMAD-owned home would be purchased from local craftsman.

When I reached the ground, the guards with me traded off paperwork and posts with the guards on the ground. Then they saluted me and returned to their ship. They would re-stock here briefly, then return to interstellar space.

I walked off the landing pad and toward the man who waited for me. The wizard was taller than I remembered. But his strength of character and seductive charisma was every bit as present as I recalled. He identified himself for my little entourage—a necessary precaution on a planet that was undergoing some not-always-peaceful transitions of power—then he stepped up and shook my hand, his magic arcing invisibly between us, giving me a warm, teasing caress. "Welcome home, Daniel."

I licked my lips. "Thank you."

The wizard was alone. Just him, his assistant, and a couple of other hired lackeys. My heart ached and my throat wanted to close up. But what had I expected? Some sort of mob of people, desperately waiting to hold me again? Nonsense.

I really was stupid sometimes.

"Shall we?" the wizard said, holding out an arm toward the sleek, round hover vehicle that waited for us, large enough to seat the wizard's people plus my guard compliment.

I nodded and followed him aboard. "I've arranged a formal dinner at the Emerald City tower to welcome you to Oz and introduce you to the new colonial heads from North, South, and East. Hopefully you can get a good read on them. I'm not quite sure of them yet. I can tell you their auras don't look *too* awful. But I know ferreting out motives and intentions is where you excel." He gave me a smile, his expression softening. "I thought you might like a chance to catch your breath after your journey, though. So, for tonight, I arranged a nice, quiet private dinner at my home. If that is acceptable?"

"Yes, thank you," I said softly, turning to gaze out the window at the brightly colored alien scenery. I had missed Oz's ridiculously loud, clashing flora and fauna. It really was a fabulous landscape. "How are the tornados?" I asked absently, recalling my first unfortunate landing in Oz what seemed like *years* ago.

The wizard snorted, but it was his assistant who answered. The man I'd enjoyed tormenting so much in times gone by. "Afraid of squishing more colonial leaders, Emissary?"

I narrowed my eyes at him. "Maybe."

The wizard laughed. "The climate control has been much more reliable since IMAD stepped in and wrested control from the North. They do still pop up once in a while—it can't be helped. But they're usually not too frequent or destructive and we have advanced warning from the climate control systems."

I nodded. "Good." So much had changed in Oz over the past six months. I knew it all on paper, but I couldn't wait to hear the wizard's real-life accounting of how things played out. I knew he and the "wicked" witch had mass-produced and dispersed their pollen antidote, with some much-needed help from an IMAD dispatch unit that I had advocated for. North and South had eventually been replaced by new rulers from their respective planets. The old rulers were currently awaiting trial for intergalactic crimes against native peoples.

One of my first tasks on Oz was to gather additional hard facts and witness statements about their misuse of power and deliver it to IMAD. I was eager to begin, to get justice for the manipulated people of this planet. But suddenly, I was just tired.

It had been a long, whirlwind few months, and I just wanted a moment to catch my breath. Preferably in the arms of people who made me feel loved and treasured. But hey, you take what you can get. At least I wasn't exiled or crash landing today.

I was surprised to find that the gates to the Emerald City were open wide, allowing anyone in without scans or security checks. As it should be, for the main hub and mixing spot for all the people of Oz. Things were slowly opening up, becoming less divided. I smiled to myself as I wondered if the standoffish witch of the west had lowered any of the safeguards around the black woods and let their shields down a little. Maybe I'd find out one day. Chances were, I'd *have* to interact with them at some point in an official capacity, if nothing else.

I imagined Lio and Crow, as I had a million times before, back among other shifters, happy and safe. Tin'amen, I had a harder time imagining…where would he go? What would he do? Was he working somewhere now, maybe in the this very city, doing something incongruous like shopkeeping, or working security at the candy factory? I liked to imagine him doing something so out of character it made me smile.

We reached the wizard's home without incident. My security detail backed off a bit, after a review of the wizard's security measures proved that I would be in good hands while I was at his home. I got cleaned up in my guest room and traded the stuffy—but fabulous—suit for an Oz-style pair of comfortable linen pants and a t-shirt. It was just me and the wizard tonight. No one to impress. It would be nice, for a while, to pretend I was no one important, just like before.

When I reached the little private dining room the staff directed me to, I froze, one foot over the threshold, suddenly unable to breathe.

The wizard sat at the head of the table, casually leaned back in his chair while the witch of the west, all blue, angular and clad in a silky, full-skirted dress that hugged their lean torso, perched a hip on the table. Vix's arms were crossed over their chest as they chatted with the wizard. But when the wizard glanced my way and smiled, the witch spun about in a sharp motion and was halfway across the room before I could remind myself to breathe.

Tin'amen, Lio, and Singing Crow all watched from around the table as the wicked witch reached me, gray eyes snapping with resolve and their entire beautiful, androgenous form *radiating* anger. "You!" Vix snapped, reaching out a six-fingered hand to grip the back of my head and give me a little shake. "How *dare* you pretend you were leaving for good!"

Then I was kissing the witch, my back bowed, hands fisted in the front of their dress as they melded their body to mine, bending me backward with the force of their sharp, biting kiss. They pulled back, leaving me breathless and shocked, then bit me on the jaw, those sharp teeth leaving a stinging crescent on my skin. I stared up into those furious, desperate gray eyes in absolute shock. "*What?*" I breathed.

They caressed my cheek and their gaze softened, showing me a wealth of nerves and vulnerability. "I thought you left me. Are you…really here for me? For *us*? Not just for the job?"

I let out a harsh breath, feeling shaky, and overwhelmed, and so, *so* fucking relieved. "Yes! Of course I am. I thought…I didn't think…."

The wizard lazed in his chair, sipping his wine. "Our dear Daniel has been operating under the flawed belief that none of you wanted him to stay."

I couldn't help the waterworks. I had been holding them back for a long time. And no one who really knew me would ever accuse me of *not* being dramatic. I cried like a baby as I was surrounded by the people I loved. I was hugged, and kissed, and petted and fussed over until finally, *finally* something inside me let loose and uncoiled, accepting that maybe, just *maybe* I really was home.

Dewin joined our knot of emoting, taking my hand and lifting it to his lips. His black eyes met mine and he winked. "I told you, didn't I? I'm the wizard of Oz. I know just want everyone needs."

Chapter 33

I couldn't get my clothes off fast enough. But I also couldn't freaking *think straight* with all the hotness around me. Tin'amen kissed me senseless, using his tall frame to crowd me backward until the back of my knees hit the wizard's big, round bed. I let out a surprised squeak and fell, landing on my back with a breathless laugh. The door clicked closed and I glanced over to see Dewin activate the lock. Good man.

Then I was being kissed silly again, Tin'amen bent over me with one hand planted on the mattress beside my head, his other hand—the flesh-and-blood one—reaching down to grip my cock through my pants. "Oh, how I've missed you," he said as he pulled away to let me breathe.

Singing Crow sat down on the bed next to me, pulling off his shirt, then leaning in to kiss me. I threaded my hands through his silky black hair, fingers smoothing over iridescent feathers as he reminded me how talented his pretty mouth was. He was grinning when he pulled away. "We've all missed you," he said, agreeing with Tin'amen's sentiment.

Lio dropped down on my other side, miles of dark brown skin and glorious muscle on display, since he was completely naked. Shifter modesty was not a thing. He petted my head with one big hand. "You can't ever go away and leave us again," he insisted.

"We'll be good to you. I promise. I'm not nearly so cowardly anymore. I'm getting better every day. And Tin'amen is downright *sweet* sometimes. You'll see. We've changed."

I pushed myself up on my elbows to look at him in shock. "What? Lio. I didn't leave because there was anything *wrong* with any of you. I just had…obligations. I had to set things right. And…well, I didn't think I meant anything to you. I *believed* all that stuff you guys kept saying about us not making promises to each other and how you all knew I was leaving, and it was just sex, and…."

Vix shoved Tin'amen out of the way and stood over me, looming, their arms crossed over their chest and gray eyes narrowed. "Idiot. They were all trying not to make demands of you. They didn't want to force you to decide between them and your career, your whole other *life*. We all thought there was nothing *here* for you, Daniel. That's why no one responded to your messages. We wanted you to be free to live the life you wanted. The one you deserve."

I swallowed hard against the upwelling of emotion that threatened to choke me. Sitting up, I wrapped my arms around Vix's narrow waist and squeezed, pressing my face to their middle, reveling in the feel of their magical aura around me. "You thought there was nothing here for me?" I muttered into the fabric of their dress. "But *everything* is here. *You're* here. I don't know if it's the life I deserve, but this is the life I *want*."

Long fingers combed through my hair, soothing, calming. Then Vix gripped my hair and tugged, yanking my head back so they could bend and deliver a biting kiss. "You're never leaving again, even if I have to lock you away in my evil tower and magically restrain you. It was a long six months."

I huffed a laugh, but Dewin had joined us, and his expression was grave. "Vix is right," he said, expression deadpan. "The witch was so upset they were *pining* and *moping*. None of us can live through that again, Daniel. It was awful. So melodramatic and over the top."

Vix shoved him, hard, and the wizard stumbled back a step, letting out a loud, deep laugh, his black eyes sparkling. "Shut the hell up, wizard," the witch snapped. "I do not pine. Or mope. You're a moron."

"There was so much moping and pining," Scarecrow whispered loudly behind his hand, as if only I could hear him. "It was sweet for all of a day or two. Then it was just sad."

He ducked behind me when Vix lunged for him, the crow using me as a human shield against the witch's fury. I caught Vix and fell back onto the bed again, taking the witch with me. "You missed me?" I cooed. "Really, Vix?"

"Shut up," they snapped. But those storm-gray eyes met mine, and I saw the vulnerability there. "I don't get attached to people. That would be absurd."

"Mmm-hmm," I murmured, leaning up to press a kiss to the underside of their jaw, where the pulse beat against that pretty blue skin. "But you got attached to *me*, didn't you?"

The muttering and swearing was cute, but when Vix finally stopped fucking around and told the truth? Oh, that was *deadly*. "You're right," they said, the tension leaving their lean frame as they melted into me. "I missed you." Sharp teeth bit down on my earlobe as they ground their hardness against my own needy cock. "Now hurry up and get naked so I can show you how much, *Daniel*."

That tone of voice. The way they said my name like it was a promise and a threat all wrapped in one—stars, how I'd missed that!

Then the witch was gone, standing and stepping away so fast my eyes had trouble following. Gray eyes met mine, and a wicked smirk slid across Vix's beautiful face. "Well? Hurry up, human."

Their long fingers went to the buttons that decorated the front of their dress, nimbly undoing them and parting the fabric. The wizard stepped up behind Vix and helped, sliding the silky layers of fabric down the witch's body, his hands trailing over all that smooth blue skin, his black eyes on me the whole time.

Holy shit. I could *not* get my clothes off fast enough. Luckily, I had Singing Crow and Tin'amen to help. Lio picked me up, and I laughed when he easily tossed me onto the center of the big, circular bed. I was happy to see that everyone else's clothes had vanished too. I was a bit surprised how no one even batted an eye over the wizard in the room. Apparently, they had all grown friendly in my absence. At least, friendly enough for Dewin to have no qualms about joining me on the bed. He stretched out his tall frame next to me, and drew me into a slow, searing kiss. His hand stroked over my body, trailing magic and pleasure as it went, moving at the same slow, patient speed as our first encounter. Like he had all the time in the world, and he would use it to drive me crazy.

He wrapped his hand around my aching cock and gave me one slow, thoroughly unsatisfying stroke, before he went back to touching my hip, my ribs, my chest. He dipped his head and trailed kisses down my throat and lower, pausing to tease one nipple with his tongue.

I arched against him and groaned, in no mood for him to tease me. I wanted them all. Now. We'd have plenty of time for exploration later. Because…this was home now.

Apparently, I wasn't the only one who was impatient with the wizard. Singing Crow and Tin'amen flopped down beside me, tangled in each other, only pausing so Crow could pull Lio in and get a hand around the other shifter's massive dick. Stars, the three of them were pretty together. But I didn't get to enjoy the view for long.

Vix climbed up the length of my body, shoving Dewin aside as the witch claimed my mouth. I gripped their slim hips, then slid my hands up their lean, toned torso to cup one set of breasts, drawing my thumbs over the hardened buds of Vix's nipples before moving upward to pay attention to their second set. Sharp teeth trapped my lower lip and the witch's cock slid along mine, the delicious friction making me arch up to get more.

The witch pulled away just far enough to whisper against my lips, their expression pure evil. "This time, I'm going to fuck you. Is that okay, Daniel?"

I huffed and drew my legs up, bending my knees in invitation. "Yes, please!"

Vix laughed softly, pausing to press a kiss to my jaw and suck up a mark on my neck before pushing themselves up and drawing those graceful six-fingered hands down my thighs. Magic sparked along my skin, different, more reminiscent of lightning, or the smell of earth after a hard rain, but no less powerful than the wizard's energy. Those intense gray eyes never left mine as the witch accepted a handful of lube from the wizard and set to work teasing me open.

There had been a time in my life when six months of celibacy would have seemed like nothing. But now, it felt like I'd been sexually frustrated for *years*, rather than mere months. I gasped and writhed, pressing into Vix's touch, wanting more, faster. I didn't care if it hurt. I just wanted them inside me. I had waited so long. Thought they were lost to me for good. That it was over. And now the thought that this was all really happening was just too much to bear.

Big hands pressed my hips down, holding me still. My eyes met the red-ringed black of Dewin's gaze and I whimpered. He bent and kissed me, as if he could read my mind. As if he knew I needed anchoring before I could completely fall apart. The wizard held me down and kissed me deeply, his tongue delving into my mouth, tangling with my own, tasting of sweet, dark wine and promise. I clutched his broad shoulders, feeling like I might fly away if I didn't have something to hold onto.

And through it all, Vix never stopped fingering me, lubing me up and stretching me out so I could take them. Maybe the others, too, if I was lucky.

I nearly sobbed when Vix withdrew their fingers, but the emptiness was quickly filled by the sensation of the witch's cock pressing home, slowly sliding into me in one smooth, steady thrust. I instinctively reached for my own cock, but Dewin gripped my wrists, sitting up so he could pin my arms above my head. "Now, now," he warned in a husky voice. "None of that."

My brain short circuited at the sight of Vix kneeling over me, all lean, androgynous beauty, their small, pert breasts bouncing slightly as they pulled out and thrust back in with sharp motion, pegging my prostate and making me see stars. Fucking *hell* the witch was hot. And the wizard holding me down like some kind of dark magic dom? Well, I never *knew* that was my kink. Until right that damned second.

The witch smiled, sultry and full of promise, their lean body moving above me at a faster pace, bracing themselves on one hand so the other could trace my chest, giving my nipples a sharp pinch, before raking their nails down my sternum. "So pretty," they whispered. "And you'll be even prettier all painted with your own cum."

I groaned pulling at the restraining grip on my arms, wanting to grab the witch and hold them close. But Dewin just chuckled. "Mmm," he said sweetly. "And he's going to come without anyone touching his dick, aren't you Daniel?"

I turned my head to look into those black eyes, surprised to find them mostly red now. The magic pouring off both the witch and the wizard combined, dancing over my skin in waves, like an added caress all over my body. "Nebulas and comets," I muttered. "You're pure evil."

The wizard smiled and looked at Vix. "He's still making coherent words, love. You need to fuck him harder."

Vix grinned, showing me sharp teeth and a promise of things to come. I gasped when the witch changed angles and slammed into me hard and fast, their long blue-black hair falling forward to hide the intense, fiercely possessive expression I could see on those beautiful features. "Now, Daniel," they whispered. The words were like magic, coiling inside me and urging me to obey.

Not that any compulsion was needed. Cause holy fuck. I came hard, feeling the warm wetness of my release hit my chest and my chin, probably the fucking headboard, for all I knew. I convulsed, wrapping my arms around the witch when Dewin finally let go of my wrists. Vix swore, pressing deeper as they came inside me, wrapping their long arms around me as they shuddered in my arms.

Dewin stroked my hair back from my face and pressed a kiss to my temple, then turned and captured the witch's lips. They were beautiful together. So perfect that my cock *almost* thought about twitching back to life.

Then Vix was pulling away with a sly grin. I found out why a second later, when I was grabbed around the waist by a pair of strong hands and flipped over. I barely caught myself on my hands and knees before Lio was there, pressing his massive, spine-covered cock into my ass.

I gasped, but I couldn't manage a protest, since I found the wizard's impressive dick against my lips. The Dewin knelt before me, gripping his dripping cock, a challenging smirk on his perfect lips. "Open up, Daniel, darling."

I groaned as Lio slid in deep, pressing me forward toward the wizard. Bracing myself on one hand, I gripped Dewin's cock with the other, pulling back his foreskin to reveal his slick, hard head. I would have liked to go slowly, maybe ask some questions about the whole alien self-lube thing. But my own dick was hard again, and Lio was about to fuck my brains right out of my skull. I opened my mouth and swallowed Dewin's cock as commanded.

Who even *knew* I was so into following orders? Not me, that's for damned sure. My dick twitched, tapping against my belly as Lio and Dewin spit-roasted me. The wizard's hands threaded through my hair and braced against one of my shoulders as he slowed my motions, steadying me so he could slowly feed me his cock one inch at a time.

Lio's grip on my hips was bruising as the big shifter tried his best to match the wizard's pace, to restrain himself. But I knew that was a lost cause the moment that fat dick filled my hole. Lio was the sweetest man I knew. But he lost it when he was in the middle of a good fuck. Turned completely beast. Not that I was *ever* going to complain about being owned by the sexy hunk of man-meat.

I had to use both hands to brace myself against the increasing strength of Lio's thrusts, so I let go of Dewin's dick, giving him free rein to do whatever he wanted. Which was, apparently, to fuck my mouth, testing the limits of my deep-throating abilities. Lio's dick swelled inside me, the flexible spines dragging against my flesh in the best possible way, and I tensed, moaning around Dewin's cock as I came again, the orgasm rushing over me out of nowhere. Lio *roared* at the feeling of me clenching around him. The big guy slammed home one last time, throbbing inside me as he came.

Beside me, I heard Crow's gasp, and Tin'amen's deep, throaty growl of satisfaction. I guess this time, it was me on display for them, rather than the other way around.

The wizard moaned, probably watching Tin'amen and Crow's show. Dewin's release flooded my mouth and I swallowed reflexively, surprised at the flavor of him. I pulled off him as Lio withdrew, then I flopped over onto my back, laughing like a crazy person, my brain completely offline.

"What is so amusing?" the wizard asked, stretching out beside me and brushing my hair back from my face. He had one eyebrow quirked, as if he was half-amused, half-concerned. "Are you broken already?"

I snorted. "No. It's just…your cum."

Both eyebrows went up at that. "My jizz is funny?"

I put a hand over my belly to stop the spasms of laughter that were starting to get painful. "Cinnamon candies. These hot cinnamon candies they have back on Earth. Why does your cum taste like *candy*?"

Singing Crow bent over me from the other side, his chin-length black hair falling forward, yellow eyes flashing. "Daniel.

Keep it together, sweetheart. Was the magical semen also an intoxicant? Are you drunk?"

Dewin huffed. "He's *fine*. He's just being Daniel."

I smacked his shoulder weakly. "What is *that* supposed to mean? Because if it means I'm being sexy, and amazing, and *fabulous*, then yes. I'm being Daniel. Thank you."

Singing Crow laughed softly and leaned in to press a sweet kiss to my mouth. "Absolutely. Now come here." He tugged, forcing me to roll over so I lay sprawled atop his lean frame.

He wasn't starving anymore, that was obvious. While still slender and graceful, my Crow had put on some weight, filled out. I pushed myself up on one hand so I could run the other over his beautiful golden-brown skin. "Good to see someone fed you up while I was gone," I said with a chuckle.

He pouted at me, running his own graceful hands over the curve of my ass. "Are you calling me *fat*, Daniel?"

I huffed. "Hardly. In fact, when I can walk again, I'm going to go find you some big, greasy cheeseburgers. Fried potatoes. Ice cream. All the best Earth foods I can cajole the staff into making." I made an exaggerated surprised face. "Oh! I think I found a new hobby. Like all those old people who sit in the parks back home…feeding birds!"

He responded by digging his fingers into my ribs, making me writhe as he tickled me mercilessly. "No!" I gasped, fighting for air. "Stop! I take it back!"

He finally relented, threading his fingers through my hair to pull me down into a kiss instead. "Food can wait," he said smugly. "Me and Tin'amen haven't had our turn with you yet."

I snorted a laugh into the crook of his shoulder. "Ha! My poor ass can't take anymore abuse. And if I come again, my dick might fall off."

The degenerate crow man just grinned at me. "Don't worry, we'll be gentle."

Tin'amen's silver eyes practically sparkled as he leaned across Singing Crow to kiss the tip of my nose. "Tell me you brought a dress or two in your carry-on."

I groaned.

Lio came to my rescue, flopping down beside us and draping an arm over my back. "Rest first. I want to cuddle."

I smiled my dopiest smile at him. "I love you."

He blinked at me, then his dark skin took on a distinctly pink undertone. "Um. I love you too."

I rolled off Crow and onto my back, putting my hands over my face as I realized what I'd just said. "Oh, stars. I'm sorry. Ignore me." We hadn't known each other long enough for me to tell them I loved them. That was just weird. I'd been with them for anywhere from weeks to days, depending on the person and where I'd met them in my journey. And I had then been away for six *months*. There was no relationship here. Just lots of mutual lust that I hoped would one day *grow into* love.

I felt like an idiot.

It was Tin'amen who spoke, surprising the heck out of me with his words. "You feel what you feel," he said softly, reaching over to tap me on the chest, right over my heart. "The heart wants what it wants, even if it is often illogical and dangerous."

I uncovered my eyes to stare at him. "You…are you talking about *emotions*, Tin'amen? Are…are you okay?"

He smiled at my fumbling for words. "I also feel deep affection for you. I'm not as familiar with love, but I think that is what I'm feeling. You are loved, Daniel. The circumstances don't matter."

They all piled around me then, this bunch of strange aliens intent on turning me into a sappy, weepy mess. “I will have to leave now and then, you know,” I informed them, trying for calm, even as someone tugged a blanket over us all and about five pairs of hands patted or stroked me, soothing and comforting. “I’ll have meetings to attend off world sometimes, and…I just…is this real?”

It was finally hitting me just how much my life had changed, how fully everything I had always wanted was just suddenly falling into place. Could I really have a useful, fulfilling career, be deserving of the love of another (or five others), *and* be myself? Was that even allowed?

The soft murmurs and sleepy kisses before I drifted off to sleep, cocooned in the arms of my lovers, in the bed of one of the most powerful people on the planet, all my hopes and dreams for the future of Oz that floated through my head just as sleep claimed me…it all said the answer was yes.

Turns out exile was the best thing that ever happened to me. I was home.

About the Author

I write quirky, pantastic romance with paranormal and fantasy elements. I suffer from what my husband lovingly calls "pan brain" and I can't choose a favorite romance subgenre, so you'll find a little bit of everything in my romance stories. Straight, LGBTQIA, monogamous, poly, you name it, whatever you're looking for, I've probably got a book for that..... The only thing I don't write is the same tired old tropes, so if you're looking for all alpha male, all the time, then I'm *so* not the girl for you.

Thank you for reading, and of course reviews are always much appreciated. If you liked this book, you should sign up for my newsletter. I release a new book every couple of months, and you can stay up to date on new releases, freebies, and more. You'll also get a free copy of my exclusive tongue-in-cheek novelette, *Mary Sue and the Petal Pink Curse*, a fun spoof story I wrote for my patrons during lockdown that pokes fun at all the usual romance tropes.

You can Join me on Patreon, where you can help me create more of what you love. There, you'll get advance access to books as I write them, listen to audiobooks before they are available anywhere else, and access and participate in Patreon-only podcasts, Q&A, livestreams, and more.

You can also find me at kayedraper.com, on Facebook and Instagram, and all the usual places. You can find more of my work on Amazon, Kindle Vella, and most major ebook retailers.

As always, thank you so much for your support and for sharing my quirky little world!

Also by Kaye Draper

The Not Quite Series

Not quite human, not quite beast. Not quite female, not quite male. Sometimes hunter, sometimes prey. Always alone. Until them.

Fiend hunter Sam "Sabertooth" Forest is used to being on the outskirts. Being a cur with a mix of shifter and human blood, Sam can't fully shift to beast but can't fully pass as human. Through sheer determination, and a desire to protect the broken shifter woman who raised them, Sam has managed to eek out a place of their own in a world devastated by the rift that allowed monsters to spill into the earth plane. Sam hunts monsters, sometimes curs and mongrels just like Sam. The work might be dangerous, and the humans might want to put the mixed breed hunter on their hitlist, but it's a job. It's freedom. Sam works alone and trusts no one.

The next hunt should bring in a big bounty—big enough to pay the pack extortion fee and keep Sam's adoptive mother safe through winter. But when a Leprechaun horns in on Sam's unicorn hunt and tricks Sam into forming a hunter's guild, Sam is suddenly burdened by an overabundance of *people*.

Setting off to hunt one-horned murder beasts with an annoying leprechaun and a nerdy half-ogre is bad enough. But when you add in a betrayal by the seductive siren Sam has loved since childhood, and the machinations of a rich human politician, well…Sam's simple, lonely little life just got a whole lot more complicated.

Printed in Great Britain
by Amazon

26381544R00175